Out with the Old

There was another brief silence before Mallory shrugged again. "It's okay. Sit there."

Phoebe sat. She examined her class schedule as if it were riveting reading. But she also stayed aware of Mallory, who continued to stand and look out the window.

Phoebe could feel the amazed stare not only of Colette Williams-White, but of her other satellites Emma Parry and Jacklyn Ivy Lurvey and Hanna Simons.

Good, she thought. Watch me befriend Mallory Tolliver. And think twice about targeting her, because you'll have to do it to me, too. And you won't.

Without rushing, Phoebe cupped her chin in her hand and held Colette's dangerous gaze. She felt herself breathing easily and deeply. Then she smiled.

I am a Rothschild, Phoebe thought, and as she watched Colette coolly, she knew Colette was thinking it too; that Colette never forgot it; that Phoebe's amazing, storied family history, wealth, and power was the only reason that borderline dorky Phoebe had ever been a desirable friend for Colette in the first place. Now, Phoebe realized, it would also get her free.

Why had she not realized this before? Why had she only felt it was a burden, being a Rothschild? Why had she wished to be ordinary?

ALSO BY NANCY WERLIN

Are You Alone on Purpose?

Black Mirror

Double Helix

Impossible

The Killer's Cousin

Locked Inside

The Rules of Survival

Extraordinary

NANCY WERLIN

speak
An Imprint of Penguin Group (USA) Inc.

SPEAK
Published by the Penguin Group
Penguin Group (USA) Inc., 345 Hudson Street, New York, New York 10014, U.S.A.
Penguin Group (Canada), 90 Eglinton Avenue East, Suite 700, Toronto, Ontario, Canada M4P 2Y3
(a division of Pearson Penguin Canada Inc.)
Penguin Books Ltd, 80 Strand, London WC2R 0RL, England
Penguin Ireland, 25 St Stephen's Green, Dublin 2, Ireland (a division of Penguin Books Ltd)
Penguin Group (Australia), 250 Camberwell Road, Camberwell, Victoria 3124, Australia
(a division of Pearson Australia Group Pty Ltd)
Penguin Books India Pvt Ltd, 11 Community Centre, Panchsheel Park, New Delhi - 110 017, India
Penguin Group (NZ), 67 Apollo Drive, Rosedale, Auckland 0632, New Zealand
(a division of Pearson New Zealand Ltd.)
Penguin Books (South Africa) (Pty) Ltd, 24 Sturdee Avenue,
Rosebank, Johannesburg 2196, South Africa

Registered Offices: Penguin Books Ltd, 80 Strand, London WC2R 0RL, England

First published in the United States of America by Dial Books,
an imprint of Penguin Group (USA) Inc., 2010
Published by Speak, an imprint of Penguin Group (USA) Inc., 2011

1 3 5 7 9 10 8 6 4 2

THE LIBRARY OF CONGRESS HAS CATALOGED THE DIAL BOOKS EDITION AS FOLLOWS:
Werlin, Nancy.
Extraordinary / Nancy Werlin.
p. cm.
Summary: Phoebe, a member of the wealthy Rothschild family, befriends Mallory,
an awkward new girl in school, and the two become as close as sisters, but Phoebe does not know
that Mallory is a faerie, sent to the human world to trap the human girl into fulfilling
a promise made by her ancestor Mayer to the queen of the faeries.
ISBN: 978-0-8037-3372-5 (hardcover)
[1. Fairies—Fiction. 2. Secrets—Fiction. 3. Best friends—Fiction. 4. Friendship—Fiction.
5. Self-esteem—Fiction. 6. Jews—United States—Fiction.]
I. Title
PZ7.W4713Ex 2010
[Fic]—22
2010002086

Speak ISBN 978-0-14-241974-8

Book designed by Jasmin Rubero
Text set in De Vine BT

Printed in the United States of America

For Jim
With joy and wonder

Conversation with the Faerie Queen, I

"You are ready for your mission, then, little one?"

"Yes. Except that I am somewhat—I am sorry, Your Majesty. Yes, I am ready."

"You are anxious. Naturally. It is a great deal of responsibility. But remember, your way has been prepared. The Tolliver woman will believe you to be her own human daughter, miraculously restored to her. Grief, depression, and loneliness have caused her to lose herself, so she will gratefully accept your guidance in all things, young though you are. Managing her will be easy for you; you will give her certain human medications to keep her under your influence, and you will use her money for all your needs in the human realm."

"I understand. And the Rothschild girl?"

"The girl is of course your main focus. You will observe her at school. I need not tell you again that everything—*everything*—depends on her."

"The stakes are high."

"Frighteningly high, at this point. It is useless to deny it."

"Thank you for your trust and confidence, Your Majesty. I am humbled by it."

"Rise to your feet, child. Bid farewell to the court and, especially, to your older brother. He is proud of you for having been chosen—and he is jealous too. Ah, I see by the flare in his eyes that I am correct. But you shall show him and all our people that I have not made an error in placing our trust in his little sister."

"Yes, Your Majesty. Perhaps I will be home again, successful, in just a few human weeks."

"Even if it takes longer, we will manage. We have three or four years left, by human count."

"I will succeed with the girl long, long before that!"

"Good. You were ever a ferocious sprout."

chapter 1

Phoebe Gutle Rothschild met Mallory Tolliver in seventh grade, during the second week of the new school year, in homeroom. Phoebe had had one of her horrific asthma attacks and couldn't start school on time, but her so-called friend had kept her in the loop about Mallory. She couldn't wait to talk about the peculiar new girl.

It was her clothing that marked Mallory out. "Every day," Colette Williams-White said to Phoebe, "she wears something weirder than the day before. Yesterday, she had on this huge old T-shirt, like she thought it was a dress. But she had it on backward, with the tag sticking out at her throat. I mean, who wouldn't notice they'd done that? And, you know what? It smelled. Or maybe that was her. Also, with it? High heels."

"Is she maybe, you know . . ." Phoebe paused, delicately. "Challenged?"

"She's in regular classes, and—no. Just no."

"Maybe she can't afford decent clothes?"

Colette shook her head decisively. "The shoes were Christian Louboutin, in this marigold color, with ankle straps. Flowers on the toes, which—I know!—sounds like too much, but trust me, it wasn't."

"Could she just be expressing—"

"Stop it, Phoebe, okay? Because, frankly? Not only are you wrong, but it's also really bitchy of you to keep arguing when I've met her and you haven't. Actually? It's bitchy *and* prissy, both."

Phoebe shut up.

Colette continued. "Mallory Tolliver is *not* making her own unique fashion statement. She just doesn't care. It's as if she throws on the first thing she finds every morning, in, like, somebody else's closet." Colette rolled her eyes. "And that somebody else, who owns the closet? Hate to say it? They're really screwed up."

Looking at the new girl now, Phoebe couldn't help herself. She exchanged a quick, incredulous glance with Colette, who had been right. Then Phoebe's gaze returned, compelled, to Mallory Tolliver.

Mallory stood at the back of the room between the windows and the last row of seats, in profile to Phoebe, looking outside toward the cars passing in the street below. She was under medium height, with long straw-colored hair that was desperately in need of a good conditioner, and she was plump, with a curiously pale face. She would have seemed perfectly ordinary, even forgettable, if not for her clothes. Today she was wearing something that looked scarily like a Disney Princess costume.

Phoebe's brow furrowed, because Mallory's outfit got stranger the longer you looked at it. It was in fact not what Phoebe had thought at first glance; not a pretty, poufy, Disney Princess dress. The costume was flimsy and crude; it tied in back with strings and had obviously been intended to be worn on top of other, sturdier clothes. Possibly on Halloween. At first it had looked similar to Belle's fabulous tiered yellow ball gown, but on closer examination, its color and shape were off. Also, the dress had a small pair of wings hanging down drearily in back. These feathery wings made it a *fairy* princess costume. A generic, tacky, cheap fairy princess.

Princess Mallory Markdown.

Phoebe caught herself a split second before she said the catty name out loud to Colette, who was gripping Phoebe's arm with one hand and had the heel of the other clapped to her mouth, her eyes alive with characteristic sharp malice. If she said the words to Colette, Phoebe knew, they would stick, and the new girl was in bad enough trouble already. The other girls were like a pack of circling wolves.

Phoebe was one of them. Or rather, she had been. However, after a long talk with her Nantucket friend, Benjamin Michaud, a few weeks ago during summer vacation, she had realized she didn't want to be, not anymore.

Benjamin hardly ever offered a direct opinion and would just listen and ask questions. And he was over a year younger and, being from Nantucket, knew nothing of the kind of big suburban middle school Phoebe went to, much less of the politics of girls and friendship. But talking with her summer friend had the ability to make Phoebe realize when she was worried. As she had gone on and on to him about her girlfriends at school, she had realized that she didn't like them, and—this was almost worse—that she didn't like herself when she was with them.

And if that made her prissy—if Colette was right about that too—well, so be it.

The problem was that Phoebe wasn't sure how to detach herself safely from her so-called friends. It had even seemed very possible that she would be a coward and do nothing, because she didn't want to be alone and friendless, and also, she really did fear Colette's sharp tongue and her power. But as she looked at Mallory Tolliver in her awful costume, Phoebe suddenly understood that she was indeed going to step out of the pack. In fact, she was going to do it this very day. Somehow. She had to.

It was as if a tight constriction around her chest began to relax, and she caught a glimpse of the truth in a conversation she had overheard her parents having about her latest asthma attack. They had said her asthma got worse when she felt stressed or anxious.

Mallory had just shifted position, moving closer to the window. "My God," Colette said to Phoebe, in a voice pitched for all to hear. "Look at the new girl now!"

Phoebe looked. Phoebe winced.

In the direct light from the window, Mallory's dress had become partially transparent. She wore nothing beneath the cheap costume. Nothing at all. And, though she had not changed position, her shoulders stiffened, and Phoebe knew that of course she had heard Colette.

Phoebe scanned the room. Everybody was looking at Mallory, and a couple of the boys had their mouths open. "My God," she muttered involuntarily to Colette. "Where's her *mother?*"

Colette snickered approvingly—and simultaneously, Mallory Tolliver whipped around. But it was not to look at Colette. Instead, Mallory met Phoebe's gaze, Phoebe's only, instantly and directly. There was no mistaking the intelligence—and disdain—and pride—in her eyes.

There was something else there too; a tiny, unmistakable flicker of recognition.

Then, just as abruptly, Mallory turned away again. Her spine was straight as a post.

Phoebe never knew exactly what it was about Mallory that

called to her so strongly. That straight back? That quick, proud look at Phoebe that held recognition? The intelligence in her face? The fear that she sensed in her, that moved her to sympathy?

I want to know that girl, she thought suddenly. I want to be friends with her. Not Colette. *Her.*

Out of nowhere, a plan came to Phoebe. It came with tidal-wave force and with the conviction and joy of a religious conversion.

Phoebe reached up and peeled Colette's hand off her arm. She walked away from her and up to the new girl.

She spoke to Mallory's back. "Hello. I'm Phoebe Rothschild. I haven't been here the last few days, but I know you're Mallory." She waited until Mallory turned. The girl's expression was now quite blank.

Phoebe nodded toward an empty desk beside Mallory's. "Is this seat free? Or did Mrs. Fraser assign seats and I should just go away and find mine?" She paused. Smiled. "Or maybe you don't want me sitting with you?"

For long seconds, Mallory didn't respond. Finally she shrugged. "This teacher lets us sit wherever we want." She had a low voice, a little flat. It was absolutely without an accent; certainly not the local Boston accent that Phoebe's mother, Catherine, said drove her crazy.

"But is it okay with you if I'm here?" Phoebe persisted. "It would be for the whole year. I'm a creature of habit."

There was another brief silence before Mallory shrugged again. "It's okay. Sit there."

Phoebe sat. She examined her class schedule as if it were riveting reading. But she also stayed aware of Mallory, who continued to stand and look out the window.

Phoebe could feel the amazed stare not only of Colette Williams-White, but of her other satellites Emma Parry and Jacklyn Ivy Lurvey and Hannah Simons.

Good, she thought. Watch me befriend Mallory Tolliver. And think twice about targeting her, because you'll have to do it to me too. And you won't.

Without rushing, Phoebe cupped her chin in her hand and held Colette's dangerous gaze. She felt herself breathing easily and deeply. Then she smiled.

I am a Rothschild, Phoebe thought, and as she watched Colette coolly, she knew Colette was thinking it too; that Colette never forgot it; that Phoebe's amazing, storied family history, wealth, and power was the only reason that the borderline dorky Phoebe had ever been a desirable friend for Colette in the first place. Now, Phoebe realized, it would also get her free.

Why had she not realized this before? Why had she only felt it was a burden, being a Rothschild? Why had she wished to be ordinary? No matter. She could use it right now, and she would. Her gaze on Colette's grew a little softer, kinder, but no less decisive. Good-bye, Phoebe thought. Good-bye.

It was so simple.

Colette's eyes dropped. She turned—stumbling a little—and sat down abruptly at her desk, her back to Phoebe.

But then things went right back to being complicated. Mallory did not sit down at the desk next to Phoebe's until the bell rang for the start of homeroom and everyone else sat down too. Phoebe was full of urgent questions about the strange new girl. Was Mallory totally unaware of what had just happened? Did she at least realize she needed help? Surely she did.

Phoebe leaned toward Mallory and dropped her voice low. "Look. Mallory. You're not wearing the right clothes. I can help you. It'll be better here—easier for you, I mean—if you don't look so different from the other girls. Okay?"

Mallory didn't even glance at Phoebe. Ten seconds passed. Phoebe waited. She thought about repeating herself, but she knew Mallory had heard her.

An astounding thought occurred to Phoebe: Was she going to be refused?

No. No! Mallory Tolliver wouldn't be that stupid.

Would she?

Tension began to coil in Phoebe's stomach. She didn't look around for Colette. It was too late; she'd chosen her path and would not be forgiven. There was nothing to do but wait and see how Mallory responded. And if this didn't work, she'd be friendless in the seventh grade.

Phoebe waited. She waited while Mrs. Fraser performed the

business of homeroom. She waited through morning announcements. All the while, Mallory kept her face turned aside.

How had the balance of power in this weird girl-game shifted in mere minutes from Colette, and then—for one brief glorious moment of power and self-assurance—to Phoebe, but then to Mallory? Phoebe didn't know. She only knew that it had.

Finally Phoebe could no longer stand it. She leaned over and spoke again, even more quietly. She didn't think she sounded desperate, but she couldn't be sure. All her newly found Rothschild confidence had ebbed away.

"Mallory? Please. Will you please be my friend?"

The bell rang to mark the end of homeroom.

chapter 2

Neither Phoebe nor Mallory moved. As the classroom emptied and the other kids started off to first period, they stayed seated.

Mallory looked at Phoebe. Her expression was different now. It was not happiness or relief, as Phoebe would have expected. It was, instead, pure panic. And for an instant, because of it, Phoebe thought her offer would be rejected. It was clear this odd girl had much more on her mind than fitting in at middle school.

But then Mallory spoke, slowly. "You want to be my *friend?*" She said the word as if she had never heard it before and wasn't sure what it meant.

"Yes," Phoebe said.

"Why?"

Instinctively Phoebe gave her the truth. "Because I need a new friend. A real one. My old ones aren't any good."

Mallory still said nothing.

What was going on with her? Did it have to do with the peculiar clothes, her uncared-for appearance? Whatever it was, Phoebe's heart stretched in empathy. She was filled with the desire to understand. To help.

A few kids had already entered the room. One of them was lingering a few feet away, quite obviously waiting to occupy Phoebe's desk.

Phoebe grabbed her class schedule and got up. "What do you have next?"

She was relieved when Mallory answered. "Earth science. Mr. Herschel."

"Oh, wow, me too. Let's go together." Phoebe began walking and Mallory came along, slowly, but beside her.

Phoebe was conscious of other kids around them in the corridor, but she kept her attention on Mallory. And eventually, Mallory said, "I've never had a friend before."

Phoebe groped for a reply. "Oh. Well. You'll like it. I'm a good friend."

Was that a smile struggling to form on Mallory's face? Yes. Yes! It was the smallest upturn of one corner of her mouth. Then she smiled outright—and it transformed her. All at once Mallory was almost pretty. In fact, the only thing that kept her from it was the anxiety that still lingered, somehow, in her face.

Phoebe smiled back encouragingly.

For another handful of seconds, they looked at each other. Mallory said, "You're sure about this? Dumping your old friends for a girl you don't even know?" A tinge of mockery entered her voice. "A girl who wears the wrong clothes? Who people stare at and talk about?"

Mallory had understood everything that had happened to her in school, then. Shame swept over Phoebe and then was washed away by relief and a kind of gladness. This girl was indeed worth befriending. She was smart, interesting, and different.

Phoebe would perhaps be able to be herself with her, like she could with Benjamin.

"Yes." Phoebe lowered her voice. "I have some stories about my old friends that I'll bore you with another time. Let's just say I need to leave them." She hesitated, waiting until they'd traveled into the next corridor, and then added bluntly, "Look, Mallory, can I ask you—what's with your clothes? That thing you're wearing, it's so awful, it should be burned. You obviously know better. So why are you wearing it?"

Mallory's right hand stole up to her shoulder and just barely touched the ragged fake feathers of one ridiculous fairy wing. Phoebe wondered if she had made a mistake in being so direct. In insulting Mallory's fairy costume. Was it money after all? It could be, even if Mallory owned a few good things, like the shoes Colette had mentioned.

Mallory said, "I actually *didn't* know better at first. I was, uh, homeschooled before this, so there weren't any other children. On the first day of school, I just put something on—anything—like I would at home. Then I saw how people looked at me here and I understood." Her voice hardened. "But I didn't care. I had other things to think about."

"I understand. But you won't mind wearing better things? Today, actually"—Phoebe took a little breath—"I wouldn't be surprised if a teacher spoke to you. It's that you're, um, not wearing underwear. Maybe you didn't realize it showed." She made herself go on. "So. I have to ask this. Is money a problem?"

"Oh. No. I don't think so. I live with my mother, and we have some."

Phoebe wasn't sure what *some* meant, but she'd find out later. She had a credit card from her parents; she could tactfully pay for some things for Mallory, if need be. Her parents would understand, she thought. "Good. I'll take you shopping. How about this afternoon? Will that be okay with your mom?"

"I have to go home first and check in with her." Mallory gestured at her costume. "This thing is actually hers. It was just, uh, something that she kept. As a memento. She, uh, she asked me to wear it and I thought, why not, if it makes her happy. She . . . she cries a lot. She sort of lives in her own world. It's hard to describe."

Interesting, Phoebe thought. Colette was right, then, with

that remark about somebody else's closet—and that "somebody" being really screwed up.

Well, Phoebe would have time later to find out exactly what was wrong at Mallory's home, with Mallory's mom—there had been no mention of a father—and if she could help.

They were now outside Mr. Herschel's class, with only half a minute before the bell. The school corridors had largely emptied. Phoebe opened her mouth to speak—

But Mallory got there first, with a rush of sudden words. "Phoebe? Listen. I'll wear what you tell me to. It obviously matters to you and that's fine. But you need to understand something." And now her face was close and her voice fierce, even though it remained low.

"I don't want lots of friends. It will just be you. I can't be part of a group. And if that's not okay, then you and I can't be friends. Sorry."

Perhaps a tiny warning bell went off in the back of Phoebe's mind. But it was faint and far away, and drowned in the class bell that went off simultaneously.

Phoebe wanted this mysterious girl as her friend. No, as her *best* friend—her confidante, the sister she had never had. She was intrigued and moved by Mallory's strangeness, and there was no way she was going to back off now.

"No problem. And we'll go shopping." She led the way into their classroom.

"You're obsessed with clothes," Mallory said as she followed Phoebe.

"I'm really not," said Phoebe seriously, over her shoulder. "I'm just looking out for you. Trust me."

Mallory did not reply.

Conversation with the Faerie Queen, 2

"But child, what you're saying doesn't make sense. You are absolutely sure the Rothschild girl is the right one? And yet you also say she is not ready?"

"Yes, she is the right one, and yes, she is not ready. That other human girl that we were watching, the one called Colette—she had not achieved what we thought she had. The Rothschild girl was fighting back. While she is not very self-assured, she has personal strength of will. Your Majesty, I now understand that when we observe human activity from outside, we can be mistaken when we try to interpret what it means."

"So you came up with this new plan, of being friends with the Rothschild girl, so that you can finish what the girl Colette started?"

"Yes."

"I sense you are holding something back from me, child."

"No, no. You have the gist of it, Your Majesty. The important part. It's only—well, I have found it not so easy to function in the human realm. At the dwelling, it's difficult to keep the Tolliver woman calm. She cries in her sleep for her own daughter, though when she is awake, it is I she thinks she loves. Or mostly so. She demands a sugary treat, but then when she has it, she becomes very strange and angry with me and—well, I will not bore you, and I assure you, I can manage her, but she is—it is not easy. Once, I must confess, I even resorted to trying to use glamour on her—you must have felt the drain?"

"Indeed. But I trusted you knew what you were doing."

"I am afraid I did not, Your Majesty. And you have my deepest apologies that I used up so much of our energy reserve fruitlessly. It turned out that because of the woman's volatile mental state, the glamour did not work well on her at all. It made her crazier and more frantic and paranoid; she screamed and cried all that night and well into the next day. And then I had to go to school for the first time, and that was fruitless too, for the Rothschild girl was not even there. She—the girl—she has an illness of the lungs and breath, called asthma, which comes and goes. And then I came home from school and the woman saw me and began screaming again. So. It is not what we thought it would be. And—and then . . ."

"Go on, child."

"At the school, I made mistakes as well. I thought I would not be there for very long, and I was tired from dealing with the woman, and thus I was careless and made myself too conspicuous. And then it was too late to undo the bad impression I made, unless I were to deploy a great deal of glamour, enough to affect everyone who saw me there. Which would cost us all too much. And then it was several days longer before the Rothschild girl even appeared at school. It—it was a difficult time, Your Majesty."

"I see. I am sorry, my child. I am glad you have told me now. Should I send your brother to you? It would deplete our energy reserves much more to have him out in the world too, for you know what he is. But if you need help?"

"No, no! I can manage. I shall manage alone, and very well too. I have found my path now at last. I am just explaining what has led to my new recommendation."

"But these details do not seem to me to have much to do with your mission."

"I—you are right. I shall not bother you with them again. I can manage. All that matters is that I now understand that if I am the girl's friend, I can influence her and complete my mission."

"Very well. When will you become her friend? Immediately, I hope?"

"It is done, Your Majesty. She approached me today, soon after she returned to school, and asked me to be her friend."

"So quickly? But I did not feel the drain of you using glamour to attract her to you."

"I did not use glamour."

"Because you were frightened that it would not work, as it did not work on the Tolliver woman?"

"No. The Rothschild girl is sane, unlike the Tolliver woman. I did not use glamour because she already liked me. On her own. She is . . . she is *kind*, Your Majesty. She is uncertain in many ways, but she has a soft heart, and I—I cannot describe it. I will get close to her."

"How long will this process take, child?"

"Just a few weeks, Your Majesty. At most."

chapter 3

Phoebe was disappointed that first day, when Mallory put off the shopping expedition, saying she needed to go straight home alone. But Mallory said that she could shop with Phoebe after school on the next day. This meant that by the time the last class ended, Phoebe was deep into trying to figure out the shopping. It was complicated, because Mallory needed *everything*. And how was Phoebe to broach the topic of money with her again? She knew it would be necessary to talk in specifics this time.

What would an entirely new wardrobe cost? There was a reality TV show in which people who dressed badly were publicly mocked, after which they were coached in how to dress well and sent out with five thousand dollars. It seemed to Phoebe that this was probably the right amount. Could she do it for less? Yes, but the thought of Colette and company continuing to sneer at Mallory's clothes made Phoebe cringe inside.

She went into the girls' room and took two puffs from her asthma inhaler.

First she would meet Mrs. Tolliver, she decided. Then she would assess the situation. Today, perhaps, they would buy just a few things. Underwear. A single pair of jeans. A couple of 100 percent cotton tees, in plain colors.

If only she dared to charge absolutely everything to her own account, and explain it to her parents later. What was that saying, that it was easier to get forgiveness than permission? However, she would also need to get Mallory and Mrs. Tolliver to agree to this. People did not always like to take handouts. And she hadn't known Mallory for very long.

Spinning thoughts like these had Phoebe roiling with anxiety by the time she met Mallory in the front lobby of their school. They went together to the car that had been sent to pick Phoebe up. "Normally I'd walk home on a nice day like today," Phoebe said apologetically. "But because of the asthma attack last week, my parents sent someone to get me."

Mallory nodded. Phoebe had the thought that she too looked tense. Well, taking your new friend home to meet your mother, who you had already implied was messed up—that couldn't be easy.

Jay-Jay was at the wheel of the car. "Jay-Jay, this is my new friend, Mallory Tolliver." Phoebe held the back door open for Mallory. "Mallory, this is Jay-Jay Epstein, who works for my parents. He mostly does the cooking but sometimes he gets roped into driving me places too. He's also a writer. He's working on a screenplay."

"I'm on my third screenplay, actually," Jay-Jay said. "Dreams die hard. Where are we going, ladies?"

"First, Mallory's house," said Phoebe. "After that, maybe Bloomingdale's. After that, who knows?"

Jay-Jay removed his hands from the wheel and turned to look into the backseat, where Phoebe, who would ordinarily have sat up front with him, had followed Mallory. "Phoebe, you're scaring me. Is this going to take all afternoon? One place after another?"

"Maybe. Is that okay?"

"No, darling, not okay. I have the dough for a couple of loaves of bread rising. I have to be back in an hour to punch it down. And then there's my halibut sauce still to make."

"All right, sorry. What if we're quick at Mallory's? And then maybe you could just drop us off at the mall? And I'll call later?"

"Now you're making sense." Jay-Jay nodded at Mallory in the mirror. "Mallory? Seat belt."

Mallory was sitting bolt upright. "What?"

"Buckle your seat belt," Phoebe said absently. She pulled on the belt she had already fastened around herself.

"Oh," said Mallory. Her eyes darted from side to side.

"It's hanging on your right," said Jay-Jay. "Yes, that's it. Keep pulling. One long smooth tug—oh, you've dropped it. It's always a little confusing in a new car. Phoebe, help her? Now you've got it. Mallory, where do you live?"

It took Mallory a moment before she recited her address.

"I think I know where that is," said Jay-Jay. "Behind Whole Foods, off Crafts Street. Yes?"

Mallory hesitated again. "My mother and I just moved there. I don't really know the neighborhood. But I know how to walk there from here."

"Direct me," said Jay-Jay easily.

A few minutes later, they pulled up in front of a normal-looking ranch house with a big driveway, a peeling paint job, and sad, overgrown bushes. The sight of the house filled Phoebe with even more anxiety about how she would get Mallory properly dressed. She chewed the inside of her cheek.

"We won't be long," she said to Jay-Jay. She trailed Mallory up the walk to the front door of the house. Mallory let them in with a key, and called out, "Mother! I'm home!"

Phoebe looked around. The living room seemed fine, even if it was the kind of fine that was completely without color or personality: white walls, beige sofa and love seat. There were no boxes or mess or other indications of the family having so recently moved in. But then again, there was very little stuff, period. No family photos or pictures on the walls.

Her gaze lingered on the sofa as a series of lumps on it stirred and then resolved themselves into the figure of a woman.

Fingertips appeared at one end of a beige blanket thrown over the sofa. As the hands pushed the blanket away, a large white face appeared, blinking sleepily. The figure beneath the blanket—Mallory's mother—struggled to sit upright. Mallory swiftly crossed the living room toward her, and Phoebe followed tentatively.

"It's Mallory," said Mallory loudly, and then added, even more loudly, "Your daughter. I'm home from school." She helped the woman to sit upright.

Mrs. Tolliver had a great big cloud of mussed, soft, graying brown hair, and heavy eyebrows that stuck out like an elderly man's. She was wearing a flannel nightgown that looked more than a little damp under her chin. "Can I have some Skittles?" she asked Mallory. Her voice slid abruptly high and whiney. "Just a few. Five. Or twelve. I've been good. I stayed right here and slept all day so you could go to school."

Oh my God, Phoebe thought.

She listened helplessly while Mallory asked her mother questions about medication and sleep, and received evasive or nonsense answers. When Mallory tried to insist that her mother eat some food, Mrs. Tolliver countered again with the statement that she was owed Skittles because she had let Mallory go to school.

Phoebe ducked her head. She chewed on the inside of her cheek. She got it now: Mallory's lack of decent clothes had been the symptom of an even bigger maternal problem than she had imagined. Mallory was in serious trouble and she, Phoebe, was totally out of her depth.

But she knew someone who wouldn't be. I'll just bring Mrs. Tolliver and Mallory home, Phoebe thought. To *my* mother. Relief filled her. It was simple as pie; simpler by far than what she had done yesterday in dumping Colette and appealing to Mallory for friendship.

And there was no time like the present.

Phoebe moved briskly to the sofa and sat down on the other side of Mrs. Tolliver, intercepting Mallory's astonished stare with an apologetic smile.

"Mrs. Tolliver? I'm Phoebe Rothschild. I'm a friend of Mallory's from school, and I want to invite both of you to my family's house for dinner tonight. You have to meet my parents. Their names are Catherine and Drew. Catherine Rothschild and Drew Vale."

"Phoebe—" Mallory began.

"You have to come," said Phoebe to Mrs. Tolliver.

"Not today," said Mrs. Tolliver dismissively.

"Yes, today," Phoebe said. "Because, um, Jay-Jay—that's our cook—he does this dessert with Skittles that you will love and he's going to make it tonight."

Mrs. Tolliver paused. "Skittles?"

"Yes, Skittles. He, uh, tosses them on top of this, this bed of homemade whipped cream. With—um, with drizzles of warm chocolate. He also puts a little dish of extra Skittles out so you can just spoon more onto your whipped cream if you want."

Phoebe felt pleased with her invention. Maybe she was destined for a future in the culinary arts. She could apprentice to Jay-Jay and never have to wonder again about her purpose in life. She would specialize in sugary desserts. Or even just in Skittles. She could invent a whole cookbook's worth of Skittles recipes. It could happen.

She raced on. "Of course, we're not allowed to eat dessert until after the entrée. That's Jay-Jay's rule. We'll all eat our—our fish, I think he's making tonight. Then the Skittles. But it'll be worth it, don't you think? Eating the fish to get to the Skittles?"

"Yes, it's worth it," said Mrs. Tolliver. She looked over at Mallory, like a child wanting guidance.

Phoebe also turned to Mallory and gave her a stare. "We'll just bundle into the car and go to my house *right now*."

Mallory's mouth opened and then closed. "No—that is, Phoebe, you don't understand."

"I do understand," Phoebe said intensely.

Mallory looked away.

"We will go," announced Mrs. Tolliver. "I haven't visited anyone for so long. It's lovely to be asked for dinner. What was your name again?"

"I'm Phoebe."

"Phoebe. Thank you for the invitation. We accept. I'll have to change." Mrs. Tolliver pushed herself upright. "It won't take me long. Mallory, you should change too. That is not a dinner dress you have on. Why don't you try the pink dress with the little Alice apron? You wore it when you were five. Remember?"

Mrs. Tolliver's face went all tender and loving. She said to Phoebe, "That dress! Mallory used to twirl and twirl in it, because of how it puffed out around her legs. How we laughed, John and I. How we laughed at our pretty little Mallory. That was before John died, of course." Walking steadily, she moved out of the room.

Phoebe's heart was aching as she looked back at Mallory. Mallory had stiffened, as if she would rush after her mother, but then, indecisively, she looked at Phoebe. Phoebe couldn't tell what she was feeling. Was she angry? Surprised? Confused? Embarrassed? Or just totally numb?

How long had Mallory been taking care of her mother all by herself?

She said, "Mallory. My mother will be able to help you. She's excellent at figuring things out. She just needs to meet you and your mom and understand the problem. So come home with me today. Shopping can wait, obviously."

"There is no problem," said Mallory.

"Oh, Mallory."

"I don't even know what you mean by problem."

Phoebe reached out in frustration and grabbed Mallory's hands. They were fists in hers. She gripped them anyway.

"Mallory. You're *thirteen*. You just can't be solely responsible for your mother and her troubles. You need to be a kid now. You need to be an ordinary teenage girl, with only regular teenage girl problems to worry about. You deserve that."

"Ordinary?" Mallory stared at Phoebe, repeating the word as if she had never heard it before. "Did you say that *I* need to be ordinary?"

"Yes. Wouldn't it be a relief?"

"I—I—no! I mean, yes! I mean—I'm not an ordinary teenage girl. You are, yes. You are. But I'm not."

Phoebe sighed. "Oh, Mallory. I understand you don't feel regular. How could you, with your mother to take care of? But it doesn't have to be that way."

"I have to take care of my people. I agreed to the responsibility." Mallory pulled her hands forcefully away from Phoebe and buried her face in them.

That was an odd way for Mallory to refer to her mother, Phoebe thought. But whatever. "Whether you agreed or not, you're too young for the responsibility," she said. "We'll—we'll arrange things. My mother is good at that. She's so good at it, you won't even believe it." And money helps, Phoebe thought practically.

She continued, "I'm your friend now, right? Friends help each other, and they *accept* help from each other."

Mallory looked up. Phoebe couldn't interpret her expression. Uncertainty? Longing? And something else too: the concentrating, calculating look of someone doing a math problem in her head.

She waited.

Mallory spoke at last, slowly, as if amazed by the words coming from her own throat. "It's all true. I *would* like to be a teenage girl for a while. To be without other responsibility." She shook her head as if in disbelief. "But also, I really want—it's strange—but I really want—just for a while—I want—" Her voice trailed off.

"What?" Phoebe asked. "What do you want?"

Mallory's fingers reached for Phoebe's hands now, clasping. Her voice held a mix of anger and wonder. "I want to be your friend."

Phoebe squeezed Mallory's hands back. And then—she couldn't help it—she reached out exuberantly to give Mallory a long, warm hug. "It'll be okay," she said. "You're not alone, you know. I won't let you be alone and in trouble."

It was like hugging someone who didn't even know what a hug was. Awkwardly, Mallory patted Phoebe's shoulder. Then, when the girls stepped away and looked at each other, and Phoebe smiled encouragingly, Phoebe saw Mallory turn sharply away.

Was she crying?

"It'll be okay," Phoebe said again, not knowing what else to say.

Mallory's reply was low and choked. "No. It is so very much *not* okay. You have no idea."

But after a couple of minutes, she straightened her shoulders and met Phoebe's gaze openly, clearly, and with determination, though her cheeks were still wet. "I'll get changed," she said. She even smiled. "We'll go to your house and do what you say, Phoebe. My friend. I'll figure out the rest later."

"With my help," Phoebe said.

Mallory turned away.

chapter 4

Within a few hours, after dinner, Phoebe was showing Mallory around her house. Things had gone just exactly as Phoebe had hoped and known they would, once her mother met Mrs. Tolliver and absorbed the story that Phoebe had told her first, privately.

"Phoebe," Catherine Rothschild had just said, "your father and I would like to sit with Mrs. Tolliver for a while and talk. Why don't you show Mallory around? You don't mind my sending the girls off, do you, Annemarie? We should discuss those ideas I have, to make your life easier."

"All right." Mrs. Tolliver was sitting upright in her chair with her hands laced in her lap, although she kept stealing glances at the little candy dish of Skittles nearby. "I'm very interested. Thank you, Catherine."

"My secretary's on her way too. You won't mind? She's so

good at brainstorming and we'll want her to make the phone calls and appointments for us tomorrow. I might actually assign her to you for a while, if you don't mind that."

"Not at all," said Mrs. Tolliver faintly.

"Run along, girls," said Catherine. "Come back in, oh, an hour, perhaps."

"Thanks, Mom," said Phoebe. She smiled at Mallory—a little sheepishly—and led her from the room.

Mallory was silent as Phoebe conducted her through the house, room after room after room. After room. Of course the Rothschild house was nothing like the ranch house that the Tollivers were living in, and Mallory's silence made Phoebe squirm inside with a familiar feeling of helplessness. When they reached the library, Phoebe was swept with a very particular déjà vu.

Fifth grade. The first time she'd brought Colette Williams-White home. They'd been in this same enormous bookshelf-lined room, with its wood-beamed ceiling and twin reading nooks and leaded glass windows and the stone fireplace that a large man could stand up in. And Colette had suddenly spun on Phoebe. "Talk about spoiled rotten Jewish American princesses!" Colette had said, her cheeks pink with fury—and then Colette had burst into tears. Which had forced Phoebe to tend to her.

"Whoa," Phoebe said now. She sat down abruptly on one of the leather chairs that surrounded the library's central table.

"What is it?" asked Mallory.

Phoebe hesitated. Mallory had been so quiet during the tour, looking around the house with interest, but with little to say. Maybe she, like Colette, had been burning up inside with envy? But if Mallory was really going to be her friend . . .

Phoebe said, "I just remembered something from a few years ago. When Colette and I were first—well, friends. If you can call it that." She related the incident.

"So you took care of Colette? Dried her tears and said *there, there?*" said Mallory. She had sat down on the chair next to Phoebe's. "You took care of her, even though she'd just insulted you?"

"I did. Yes."

"Why?"

Phoebe knew the answer. She had thought about it. She had talked about it with her friend Benjamin. "She made me feel ashamed. Of—" Phoebe waved a hand at the room.

"Of having so much," said Mallory.

"Yes."

"Colette doesn't seem to me to be in any need," observed Mallory. "Am I wrong?" She smiled a twisted smile. "Did you go home with her and find that her mother was a wreck and she was the only one taking care of things?"

Phoebe met Mallory's gaze and smiled back awkwardly. "No. Colette's home is fine. Her parents are lawyers. She has everything she wants. Including two adorable little twin sisters, by the way. But her life isn't, well, you know." She waved a hand again.

"It's not like this."

"Right. And, like I said, it made me ashamed."

Mallory tilted her head to the side. "Did she make you feel like you'd rather be more like her? Not be a Rothschild, not have everything else that goes with it?" She leaned toward Phoebe. "Would you rather be regular and ordinary?"

"At that moment I felt that way."

"But you don't feel that way now? You're over it?"

Phoebe nibbled thoughtfully on the inside of her cheek. "It's complicated. I'm not a princess type. At all! You don't know me yet, but believe me. And my dad is a regular person. But when your family is like mine, I guess nobody in it can be regular in the, uh, regular way." She paused. "Also, my mother is amazing. She'd be amazing even without being a Rothschild. She's just so brilliant. You've only just met her, but—"

"I have an idea. Just from tonight."

"Yes. I wanted to fit in with Colette and the others, for a while there. But now you're my friend, right? I don't have to care about them anymore." She was suddenly aware that she sounded a little . . . well, needy.

Was she buying friendship, again? Was that what had happened with Colette? Was that what was happening here too? Phoebe wasn't sure. She hunched her shoulders. Maybe she would call Benjamin tonight . . .

She looked warily at Mallory. Mallory was smiling, but her eyes were sad.

"I am your friend," Mallory said. "I want to be, and I am. And so, as your friend, let me tell you something important. It's that you decided to get out of that bad friendship with Colette by yourself. I just happened to come along to make it easier. But you could have done it alone if you had to. And you would have. Right?"

"I wanted to. I—I'm not sure I would have actually gone through with it."

"You would have."

"Maybe."

An awkward silence came over the girls. Mallory got up and wandered around the room, finally coming to a stop at the wall next to the stone fireplace, where a portrait from the nineteenth century hung. It showed the upper torso of a man in a white shirt and black coat. He was bald with fluffy tufts of gray hair sticking out on either side of his head and had the kind of expression that was impossible to read. "Who's this?" Mallory asked.

"Oh. He's a Rothschild ancestor. That's a copy, actually, not an original painting."

Mallory came to attention. "Which ancestor? Is it—is it Mayer Rothschild?"

"You know about him?" Phoebe asked, surprised.

"Well, I read a little online. After I met you yesterday. I was interested in the family founder and the story and all."

"Oh."

"I'm not jealous like Colette," Mallory said. "I promise. I wanted to know more, that's all. Your ancestor Mayer Rothschild sounded like a fascinating man. You should be proud of him, by the way. Not ashamed."

"I am," said Phoebe, stung.

"Good," said Mallory smoothly. "So, who is this, then, if it's not Mayer?" She indicated the portrait again.

"That's Nathan Rothschild," said Phoebe, glad to move on to talking about something factual. "He was Mayer's third son. The third of five sons, did you read about that? There were five daughters too, by the way, though they hardly ever get mentioned. My mother is descended from Nathan's branch, which is the English one."

"Is there a portrait of Mayer himself?"

"No. There are a couple of historical paintings, scenes that include him, that were done many years after his death. My cousins in Paris have them—or copies of them, I'm not sure which. Anyway, Mayer is represented in them, but it's really the artist's imagination at work."

"Oh. I was hoping for something that would show what he really looked like."

"There's nothing like that," said Phoebe. "There was no photography then. The five sons all sat for portraits, but not Mayer. He was supposedly a very modest and humble man, so it wouldn't have been like him to commission a portrait, I guess.

"I don't know how much you read about him, Mallory. It was his sons who, well, who rose in the world. And that was how he wanted it. He stayed in Frankfurt in a small house, with his wife—I'm named for her, my middle name, Gutle. Anyway, he stayed there his whole life, even after becoming rich and powerful."

"In the Jewish ghetto?"

"Yes. It was a terrible place. There are pictures of that, if you want to see them."

"I would," said Mallory. She looked again at the portrait of Nathan Rothschild. "Do you ever wish you could go back in time and meet Mayer?"

Phoebe had never thought about that before. But after only a second, she shook her head. "Only if I could be really certain of coming back here afterward. Mayer's time was *not* a good time to be a Jew in Europe."

"Even if you were a Rothschild?"

"Well," Phoebe said awkwardly, shyly, "the name meant nothing until Mayer and his five sons *made* it mean something. And it wasn't about building power and money. Those were just the tools. Underneath that, it was all about safety and survival.

"I guess . . ." Phoebe paused. "I guess that's why what Colette said—about my being a spoiled princess—that's why it really hurt. She just didn't understand. But it's my fault, in a way. I couldn't explain. I barely can now." She shrugged. "Well. Anyway. Let's go see the rest of the house."

"Okay," said Mallory. "But Phoebe?"

"Yes?"

"I understand what you're saying. About survival."

"Well, it was a long time ago. I don't mean to be so dramatic. It's not like I'm personally in any danger. It's the history, that's all. Family history and world history and, well, Jewish history."

"History affects the present." Mallory caught Phoebe's gaze and held it. "The history of our family and our people affects who we are in the present."

"Yes," said Phoebe. "It does! Even if you really wish it didn't."

"Even if you really wish it didn't," echoed Mallory.

Conversation with the Faerie Queen, 3

"This is a risky path that you recommend, child, and requires so much time that it frightens me. Only yesterday you said you would be done in a few weeks. And now you say it will take *years?*"

"Yes, Your Majesty. I am sorry. I did not fully understand the girl when I made that first rash estimate. But you told me it was safe for a few more years?"

"Yes. I did. And it is. But—"

"She is our best option. She and no other. She is the one we need. She is! Just not yet."

"I see. I should have expected it would not all go exactly as we had planned. I should even have expected she would not be so easily led; she is a daughter of Mayer, after all."

"I am sorry, Your Majesty. I will not fail you. I promise. It will just take me more time. More time as her friend."

"I understand. Do not be sad, child. I am proud of you. It seems you have adjusted well to the initial difficulties of which you told me, and come up with another plan. And of course, I too understand what it is to make initial errors in judgment. As you know. It was my own mistake that brought us to this precipice."

"Yes, Your Majesty. Phoebe—the girl—we are best friends now. That is what humans call it: best friends. With time I will be able to make her do exactly as we wish. But Your Majesty! I have tired you. Would you rest now? I can come back."

"I am only a little tired. I am not so sick yet, my child. Very well. You may have the time you say you require. It will not, after all, be the longest time that a faerie has ever masqueraded as a human."

"Thank you, Your Majesty. This is just a delay. I won't fail you or our people, I won't. You may rely on me. In the end I will do exactly as I have promised."

chapter 5

"Oh, no! It looks too utterly slutty!" called Phoebe to Mallory, who was just outside the dressing room.

"Are you sure?" said Mallory. "I don't trust you."

"See for yourself." Phoebe opened the dressing room door so Mallory could slip inside. After only a glance, Mallory laughed.

"I know!" said Phoebe. "So much for push-up bras. And stop laughing, you—you perfect C-cup, you. It's just so not fair."

It was more than four years later—four good, solid years of best-friendship later. It was the middle of January and the girls were in their junior year of high school. Mallory was seventeen and Phoebe had just turned eighteen and they were at the lingerie store in pursuit of the perfect bra for Phoebe. They had taken possession of a large dressing room, but were getting, in Phoebe's view, absolutely nowhere.

"No, no," said Mallory, sobering. "Don't give up."

"I've already had on a dozen. The problem is that I'm between sizes. Just like the salesclerk said."

"The problem isn't you. It's that *thing* you picked out. It's got way too much padding. Look, Phoebe, there are so many styles and we're just wandering around grabbing random bras off the rack. It's crazy. Let's ask that salesclerk for help."

Phoebe shook her head stubbornly. "No. I don't want her in here with her tape measure and glasses and her professional knowledge of—of—"

"Of exactly what bras she has in stock?"

"Of mammary inadequacy!"

Mallory snickered, and a second later, so did Phoebe.

"Try putting on a shirt," Mallory suggested. "See how it looks underneath. It's not like you're going to go parading around just in the bra."

Phoebe sighed, but obediently reached for her shirt and put it on. She scrutinized her image in the three-way mirror. "No. They're in a weird position. Like I had surgery that went all wrong." She met her friend's eyes in the mirror. Suddenly what had been meant as a fun shopping trip felt horrible. She felt horrible. Her shoulders slumped.

"Stay here, Phoebe," said Mallory decisively. "Let me go pick something out for you. I bet I'll have better luck."

"Maybe I should have surgery."

"Don't even think that! You're fine. Besides, your mother would never let you. Actually, neither would I."

“I don’t really mean it.”

“Good. Stay here. I’ll be back in a few minutes.”

“Don’t you ask that salesclerk!”

Mallory didn’t answer as she shut the door behind her. Alone, Phoebe looked again at herself in the mirror. But it was Mallory she saw in her head. Her friend Mallory.

Her gorgeous friend.

Mallory had changed so much in the last few years. At five eleven, she now towered over Phoebe’s five two. And Mallory, not Phoebe, was today the girl that other people noticed when they were together in public. Often people even thought Mallory might be a model, which was not so much because she was tall and pretty as it was because she was striking and confident and held herself well. Her long fall of silky hair, ivory skin, and oval, deep-set eyes didn’t hurt either. It was strange to compare Mallory’s current grace and style and beauty to the defiant, plain-faced ragamuffin she once had been.

Phoebe faded away next to Mallory now, and she knew it. In part, this was because of her decision last year to wear only black clothing. It wasn’t really a goth look, because of Phoebe’s thick, reddish brown hair, soft gray eyes, and scattering of freckles, and also because she couldn’t be bothered with much makeup. But it also had the effect of making Mallory stand out as the sophisticated, put-together, worldly one.

Phoebe didn’t mind, actually. She got enough attention in the world already, when people heard her last name. “This is one of your ways to try to fade into the background and not be noticed," Mallory had observed to Phoebe about her clothing.

"No, it's just what makes me feel comfortable," Phoebe had said. "So please, Mallory, don't give me that lecture about standing up for myself again."

"That lecture" was something that Mallory trotted out occasionally, and which Phoebe had come to find slightly annoying. But she knew Mallory meant well.

And Phoebe had to admit to herself now that she had sort of wanted an amazing bra. She had wanted to believe the ads she'd seen about this one particular miracle bra and how it could change your life.

Make you sexy. Make you feel delicious. Make boys notice.

Oh, well. Phoebe rolled her eyes ironically at herself. She took off her shirt and the miracle bra that had been so terrible on her. She put her own bra on and sat down on the bench in the corner of the dressing room while she waited for Mallory to come back.

It was a good thing she had, too, because it was a long time, twenty minutes at least, before Mallory returned, carrying a single bra on a little hanger.

"There you are." Phoebe jumped up. "Why didn't you answer your cell phone? I was just about to come out and hunt you down."

"Sorry." Mallory sank down almost heavily on the bench that Phoebe had just vacated. She handed the bra to Phoebe.

"This is it?" Phoebe said. "This is what took you, like, half an hour of searching to find?"

“Yes.” Mallory leaned her head back against the wall and closed her eyes.

“Hey. Are you okay?”

“I’m a little tired, I guess. I didn’t sleep well last night. Try on the bra, Phoebe. I think it’s really cute. I think it’s just right for you.”

Phoebe looked again, dubiously, at the bra. It was beige and lacy, and she supposed it was pretty, but it was understated and it didn’t have any of the underwire or padding that absolutely would be needed, architecturally speaking, to make her look a size bigger. She was about to say this, but another glance at Mallory changed her mind. Mallory had wrapped her arms around herself, and actually looked somehow shrunken as she sat, curled up now, on the bench.

“Try it on,” Mallory said again, without opening her eyes.

Phoebe did. And stood amazed. The little bra fit perfectly and delicately. No, it did not make her look any bigger. But it was nice. And pretty. And maybe even just the tiniest bit sexy too.

She put on her shirt and looked again.

“All right. I’ll get it,” she said.

At that, Mallory opened her eyes. She smiled, though she still looked tired and almost sad. “You’re going to get six, my friend. Two beige, two black, one hot pink, and one blue. They don’t have them all in stock, but that clerk will order them for you. I already asked her.”

Mallory remained unusually quiet, however, not even crow-ing in triumph as Phoebe did exactly as she had been told, until the girls had left the store and gotten into Phoebe's car in the parking lot. Then she reached out a hand and stopped Phoebe from turning on the ignition.

"There's something I have to tell you, Phoebe," Mallory said. "It's good news, but I'm afraid you're going to be mad at me. So please don't be. Please?"

"What is it?" Phoebe wasn't sure if she'd ever heard Mallory sound so—so odd.

Or maybe she had. The combination of strain and relief was actually similar to how Mallory had sounded way back when, at the beginning of their friendship, on the day that the home health care agency had begun managing Mrs. Tolliver's care so that Mallory no longer needed to be responsible for it.

"What's going on?" Phoebe said again, because Mallory hadn't answered her.

"It's my brother," Mallory said. "My brother is coming to live with me and my mother."

"What?" Phoebe stared at Mallory, whose face was averted. "What are you *talking* about, Mallory? You don't have a brother!"

There was a little silence.

"That's why you're going to be mad," said Mallory. "I've never told you about him. But he does exist. He's my half brother, actually. We have the same mother."

Phoebe shook her head in bewilderment. "I'm—I'm shocked!"

"I knew you would be. I'm sorry. I should have told you."

All at once Phoebe realized she was more than shocked. She was furious. She unbuckled her seat belt and leaned close to Mallory, who would still not meet her gaze.

"Uh, do you care about your brother at all? Does your mother? Just wondering. Since neither of you ever mentioned him before. What did you say his name was again?"

Now the strain was even more evident in Mallory's voice, though she was able to turn and glance into Phoebe's eyes for a second or two.

"Of course I care about him. And I didn't say his name. He's Ryland. Ryland Fayne. He and I have different fathers, like I said, so we have different last names. I'm really, really sorry I never told you about him, Phoebe. I can explain."

"Go right ahead," said Phoebe. "Honestly, I can't wait. And by the way, feel free to share any other big secrets you might have been keeping from me. Any year now is fine. Let me just turn the car on so we have some heat while you tell me everything. Everything, do you hear me? Everything! I still can't believe it! This is so crazy!"

But her astonishment and outrage faded as Mallory talked and Phoebe watched her. Mallory had always been odd and different, after all. And as she began explaining about her older half brother—Ryland was twenty-four—and how he'd been working in Australia for a few years, and in college in England before that, well, it was almost logical that she hadn't mentioned him before.

Almost.

"I missed Ryland too much to even think about him," said Mallory, talking rapidly. "So I tried not to. And maybe I was a little angry at him too, for—for leaving me alone."

At least that makes sense, thought Phoebe.

Mallory went on talking and Phoebe listened. Ryland worked doing something good-for-the-earth involving desert water conservation. He was very committed and he just hadn't been able to visit his mother and sister.

"He didn't get a lot of vacation time, and you can't just come and go between Australia and Massachusetts in a long weekend. Plus, it's important, intense work, and other people are involved. Other people's welfare. Ryland told me in advance how it would be. It was outside of his control. And he keeps in touch when he can."

"I'm so happy for you," Phoebe said at last, because what else was there to say? "Did you say when he's coming?"

"No, I didn't. It's tomorrow. Listen, I'm going to stay out of school to make sure I'm home when he arrives."

Mallory went on and on, the details coming out almost in a frenzy, as if she were trying now to make up for past silence. Ryland had finished with his job in the Outback. He wasn't certain what he would do next with his life. He would stay with his mother and sister while he figured things out. It was going to be so, so fantastic. Also, Phoebe was just going to love him!

"You know what, Phoebe? You can see a picture of him. Hang on just a minute. It's on my phone. Here."

Phoebe leaned over to look. She couldn't deny that she felt great interest.

And Ryland was attractive, Phoebe thought. He seemed tall—like Mallory—and lanky. In the picture, she could see that he had thick lion-colored hair, darker than his sister's. But Phoebe couldn't see his features clearly because he wore large sunglasses. She couldn't tell if he looked at all like Mallory.

"Is this a recent picture?" Phoebe asked.

"Uh. Yes."

"Huh." As Phoebe looked, and as she felt Mallory's anxious gaze on her, thoughts tumbled through her head. It was all so strange. *Phoebe* had been Mallory's sibling, these last years. She felt like she had done a good job. But maybe she wouldn't be wanted now. Had Phoebe just been a substitute? A substitute for this irresponsible loser who had left his little sister all alone to take care of their unstable mother? And would Mallory stop visiting the Rothschilds so much now? Would she no longer occupy the little turquoise bedroom across the hall from Phoebe's, the room that, to all intents and purposes, had belonged to her for these last years?

She managed to focus once more on what Mallory was now saying.

"Mother actually spent the weekend getting the spare bedroom ready for Ryland! She's so happy. I think she did sort of forget he existed. You know how she is. But she remembers now."

Phoebe looked up from the picture. "Your mother actually did physical *work*?"

Mallory laughed shrilly. "God, no! Mother directed *my* work. But still, it's a change from lying on the sofa sleeping or eating Skittles. Maybe, with Ryland here, she'll wake up. Be more active."

"Do you know how long he'll stay?" Phoebe asked.

"No. But a while. He says he's earned a long vacation."

Phoebe was dying, suddenly, to go home—alone—and find her parents and spill it all to them. They'd be amazed!

"Phoebe," said Mallory quietly. She reached out and put a hand on Phoebe's arm.

"What?"

"Phoebe. Could you just—"

"Just what?"

"Be happy for me? Be happy that I have a brother who's coming to be with me?"

Phoebe was stricken to the heart. "I'm sorry," she said.

"Will you be nice to Ryland? Make him feel welcome? For my sake?" Mallory's eyes were huge. If she hadn't known better, Phoebe might have thought she was holding back tears.

"I—of course I will," said Phoebe, thoroughly abashed.

"Promise?"

"I promise," said Phoebe.

chapter 6

After she dropped Mallory off, Phoebe went home and peeked into her mother's office. Catherine was taking a meeting on her computer, probably with people in Tokyo or Taiwan or someplace else where it was already Monday morning. Maybe even Australia.

Professor Catherine Rothschild, whose only official title was Senior Lecturer in Economics at the Massachusetts Institute of Technology, was actually at the center of an enormous, intricate global web of money, power, and influence. Being her mother's daughter was, Phoebe thought, a little like being the daughter of the U.S. president, except that Catherine's position in the world was neither dependent on elections nor subject to the scrutiny of the media. Catherine's power was like a swift, wide, underground river, fed not only by family wealth and history, but by decades of personal accomplishment and connections.

Phoebe had done an Internet search on her mother once and gotten hundreds of thousands of hits, almost all on pages having to do with finance and monetary policy. There was much more information online about Catherine than there was about her ancestor Mayer Rothschild, who—with his five extraordinary sons—had established the family empire in Europe two hundred and fifty years ago.

There had been one blog where it said that Catherine had won a top-secret penny-poker tournament that had happened during the wee hours of a weeklong world economic summit. There was even a ten-second section of a video, showing her grinning, her white-streaked hair rumpled, while she raked in an enormous pile of pennies and the president of the World Bank bellowed in mock outrage. The next time Phoebe looked for it, though, the video had disappeared.

Occasionally Phoebe had talked with Mallory about her mother's place in the world. Mallory liked to ask probing, even disturbing questions about how having such a mother made Phoebe feel. But Phoebe could only guess as to how her mother's reputation might affect her own future life and choices.

"I wonder," Mallory had said, "if you're going to be vulnerable the way a child movie star is. You know. People will want to get close to you because they want something, not because they like you."

"Maybe gorgeous international playboys will want to marry me for my inheritance," Phoebe said. "They'll line up for my approval like in a beauty pageant. It would

Then Phoebe had felt compelled to

actually know if I will inherit much money.

ideas about how you have to earn your own way

How each of us has to contribute, and how you especially

to do that if you're, well, privileged. The more you're given, the more you owe, that sort of thing. And she supports a lot of good causes that need her money."

She groped for words. "She'd be so angry at me if I wanted a life where I just, I don't know, went to parties and shopped. Or even if I chose a career that she thinks is frivolous, like acting."

"You don't want to be an actress anyway," Mallory pointed out. "You sounded like a robot when we had to read *Julius Caesar* aloud in English class."

Phoebe laughed. "That's just an example. What I mean is that I can't take anything for granted with my mother. She wants me to be worthy. I have to live up to her and everything she's given me. I have to make her proud."

"Do you really?" Mallory asked. "Be honest, Phoebe. Sure, your mother probably wants you to have a career and all that, to use your mind and contribute, like you said."

Mallory's voice got a little tight. "But she's also just so—so motherly. In her own way. So you'll have things to worry about in life, sure, because everybody does, but for one thing, there's no way you'll ever worry about money. She'll make sure you're right, always, just like she does with your dad." A tiny pause. "I mean, he's a really nice guy and you know I just love him. And he's a great father and all. But he's not, you know, your dad's not—he's sort of ordinary. You've said that yourself about him. I mean, compared to your mother and her family and all."

Phoebe shrugged.

"I'm sorry, Phoebe. Maybe I shouldn't have said that. What I'm trying to get across—and doing a terrible job, obviously—is that your mother will always love you. Even if you turn out to be ordinary. You have the freedom to be ordinary. That's all. I'll shut up now."

"I know what you mean," said Phoebe. And she did. She knew she would always be loved. But that was not what Phoebe had been talking about, when she said her mother had expectations of her.

So Phoebe had changed the subject, because there was no way that Mallory was ever really going to understand this, and maybe also it was a little bit hurtful to even try to talk about maternal expectations and pressures with Mallory, given how different Mallory's mother was from Catherine.

Phoebe had been standing in Catherine's open office doorway too long. She saw her mother feel her presence, and look up from her meeting, the crow's-feet around her eyes and mouth deepening in a smile as she met her daughter's gaze. Catherine lifted one hand to indicate that she was going to be busy for a few more minutes. Phoebe nodded, made a "don't rush" motion with her own hand, and moved on into the family room, where she found her father standing tensely in front of the television.

Drew Vale claimed that he was a rational being who knew perfectly well he couldn't control the play in a football game by standing in front of the TV shouting. But you wouldn't know this from watching him.

Phoebe was used to her dad. She noted that the Patriots were ahead and sat down on the sofa to wait for a commercial so she could tell him about Mallory's brother's impending homecoming. He would be interested, she knew. Both of her parents would be. They were fond of Mallory and understood how important she was to Phoebe.

What Mallory had said about Phoebe's father was mostly true. He was fifteen years younger than his wife. He worked—not terribly often, to be truthful—as a producer of documentaries. People sometimes whispered that he was really a sort of peculiar boy-toy who had had the good luck to meet the extraordinary (but not exactly sexy or beautiful) Catherine Rothschild when she was past forty and wanting to marry and have a child. There had been all sorts of talk. But the bottom line was that Catherine and Drew's marriage worked, even if outsiders found it odd, and even if some people sneered at Drew. (Nobody ever sneered at Catherine; not even, at this point, behind her back.)

One reason the marriage worked was that the couple shared a near-complete indifference to what other people might think. Catherine Rothschild had trained herself to feel that way, but Drew Vale came by it naturally. It was, in fact, the quality in him that had originally caught and held Catherine's attention.

Phoebe was not like either of them in this. She knew it too.

A commercial came on. Drew turned to his daughter and listened with interest while she told him about Ryland. "Mallory thinks maybe her mother will perk up once he's here," she said. "But isn't it weird he was never mentioned before? And it makes me think he's got to be good-for-nothing, that he hasn't been around."

"Yeah," said Drew. "Although sometimes people need a while to grow up. I was pretty bad too, until I met your mother. Speaking of whom, is she still in that meeting?"

"As of five minutes ago."

"Okay. Are you hungry?"

Phoebe considered. "Yes."

Drew switched off the TV. "Let me watch this on the kitchen TV while we eat. Catherine will come when she's done."

In the kitchen, they found roasted chicken and salad that Jay-Jay had left for them, along with strawberry rhubarb pie for after. As Phoebe ate, she thought about Mallory's brother. Mallory had asked her to be nice to him, to make him feel welcome.

When the next commercial break came, Phoebe asked her father, "Can we invite Mallory and Ryland over for dinner once he's here? And Mrs. Tolliver too, if she wants to come."

"Sure," said Drew. "Just say the word." He reached over and patted Phoebe's hand. "Don't worry, honey. We'll go right on keeping a good eye on your friend. Brother or no brother."

Conversation with the Faerie Queen, 4

"Your Majesty, please, listen to me. Please change your mind. Don't send my brother! Listen to me—it's useless now. Phoebe isn't vulnerable as I thought at first. My brother won't succeed! I've been wrong all these years. I'm sorry! But there are two other Rothschild girls, Phoebe's cousins—they're old enough now. Send my brother to one of them instead. Or you could send me too. We would work together, fast—"

"No."

"But I'm begging you—"

"Stop. You are grabbing at shadows. And you have wasted four years. Four years, child! If it is not this girl, we are all doomed."

"I don't agree at *all*—"

"Do not contradict me. Do you think I know not of what I speak? You, who have been given borrowed strength from the court, you have forgotten how time is slipping away for the rest of us."

"No, Your Majesty. I haven't forgotten. I swear I

haven't. Your suffering tortures me. Let me explain what happened. You see, most human beings would feel ordinary next to her mother, and I thought for a long time that I simply needed to reinforce those feelings. But I know her better now, and—"

"Cease your babbling! I have little faith in your judgment anymore. This mission is now in your brother's purview. He will succeed in this where you have failed. She is old enough now to be vulnerable to a man, and from what you have told me, she has become wistful after love like most maids. Even if she has this inner strength you speak of, he will crush it."

"But, Your Majesty, it will drain off even more energy to send my brother and glamour him to appeal to her! He is so far from human in appearance and—"

"It matters not."

"Your Majesty—"

"I have decided. I would in fact bring you home now if you were not still necessary to the mission. You will now help and support your brother in every possible way to gain the girl's confidence and love. You shall do exactly as he says. He is now in charge. You will obey me and him."

"Yes, Your Majesty."

"You have both disappointed and exhausted me. Go prepare the way for your brother."

"I've started doing that. But you see, she thinks it's weird that suddenly I have a brother I never mentioned before, and my mother—I mean, the Tolliver woman—she never had a son, and—"

"All these small problems your brother will handle with glamour. We will spare no expense. You are dismissed."

"But—"

"Go!"

chapter 7

Mallory, her mother, and her brother, Ryland, came to dinner at the Rothschilds' the following Saturday night. That Mrs. Tolliver came too was a surprise because originally she had declined. But when the doorbell rang, there she was, flanked on either side by her son and daughter, and looking unexpectedly beautiful in her large, puffy way. She wore a violet silk dress with an enormous matching shawl, and she swayed slightly as she stood in the foyer in her backless high heels with their sharply pointed toes, her winter coat falling from her shoulders to the floor.

"My son is home now too?" said Mrs. Tolliver. Her voice rose in that insecure way of some women, making a question out of a statement.

"Yes, and we're so happy you can come celebrate with us," said Catherine. Phoebe's father echoed the welcoming words with something Phoebe didn't catch because she was intercepting a significant glance from her mother. Phoebe contained a sigh, smiled quickly at Mallory, who waved back, and then slipped away to do what her mother wanted: Set another place at the dining room table and inform Jay-Jay that they needed Skittles.

It was frustrating. Phoebe hadn't had time for more than the tiniest look at Ryland, and had only gotten a vague impression of him.

She lingered in the dining room, setting another place at the table, not wanting to face the cook yet. Jay-Jay was going to delegate her to go to the grocery store for the Skittles, she knew it, and Mallory, who had not even come to school the last few days, wouldn't want to leave Ryland to go with her.

Out in the foyer, Phoebe could hear the murmur of her mother's voice, talking to Mrs. Tolliver, but she couldn't make out what was being said. An otherworldly feeling slipped over Phoebe. They were all out there, and she was apart from them. It felt like the kind of spooky distance from the world that you sometimes experience when you have a fever.

Then a voice—smooth, deep, unfamiliar, utterly clear—cut into the distance. "Let me put away your coat, Mother. And yours, Mallory. Ms. Rothschild"—and now the voice moved closer—"do the coats go in here?"

Phoebe looked up.

Ryland Fayne was standing in the dining room archway, women's winter coats heaped in his arms, gazing straight at her with a pair of cool, analytical, unsmiling green eyes that reminded her, not in their shape or color, but in the quality of their calm gaze, of his sister.

He was tall and slim, but she had known he would be. Tawny-haired, like a lion; yes, she'd known that too, from his picture. His mouth was set a little crooked in his tanned face, and Phoebe vaguely recalled that it was now summer in Australia, from where he'd come.

Ryland Fayne was not handsome in any conventional way. His sharp nose and high forehead and thin, mobile lips were too individual for that. But he had a confidence about him, a presence. In this he was like Mallory, only more so. He was a male Mallory with more maturity and experience. And all of it, together—the full package that he was—it was—he was—

Phoebe felt like she'd been hit by a brick. Time seemed to freeze before she came to herself enough to speak.

"Hi," she said. Or at least, she felt her lips move. But she wasn't sure any sound actually emerged.

He was smiling at her. The impact of the smile, cool and reserved and watchful though it still was, stunned like a second brick. Phoebe flattened her hands on the polished dining room table to help support her legs.

She thought about looking away—she knew she needed to go to the kitchen—but she couldn't.

Like his mother, Ryland had dressed for the evening. He had dressed like an adult, in pants and dress shoes and a white oxford shirt with a wool suit coat. At least he was not wearing a tie. This was good because Phoebe was suddenly, horribly aware that she was not only dressed like a kid, but was also sort of a mess.

She had dressed casually on purpose, thinking it would be more welcoming, more like family. Why, why, why had she thought this a good idea? She could not remember; it now seemed like the purest disrespect and rudeness to their guests. Here she stood, shoeless and flat-footed in her black tights (which at least had no runs in them; she'd had to throw out two pair before she found whole ones), with a jeans skirt that she'd paired with a black sweater. While she loved the sweater, and even felt pretty in it, it was undeniably past its prime. In fact—Phoebe pulled her arms in tight to her sides—it was beginning to pill in the underarms.

But if she raced upstairs to her room and changed, he'd know she'd done it. Those eyes would miss nothing. Would that be bad or good? She didn't know, and anyway, she still had to tell Jay-Jay about Mrs. Tolliver and the Skittles. And no doubt she would have to race out to the grocery store too.

Ryland might already have returned her inarticulate greeting, might have said her name and hello and how nice it was to meet her and all that. Phoebe's mind was swimming so much she couldn't tell. He was still looking at her in her all-wrong clothes, though, and never, Phoebe thought, never had she been examined so carefully.

Not even by Mallory, back at the start of seventh grade,

when she had been deciding whether she would allow Phoebe to be her friend.

This was the thought that finally snapped Phoebe back to herself. Because it was funny, wasn't it? She'd been so vehement about telling Mallory how to dress, back then, and now it was Mallory who was stylish and she who was the ragamuffin. And here she was just about ready to beg Mallory's brother for friendship too . . . something about him . . . she wanted—wanted to please him—

No! No, she didn't. And she wouldn't.

She was not in seventh grade anymore. She was eighteen and she was not needy and she was not desperate.

Phoebe straightened her back and lifted her hands from the table. "There's a coat tree just over to the left, in the foyer, Ryland," she said. She gave him a professional smile as cool as his eyes. "Now, if you'll excuse me for a minute. I have a couple of things to do." She turned and went to the kitchen without looking back.

The shameful thing was that she hoped he was watching.

chapter 8

Phoebe never knew what her mother's original intended seating arrangement for dinner had been, because as they all moved into the dining room to sit down, Ryland turned to Catherine and explained that he'd had some back problems as a result of the long cramped flight from Australia. Could he please sit at the foot of the rectangular table, where the chair was taller and had a straight wooden back? This resolved itself into Phoebe, Ryland, and Mallory sitting at one end of the table, with their parents grouped at the other.

It also meant that for large portions of the meal, there were two entirely separate conversations going on, in part because Mrs. Tolliver had a dull, sad, whispery monotone of a voice that required concentration from Drew and Catherine even to hear. She was so unlike her daughter—and her son. It was amazing to think how different family members could be, not only physically, but in terms of personality.

On the other hand, Mrs. Tolliver took a lot of medication. So the Mrs. Tolliver they knew wasn't who she might have been. "If life had been kinder to her," was the phrase Catherine used.

Phoebe sat on Ryland's left, directly across the table from Mallory. From this position, she could glance at him now and then, but didn't have to look at him directly, which was a relief. She felt shy, even tongue-tied, which was ridiculous and she knew it. She had watched her mother orchestrate formal dinner conversation often, and understood the principles of small talk, of encouraging others to speak by asking them questions about themselves and their experiences. She had become decent at it and often even enjoyed it.

Yet tonight she couldn't think of anything to say. For a second she thought of catching Mallory's gaze across the table and mouthing, "Help me! Say something!" But she couldn't do it. She didn't want Mallory to know how uncomfortable she was with her brother.

If discomfort was what she was feeling.

And if it was something else—if it was—well, Mallory couldn't be allowed to know that either. It would have to be Phoebe's secret until she could talk herself out of it. Because it was ridiculous. Ryland was too old for Phoebe; she was too young for him. He would never be interested in her. And her parents would be shocked. She had to stop thinking—feeling—this way. Right this very minute.

Please, God.

Phoebe picked up the basket of warm whole-grain bread and passed it to Mallory and then to Ryland. To her relief, Mallory began talking about Jay-Jay.

"He's the cook, Ryland, and he's great. You'll meet him later, right, Phoebe? Anyway, he never forgets that I'm vegan. There's always at least one dish I can eat."

At least this gave Phoebe an idea for something to say. She looked toward Ryland, if not directly into his face. "Jay-Jay's afraid Mallory doesn't eat properly, so he tries to make up for it when she's here. He's made a vegetable curry tonight, Mallory. I think there's pineapple in it, and coconut milk."

"Yum." A shadow passed over Mallory's face, though, and she sent a glance toward the other end of the table for just a second.

"There's also going to be Skittles for your mother, after," Phoebe said.

Mallory smiled. "Did I already say Jay-Jay is great? And you."

"No problem." Phoebe was pleased. She hadn't waited for Jay-Jay to ask her to go to the store; she had volunteered.

Phoebe wondered if Ryland had noticed that she had also changed clothes. No, probably he had not. One item of black clothing would look the same as another to most guys, wouldn't it? Which was good, right?

But maybe she should give up wearing all black. Introduce

a little green, even just in the accessories. Or gray. Gray would be more subtle. She'd just die if she were obvious.

Stop! She had to behave normally, or she'd embarrass herself.

Phoebe forced herself to turn to Ryland. She tried to imitate Catherine and talk graciously, with dignity. "Are you also a vegan? Or just a vegetarian, maybe?"

"No," said Ryland easily. "I eat meat. Quite happily, in fact." He seemed to feel no need to add anything else, even though he was looking directly at Phoebe, examining her face. Phoebe felt herself blush. She ducked her head. She picked up her bread and unconsciously began to pull it into small pieces.

At least Mallory was talking now. "Phoebe, what did I miss at school this week?"

"Oh. Well. I, uh, I think there was a quiz in American history—but wait. You're not in that class with me. Um, in Spanish, that dialogue is due." She tried to remember. "Or maybe that's not until Tuesday. We should work on it, though. And then in chem—"

It was a relief when Ryland interrupted, in a drawl that had more than a hint of amusement. "Girls. No more. Please. Keep the details of high school to yourself."

Phoebe said happily, "It's a deal." And then, to her surprise, she found herself able to smile at him and add, with fair composure, to Mallory, "You know what? I'm having trouble *remembering* what happened at school this week. It's dull. And you just got your brother back and everything."

Mallory smiled, a little stiffly. "That's sweet of you."

Phoebe felt Ryland's gaze still on her. She turned to him.

"Do you always find school dull, Phoebe?" He asked as if he really wanted to know.

"Well. It's a good school," Phoebe said. "It's one of the best public high schools in the state."

"I know. Still, you might be bored and ready to move on to something else."

Phoebe wanted suddenly, urgently, for Ryland to think she was extremely smart, like he obviously was. Of course, she knew she was far from being as smart as her mother. But still, she was intelligent. She read all the time, even if it was mostly novels, and that had to count for something.

But she didn't know how to get this across—how to impress Ryland—especially given that right now she was having trouble putting together a coherent thought. She wasn't even sure she could name the novel she was currently reading. It wasn't anything impressive anyway; that she knew.

Luckily, Jay-Jay arrived with little vegetarian eggroll-type things with a spicy dipping sauce. There were introductions while Jay-Jay passed the food and dictated exactly how they were to eat it ("Fingers! Don't be shy!"). But once they had settled down again, Ryland immediately turned back to Phoebe and repeated his question.

"Yes, I guess I do mostly find school boring," she said at

last. "The subjects I'm taking are just prerequisites for college. But I might as well be in school as anywhere else. It's okay for now. Probably college will be more interesting, but I don't feel like I'm in any big rush to get there."

She shot a glance toward the other end of the table. What would Catherine think if she heard what was practically an admission of laziness? But her parents, thankfully, appeared to be fully occupied by Mrs. Tolliver; they were leaning in to hear something that she was saying. And if Drew was rubbing his forehead as if he might be getting a headache, well, that was only to be expected.

"Phoebe likes to keep a low profile," Mallory said. "She doesn't make waves. She does a good job at everything, but not *too* good a job. Except in English, of course. She doesn't even have to try there, she just loves it all." A hint of mockery—loving, teasing mockery—entered her voice. "Teachers love her."

Ryland laughed. "But you're more of a troublemaker, is that what you're saying, sister dear?"

"I am," said Mallory. "Question authority. Push back, that's my motto."

"I believe you," said Ryland. For a long moment, Phoebe watched as the brother and sister stared at each other. Then Ryland looked again at Phoebe. "But Phoebe doesn't like to be pushy."

Phoebe shrugged.

He leaned toward her. "What about when something bad is

happening? Something you have to take action to stop? Would you speak up then?"

Was she being accused of something? Cowardice? Not having principles? Phoebe put up her chin. "Mallory does it for me."

The other two laughed. But then Mallory leaned forward and began to tell Ryland about how Phoebe had "rescued" her back in seventh grade. "She was all ready to save me from the Big, Bad Seventh-Grade Girls," she said. "Take me under her protective wing and all. So, you see, Phoebe speaks up and acts when she feels she has to." Her voice was a little shrill; Phoebe gave her a careful look.

Ryland put a hand on his sister's shoulder, squeezed it, and smiled at Phoebe. "Thank you for looking out for my sister. Especially since you went against your more shy and retiring nature to do it."

"Oh," said Phoebe. She wasn't sure what her true nature was, to be honest, but she liked that he had praised her. In fact, she was blushing again; she could feel it. "Mallory looks out for me too."

Ryland's eyes were the color of dark seaweed. "You think so?"

"Yes. I tell Mallory everything," said Phoebe. "Sometimes I think she knows me better than *I* know me. That's what it means to be best friends." She paused, and then added, awkwardly, honestly, "And I don't have a sister. So Mallory—well, she's like the sister I would have chosen if I could."

"I see," said Ryland. He smiled a slow smile as Jay-Jay

came in with the vegetable curry and a spinach salad. "But I assume you're not also looking for a brother. Brothers are trouble. Right, Mallory?"

Mallory laughed, which helped Phoebe not to have to reply. Which was good, because any reply she might have made had frozen in her throat.

No. She definitely did not want Ryland as her brother.

By then, the whole table was occupied with the new food. Also, Catherine had taken control of Mrs. Tolliver and firmly begun a conversation that involved everybody, about the Passover seder she planned this year, to which all the Tollivers would be invited. It turned out that Ryland had never been to a seder before.

So the moment passed without Phoebe having to answer. But she had a feeling that Ryland hadn't needed to hear her say anything aloud anyway. That he'd read her answer on her face and tucked it away in his pocket.

CONVERSATION WITH THE FAERIE QUEEN, 5

"An interesting report. Your perception of the Rothschild girl differs from what your sister has said."

"Naturally, my queen. The girl will be quite easy to seduce and guide. I will be kind and say that my sister was perhaps blinded by spending so much time in the human world. However, she is yet of use to me."

"You are pleased then with your sister's cooperation?"

"So far, she has done everything I asked in introducing me to the girl and her parents, and in explaining the habits of humans to me. She has also obeyed my instructions for her future behavior toward the girl. There is subtle groundwork to be laid for me, and my sister shall do it."

"Yet you are frowning. Something displeases you."

"A small matter. My sister coddles the Tolliver woman. She suggested that I go with her to the woman's doctor. She said the doctor was dismissive of her, as a teenage girl, and might listen to me. She even presented me with a list of questions she wished me to ask this doctor."

"Did you do this?"

"Of course not. Waste precious time on the Tolliver woman? She is fed and housed in comfort and needs no more. There were even strangers coming and going to attend to her, which my sister had never mentioned to us. That is over now. I have dismissed the strangers and helped my sister remember that the woman is not really her mother and that we can give her no particular special care. We have a larger mission."

"Remind her also that the woman gains greatly in that she is allowed to live her fantasy of having family."

"True, my queen. And now I have tired you."

"Yes, but it was necessary. I shall rest soon."

"I shall work as rapidly as possible, my queen. This I promise you. Soon I will have the Rothschild girl secure."

"I know. We depend on you now."

chapter 9

A week passed. Phoebe didn't know whether to be glad or sorry that she didn't see Ryland and that life returned to its usual pattern. The only difference was that Mallory now talked about Ryland often, reporting his activities and talking about his character and past.

Phoebe couldn't hear enough about Ryland. But she tried to exercise self-discipline. Once, she even changed the subject when she thought they had talked about him too long. She was determined that Mallory never know how interested Phoebe was in Ryland. She would just be a good friend, she told herself, and let Mallory talk about him as much as she liked. Which, luckily, Mallory seemed to want to do.

The more she heard, the more Phoebe understood that her initial reaction of astonishment and anger at how Ryland had been away for the past four years had been misplaced. She hadn't understood. Ryland's father was not Mallory's father, for one thing, and there was apparently some divided loyalty on Ryland's part about that. "Long stupid story," Mallory said. And then Mrs. Tolliver at a different stage of instability had told Ryland she never wanted to see him again and he wasn't welcome in her house. Also, Mallory had been too proud to ask Ryland for help with their mother, which, Mallory said, was entirely her own fault. The bottom line was that Ryland was not to blame for having been absent.

But on the other hand, it wasn't like Mallory praised her brother all the time, either. Ryland was a complex individual, not some idealized figure of a perfect older brother.

"I'm so angry at him," Mallory said one evening. She had come home with Phoebe after school to study and stay over for the night, and they settled down in the library at the big worktable there, with their laptops. "Wednesday night, he just never came home."

"Oh," said Phoebe neutrally. Did Ryland have a girlfriend? So fast? Or maybe he had just hooked up with someone? He was so attractive—

She looked down at her laptop. "Do you know where he was?"

"No idea," Mallory said.

"Did you ask him?"

"Do you think I should?"

"I don't know," said Phoebe. "I guess not. I—did you call him? Or text?"

"Yes, I did, but that's no good. He likes to turn his phone

off. And then he forgets to turn it back on. For hours. I mean, is that responsible? Shouldn't you at least check messages every so often? Or maybe he is checking, and he's just ignoring me. Either way, I don't like it."

"Yes," said Phoebe. "You're right. What if there were an emergency and you couldn't reach him?"

"I know." Mallory, who was enviably good at multitasking, squinted at her laptop for a minute, and then sighed deeply. "But he won't listen to me. In his mind, I'm still twelve. Sometimes I feel like I need someone to be a go-between. Someone who will explain to him that I'm a grown-up now."

Phoebe's stomach fluttered. "Do you want *me* to do that?"

Mallory was gratifyingly open to the idea. "Do you think you could, Phoebe? You wouldn't feel funny doing it?"

"Maybe a little. But I could try. I'm willing."

"Well, it's up to you. I'll send you his phone number." Mallory lapsed into silence and focused again on her laptop.

Phoebe chewed on the inside of her cheek. She had permission from Mallory to call Ryland! But did she dare? She didn't know. Maybe. After all, she had practically promised Mallory she would. She wouldn't want to let Mallory down.

Phoebe forced herself to work on her essay for English for a while. Eventually, though, she sighed and said, "Five whole pages on *The Great Gatsby*. I don't know if I can do it."

Mallory didn't answer for a minute, and Phoebe had to repeat herself.

"Of course you can," Mallory said. "You're great at that stuff. What's your topic?"

"I don't have one yet. Got any ideas?"

Mallory frowned. Then, slowly, she nodded. "*The Great Gatsby*. Actually, I do. Write about the significance of Daisy Fay's name."

"What *is* the significance of her name?"

"You tell me."

"Daisy. That's a flower. She's little and pretty and—oh, only blooms in the summer. Maybe that means she requires wealth and privilege to exist. No wait, a daisy is actually pretty tough, almost a weed, which is even more interesting. You know, you're right, Mallory. There's something there. I don't know if I can spin it out for five pages, though."

"What about her last name?"

"Fay. Oh! You're brilliant, and I'm a complete idiot. Fay spelled with an *A*, which is a homonym for fey spelled with an *E*, which is another word for fairy."

"The author meant that Daisy Fay is literally a fairy?"

"Don't make fun of me. It's metaphorical. Daisy is ethereal and unreachable. Gatsby will never ever have Daisy the way he wants. She will never love him. And also, probably, F. Scott Fitzgerald means the name to indicate that Gatsby doesn't really know her at all. She's rich, so that's the same as if she were a different species from him. Again, metaphorically."

"You're all set," said Mallory. "Five pages is nothing. Throw in a little Shakespeare quote at the beginning. What's in a name, and voila." Mallory smiled. "Fay, Fay, Fay," she said.

A thought struck Phoebe. "Hey, Mallory? Ryland's name is Fayne, which is close to Fay. Is your brother unreachable and ethereal? Or a fairy, or—" She stopped talking and then, she couldn't help herself, she looked at Mallory and blushed. Was Mallory trying to hint to her that—

"I know just what you're thinking," said Mallory. "No, my brother isn't gay."

"I didn't say—and it would be fine—"

"You were wondering." Mallory went on rather intensely, "So, since he's not gay, with a name like Fayne, that must mean he's literally fey. Unlike Daisy Fay, who is only fey metaphorically."

Phoebe laughed. "I'm definitely writing this up," she said. "But without the part about your brother."

Mallory lapsed again into silence. Phoebe typed hard on her essay, the words coming to her easily now that she had the full spine of her argument. She even took some delight in saying in her concluding paragraph that she, personally, thought that F. Scott Fitzgerald was hitting the reader over the head with the name "Fay." A better writer would have been more subtle. She shared this excellent tidbit with Mallory.

But Mallory said, "I bet he didn't want to be subtle. He wanted the reader to know and used the name as a deliberate clue. And by the way, a few minutes ago you hadn't thought of it. So it wasn't all that obvious after all, was it? I had to tell you to think about the name Fay."

"But now I think it's too crude," said Phoebe. "From a literary point of view."

She finished her essay. When she looked up, satisfied, she saw that Mallory was again staring into space.

"Mallory? Are you okay?" Phoebe drew in a little breath and then dared say, "You're thinking about your brother again, aren't you? Worrying?"

"You think so?" snapped Mallory. Then she sighed. "Sorry. I'm actually thinking about my mother." She began talking rapidly. "Mother's been so obsessed with her gardening magazines. She's got a whole pile of pictures of herbs and flowers. And Ryland is into planting, why couldn't he help her plan a garden? It wouldn't take him long, and it would make her so happy."

"What does Ryland say?" Phoebe asked.

"He says she wants to dream. She doesn't want reality." She hesitated. "Phoebe? Don't take this the wrong way, but Ryland has dismissed the home health agency. He says that now he's home, he and I can take care of Mother together."

"What?!" Phoebe sat up straight. "Mallory! He can't possibly understand. He hasn't been here long enough."

"Well, the thing is, our family has leaned on yours enough. Too much. It's not right, Ryland says."

"No, Mallory! Listen, I'll talk to your brother. I'll make him see that it's no burden on us—it's just money, you know—and your mother's health is at stake here, after all. And yours, in a way. If he doesn't believe it from me, then my mother will talk to him."

"Phoebe! Please don't involve Catherine. She's done enough."

"But I can talk to your brother about this?"

"Yes. Yes, that would be okay."

"Then I will." Phoebe felt filled with righteousness. "I'll call him tonight."

Mallory bit her lip. "Phoebe, not tonight. He's got something going on tonight. I'll tell you when it's a good time to call. Just wait for me to tell you, okay?"

"I can just text him and ask when's a good time to talk."

"No, no, he never responds to text messages. He hates them."

"Really? That's weird."

"He hates the phone too. He only uses it because he has to. I'll let you know when to call."

"Well, okay, but it should be soon, right? For your mother's sake? The home health care people have to be called and everything."

"Yes, but—but I don't want my brother angry at me because I went to you about this."

"You're worried," said Phoebe compassionately. "Please don't worry. I know I can make him understand." She felt her heart rate speed up. She could. She knew she could.

"I won't worry." Mallory leaned over her computer again. "I

just—you know what? I've changed my mind. Please don't call him. I'll handle it. I'm sorry I brought it up."

Phoebe was silent.

"Please," Mallory said urgently. "Promise me you won't tell him I told you about this. Promise you won't call him after all."

"But Mallory—first you wanted me to talk to him about you being a grown-up, and then about this, and now you say—"

"Promise me! This conversation never happened. Promise me! Don't call him!"

"All right," Phoebe said finally, reluctantly. But she knew she was lying. She would talk to Ryland. It would be for Mallory's own good, and Mrs. Tolliver's too. And she'd apologize to Mallory later. This was yet another situation in which she knew better than Mallory what should be done, just as she had known four years ago.

She would call Ryland.

Her heart beat quickly, quickly.

chapter 10

Phoebe didn't feel comfortable contacting Ryland that same night, not with Mallory sleeping across the hall in the turquoise bedroom. But the next day at school, during her morning study hall, she slipped into the girls' restroom. Fingers trembling slightly, she texted him.

Need talk to u privately about something v important.

A moment later, she remembered that Mallory had said Ryland didn't respond to text messages. But the actual truth must have been that Ryland preferred not to answer *Mallory's* texts, because not two minutes later, Phoebe's phone trilled to signal a call.

And it was him.

Phoebe had not expected such an immediate response. She had a moment of panic. Then she sent up a quick prayer of thankfulness that she was alone, and also that she had fifteen minutes left of her study hall. "H—hello?"

Ryland's voice was deep, resonant, and faintly amused. "Hello, Phoebe Rothschild. What's so v. important?"

Phoebe had to struggle to remember. "Um, your sister—Mallory—she said something about, uh, about your mother's care. I wanted to talk to you about it."

"Did she?"

"Yes." Phoebe tried for a crisp, businesslike, adult manner. "Mallory said you've canceled the service that checks on your mother a few times a week. But they're needed. They make sure your mother is doing okay on her medications and eats enough and goes for a walk now and then, and, you know. Washes. They take her to doctor's appointments and things too. They make sure there are groceries in the house." She paced the restroom while she talked.

"Mallory and I can do all of that. We don't need to be paying strangers for it. Or perhaps I should say: your family shouldn't be. I'm grateful. I'll thank your parents as well. It's not that I'm unappreciative. But you've done enough."

Ryland sounded so reasonable that Phoebe almost found herself agreeing.

But she didn't agree, and after a moment, she recalled exactly why. "No, please, can't you understand? I mean, yes, Mallory can do those things for your mother sometimes, but it's such a relief to her to know there are professionals helping. She needs to be able to take care of her own life without worrying. She has to be able to go to school and study."

"And she needs plenty of time to be visiting with you overnight too?" said Ryland. "Which is where she was last night, correct?" There was a little teasing note in his voice. But there was also—also—

Phoebe felt her face heat up. "What are you saying?"

"What do you think I'm saying?"

Now Phoebe was embarrassed about her embarrassment. She did love Mallory, and why should she care what Mallory's brother thought about it? He could ask Mallory herself; that was what he ought to be doing.

But—but she did care what he thought. Suddenly, she cared terribly. She wanted him to be clear on this point. Clear about her.

She said, "Well, Mallory does come and stay often with me, but that's just because, you know . . . we're such good friends . . ."

"But what does it mean to be your friend, Phoebe?" The teasing note in Ryland's voice was paramount now; that other insinuation had vanished. Maybe she had imagined it?

Before she could reply—assuming she could even have thought of a reply—he went on. "I'm told that you have one other really good friend, a boy named Benjamin. But Mallory says she's never met him. Are you different with your male friends than your female friends, Phoebe? I wonder."

Was he—could he be—was Ryland *flirting* with her? No, no. Not possible. And yet—

Excitement began to flutter in Phoebe; she couldn't control it even though, in a way, it horrified her. She tried to calm herself down. Ryland was just asking a question.

"You mean my friend Benjamin Michaud? He lives on Nantucket. We have a vacation home there, that's when I see him. Mallory hasn't ever been able to come with us, even though I've asked her. She's never wanted to be that far away, in case something happened with your mother."

Phoebe discovered she was gripping her phone hard. "Benjamin's younger than me," she added, for no reason.

Ryland's voice, when he replied, sounded almost caressing.

"So he's just a friend, then, this Benjamin Michaud? Not your lover? And my sister, she is not your lover either?"

Phoebe was speechless. Her hand, where she held the phone, was sweaty.

"The answer to both of my questions is clearly no," said Ryland's voice.

Now it seemed almost as if his words caressed the rim of her ear before entering it and translating into sense.

"And I can also tell that I've shocked you. I apologize, Phoebe. You haven't had any lovers at all, have you? Not yet."

Phoebe tried to say something—anything—but all that emerged from her throat was a little croak.

She discovered that she had at some point stopped pacing, and that she now stood in front of the row of sinks. She was staring at her own face in the mirror. Her cheeks were flushed; her eyes were huge . . . her body felt—felt—

"I apologize again," said the voice. "I wanted to know, Phoebe, and so I asked. It was wrong of me. Can you forgive me for shocking you?"

"Oh," Phoebe managed at last. "O—okay."

"Really? Is it okay?"

"I—yes."

"Truly? Say you forgive me." Ryland's voice was a spectral finger that had reached out to trail down her bare spine. "I need to hear the exact words."

"I forgive you," Phoebe whispered.

"Do you? Say it again."

"I forgive you."

"What you say three times is true. Say it once more, but say it with my name, so that I know you mean it. Say, 'I forgive you, Ryland.'"

"I forgive you, Ryland," said Phoebe.

"Good," said the voice. "And now—"

The bell for the end of class rang, loudly, jangling, startling Phoebe so that she literally jumped. The next second, the door to the restroom slammed open and two girls came in. They looked at Phoebe indifferently as she stood clutching her cell phone, and then once more the door slammed and three more girls piled in, talking, laughing—

It was like being shaken awake from a dream.

"I have to go now," Phoebe said. "I have a class."

"All right, then," said Ryland easily. "I'm glad we talked, aren't you? Let's talk again. Call me. Will you?"

"Yes," said Phoebe. "Good-bye."

"Good-bye."

Phoebe held the phone to her ear for another long second.

She was sleepless that night. Turn and reposition though she might, she couldn't seem to find a cool spot on her sheets. She got up once, in the middle of the night, to turn on the light and stare at herself again in the mirror.

She wasn't beautiful, she knew, but was she pretty at all? Sexy, desirable?

Had Ryland really been flirting with her? Had he really asked the intimate questions that he had asked? Yes, he had. He had. She ought to be repulsed, because he was six years older. But he was gorgeous, and his voice—oh, his voice . . .

Her blood pulsed through her body. When she put a hand on her chest, she felt her heart thump. She couldn't stay still; it was as if she needed, *needed*, to climb right out of her own skin. Would she ever sleep again? She didn't see how.

What next? He had asked her to call him again. If she didn't, would *he* call *her*?

How would she feel when she saw Mallory again tomorrow? She had avoided her friend after the phone call. She hadn't felt ready to talk normally with her, after what Ryland had said about her and Mallory.

Benjamin too. Ryland had asked about Phoebe and Benjamin. Imagine that. It was as if he could not conceive of a friendship that was not, in some way, sexual.

Phoebe went back to bed but still did not sleep. After a while, she crept into her bathroom and had a long, hot bath, with bubbles and scented soap and bath oil from France.

Finally, finally, morning came.

Conversation with the Faerie Queen, 6

"Yes, Your Majesty. Ryland is—well, it's working. Phoebe's becoming obsessed with him."

"And Ryland, what is your opinion?"

"My sister is telling the truth, my queen. We have made excellent progress. The girl is fascinated."

"And your sister is cooperating? She is helping you?"

"Yes. Soon I will not need her anymore."

chapter 11

It was the first official day of spring in the month of March, but Boston was greeted by a gentle snow shower that scattered a light dusting of white on the landscape.

Phoebe enjoyed snow, especially when it came down all soft and unthreatening as on this particular March day. But knowing how Mallory loathed it—Mallory complained bitterly about every aspect of winter weather—Phoebe wasn't surprised to find that her friend had declared a personal snow day and not come to school. She was relieved too, because she still didn't quite feel able to face her. Out of guilt, she sent a stream of text messages to Mallory during the day. But as the day wore on and Mallory failed to respond to even one of them, Phoebe, vaguely, thought it was odd.

But the forefront of her mind was occupied with its own separate tug-of-war.

I won't call him, Phoebe thought. I won't, I won't, I won't.

I want to.

I won't.

And she didn't. But after school, she got in her car and found that, instead of driving home, she was on her way to Mallory's. She would just check in on her friend, she told herself. She would drag Mallory kicking and screaming out into the land of the living, even if there was snow on the ground there.

The Tollivers' driveway was empty, which meant Ryland was not home. Phoebe repressed disappointment, even though she acknowledged, in that moment, that she had really come to see him.

But it was Mallory she ought to see. It was Mallory who was her friend. She was lucky, really, that Ryland was not home.

She rang the doorbell and waited patiently, swinging her backpack in one hand. There was a light on inside, and Phoebe could hear the irritating elevator music that Mrs. Tolliver liked. Mallory would no doubt be wrapped up in bed in three or four quilts, pretending she was going to die of the cold. Since Mrs. Tolliver never got up from her sofa unless she had to, she'd be whining pathetically for Mallory to get the door.

But when Phoebe had rung three times without success, she gave up and reached for her phone. It was then that the door opened. And it was Mrs. Tolliver, not Mallory.

It was Mrs. Tolliver in a terrible state, her face streaked

with tears and her shoulders and chest heaving in loud hiccup-like sobs.

"Mrs. Tolliver, what is it?"

Mrs. Tolliver had already turned and walked unsteadily back into her living room. Phoebe followed her to the sofa, where Mrs. Tolliver collapsed and said something that the volume of the awful music drowned out. Luckily, the music player was within reach, and it only took Phoebe a second to turn it off.

"I'm alone," said Mrs. Tolliver to Phoebe. "I have nobody. I have nothing." Without the competition from the music, her voice emerged powerfully. It was very different from the dull, tentative voice she usually used. Hearing it seemed to startle Mrs. Tolliver; her body jerked as if in surprise.

Phoebe knelt beside the sofa, dropped her backpack onto the floor, and put a hand on Mrs. Tolliver's arm. "Now, you know that's not true. You have Mallory and Ryland."

Mrs. Tolliver blinked at Phoebe. "My daughter Mallory is dead," she said. "She died years ago. Who is this Ryland? And who are you?"

"I'm Phoebe, Mallory's friend. We've met many times. And Ryland is your son. He's been away for a few years, though. Remember? And Mallory isn't dead. She lives here with you."

"Oh." Mrs. Tolliver blinked at Phoebe. "Mallory didn't die of leukemia?"

"No! Of course not. Mallory is just fine. Mrs. Tolliver, were you asleep? Did you have a nightmare?" Then Phoebe had another thought. "Have you had your medication today?"

A sly expression slid across Mrs. Tolliver's face. "I had my Skittles. I'd rather have Skittles than any other pills. They help me more."

"I see," said Phoebe. This was by far the worst she'd ever seen Mrs. Tolliver, and she was a little frightened. The woman was totally disconnected from reality. She needed those home health care people! "Well, listen, I'm going to go get Mallory."

"All right." Mrs. Tolliver seemed suddenly to see Phoebe anew. "Wait. I remember you now," she said. "Mallory's little friend. It must be true, then. Mallory isn't dead. Thank God." She smiled warmly, all at once returning to apparent stability.

Phoebe was relieved.

"It's true. I promise. Mallory's alive." She's just sleeping like she's dead, Phoebe thought. "I'll go get her now."

"Oh, good, dear. Thank you!"

Phoebe escaped down the hall toward Mallory's room, the door of which was closed. She rapped on it, and when there was no answer, turned the knob and eased it open an inch. "Mallory?" she said. "It's Phoebe. Are you sleeping? It's after three! You have to get up! Your mom isn't doing well. She says she didn't take her medication, but I don't know what to get her, or what to do."

There was still no answer, so Phoebe went in.

She had visited before, but not often, and always in a rush

because she and Mallory were on their way somewhere else. So she had never really paused to reflect on the bare white walls of Mallory's room, the lack of any dolls or stuffed animals or other totems from childhood, except to think smugly about how different the room was from Mallory's other room at Phoebe's house.

But now it came to Phoebe as she glanced around that the two rooms were not really so different. Yes, the turquoise room at her house was cozy and warm and beautiful, while this room was white and barren. But in both, Mallory lived without leaving much of a personal mark beyond the occasional set of crumpled bedcovers. And in both, Mallory lived completely without items from her past.

Sad. And also weird?

Maybe there were still things about Mallory that Phoebe didn't know?

Phoebe looked past the barren room to the huge heap of quilts on the bed. At first she had assumed that Mallory was beneath it, asleep. But when she put her hand on them, the quilts collapsed into air.

The bed was empty.

Phoebe thought of Ryland's missing car, and of how Mallory had not returned messages all day. And she realized: Mallory's unauthorized snow day hadn't been about her sulking at home in bed. She had instead gone off somewhere with her brother—leaving their mother home alone, confused, no health care worker, and not taking her medication.

Phoebe sat down on the edge of Mallory's messy bed. She took in a shallow breath. Indignation and confusion filled her. She had spent an entire day obsessing over yesterday's conversation with Ryland, but somehow she had lost track of what she had originally meant that conversation to be about.

Until now.

She tried to think. First, she had better go back to Mrs. Tolliver and see if she could figure out the deal with the missed medication. Then, when the woman had calmed down a little, she would try calling Mallory again. Or—or she'd call Ryland. She'd scream at him this time. She'd tell him exactly what she thought. She wouldn't get distracted by his voice.

She got up to leave Mallory's room, to return to Mrs. Tolliver, and she looked around for a moment and noticed, once more, how barren it was.

And then Phoebe wondered: What did Ryland have in *his* room?

chapter 12

One moment, Phoebe was in Mallory's bedroom. The next, she was standing in the hall before the room next door, which she knew belonged to Ryland. His door was closed.

There was an instant during which Phoebe imagined being caught by Mrs. Tolliver. How embarrassing would it be if Mrs. Tolliver actually found her snooping in Ryland's bedroom? Or even outside, in front of it, with her hand on the doorknob?

Combined fear, shame, and excitement made Phoebe's heart beat fast. She knew she shouldn't do this. But she turned the doorknob anyway, because it was only going to be for a minute. Because she'd just take a quick look and do no harm. Because Mrs. Tolliver was totally out of it and Phoebe would never be caught.

Because she wanted to.

In a second, she had closed the door of Ryland's room gently behind her.

The room was dark, with only a small amount of daylight filtering in from around the edges of the window shades. Phoebe groped automatically for a light switch on the wall and pressed the one she found. When nothing happened, she thought it hadn't worked, and then realized that the room was indeed brightening, filling almost imperceptibly with a soft, warm, growing light.

The room and its contents gradually materialized before Phoebe's eyes. But it was not as if they had been there all along in the dark and were now revealed. It was as if they were budding right now, fed by the light itself, taking shape and form out of nothingness—first slender, shapeless shadows, then developing edge and texture, then seeming to enlarge, and then to subtly tighten, now taking on color, then depth, and then—then—

Phoebe gasped. She was no longer standing on the Berber carpet of a small suburban bedroom. She stood instead on an enchantingly worn stone path that lay just inside the archway of a private little walled garden.

Such a garden.

Although not large, the garden was bigger than the bedroom into which Phoebe had slipped. Beyond its low walls, which were covered with delicate new spring ivy, the vista of nature seemed endless, with purple hazy mountains in the far distance and a green forest in the near. But these only provided backdrop to the garden itself, for it was breathtakingly beautiful and yet cozy and welcoming; the kind of garden that seems the ideal mix of planning and accident, of wild nature and cultivation.

Sunlight flowed down on the garden from the clearest of late spring skies overhead; Phoebe could feel it warming her shoulders through her sweater. Just inside the garden walls were deep raised flower beds bursting exuberantly with lilies, daffodils, larkspur, sweet William, poppies, daisies, freesia, and anemones. Their scent drifted to Phoebe on a little breeze. Were these flowers even supposed to bloom at the same time like this, Phoebe wondered. Then she thought of Mrs. Tolliver's garden dreams. Surely this room, down the hall in her own home, was exactly what Mallory's mother longed for?

The strangeness of it all hit Phoebe. She felt her knees weaken. She reached out and found and gripped the stone archway, feeling its rough-hewn texture and its covering of ivy beneath her palm and fingers, and then against her back and head as she leaned on it.

The flowers. Their colors whirled before her eyes; their scents dizzied her. A few bees seemed to levitate above them; one drifted down into the petals of a half-open rose as if hypnotized, and Phoebe thought dazedly, *Me too*.

Nothing that the Rothschilds' own gardener had come up with was ever like this.

Finally she tore her gaze from the flowers and looked down. Yes, those were her feet. Her own regular size seven feet. She was wearing clunky red clogs that long ago, this morning, she had thought fun yet practical for a light snowy day, and a good way to start edging out of dressing entirely in black. But now, looking at them, Phoebe was forcefully reminded of the feet of the Wicked Witch of the East, which had stuck out beneath Dorothy's house in Munchkinland and looked so completely ridiculous that it didn't matter to you that she'd been horribly, brutally killed.

Had Phoebe now somehow entered Oz? Some magical place? But there were no such places. Not in the real world. Cautiously, Phoebe put more weight back against the archway. It felt solid and real. It was supporting her . . .

She closed her eyes and rubbed them. Dropping her fists, she kept her eyes closed because, when she did open them, she decided, she would be in a regular bedroom, Ryland's bedroom. With her eyes closed, plausible theories came easily. Mrs. Tolliver had slipped her a hallucinatory pill. Somehow. For some reason. Or maybe Phoebe was actually home, in bed, and asleep. With a fever.

Did dreams have scents? Did hallucinations? Phoebe could smell the flowers, feel the breeze and the sunlight, hear—was it birdsong? Insect buzz? Both? Yes.

"One, two, three," Phoebe whispered, and then she opened her eyes. There were her red feet again, solidly planted, and beneath them, the stone path. She turned to look at where the door of the room ought to be, just behind her. It was still there, weird in its ordinariness. She reached back for the knob and kept her hand—one hand—securely upon it.

Then she looked out again at the garden.

In the very center of the garden, ringed by the flower beds, lay a circular clearing or terrace, paved with the same mellow gray stone. Just beside this terrace, a large oak tree lofted its shapely branches high into the sky. And beneath those branches, in the perfect place for a little pagoda or a small pond or even a simple bench, stood a throne.

Once you saw the throne, you couldn't believe you hadn't noticed it before, for it was imposing; it commanded attention. Yet at the same time it fit completely and easily into the landscape, for it was made of trees and flowers.

A little table sat beside it, and on that table were a couple of stacked books. And as Phoebe stood with her mouth open, a plump little hermit thrush alighted on the top of the books and cocked its head to the side, its bright black eye seemingly fixed upon her.

Something about the bird jogged Phoebe's mind, and, one-handed, she groped for her phone. Click. The bird flew as she photographed the throne, the oak tree, the flower beds, and her red shoes on the path. Click, click. More flowers. The mountains in the distance. Click. She even stuck her arm out and got a shot of herself before the stone archway.

Taking the photos steadied Phoebe. She checked to make sure the camera had worked properly and that she had the pictures—she did—and then she released the doorknob behind her. Still clutching her phone, she stepped forward into the garden, slowly but compulsively following the stone path down the short flight of steps onto the terrace and up to the throne.

Her gaze was drawn to the books on the table. The one on top was familiar: *The House of Rothschild, Volume 1: Money's Prophets: 1798–1848*, by Niall Ferguson. Beneath it she could see *Volume 2: The World's Banker: 1849–1999*.

Of course these were books she knew.

And now, finally, she was afraid. She was overwhelmed by fear, in fact; it swelled inside her throat. She had meant to take one more photograph, a close-up of the books, but she didn't. Instead, Phoebe turned and fled. Reaching the archway, she grabbed the doorknob again—miraculously, she remembered to grope for the light switch and press it off—and she was out. She was back.

Back in the dim hallway of Mrs. Tolliver's normal little ranch house.

chapter 13

Once Phoebe was back in reality, she was tempted to whip around, reopen the door to Ryland's bedroom, and peek in again. Instead she clutched her phone more tightly in her hand. She had evidence.

It was then that she realized she was wheezing, and that her chest felt tight. The next second she remembered that she didn't have an EpiPen with her. Where was her inhaler? At least she had that, but where? In the little front pocket of her backpack, which was, where? Phoebe remembered taking the backpack from her car. She'd had it with her on the doorstep outside the house when she'd rung the bell. Then Mrs. Tolliver had opened the door, and she'd come in—and she'd dropped the backpack in the living room.

She felt dizzy. With one hand on the wall, she walked rapidly toward the living room and Mrs. Tolliver and her backpack. She knew better than to panic. Panic made things worse. And there was no cause for panic; she knew what to do. The only thing that made this asthma attack different from any other time was that she'd just been in that magic garden—or that she had just hallucinated a magic garden—or dreamed it—or whatever.

Maybe she was allergic to something in that garden. Did that mean the garden had to be real? Could asthma be triggered by something imaginary? Actually, yes. Because wasn't anxiety imaginary? And anxiety had always been able to trigger Phoebe's asthma.

She reached the living room, and none too soon, either. The wheezing had stopped—she did not have enough breath to support it.

Which was bad, bad, oh, very bad.

Blurrily, Phoebe saw Mrs. Tolliver lying on the sofa, curled up on her side facing away from Phoebe. Phoebe ignored her and scanned frantically for her backpack.

There it was, a black lump on the beige carpet. She collapsed on the floor beside it and pulled it toward her. There were excruciating seconds of groping blindly inside before she closed her shaking hand around the familiar shape of her inhaler, dropping her phone in exchange.

Now, okay. Now she knew what she was doing. Sit up. Secure the spacer on the inhaler. Breathe out hard. Raise head. Lips around spacer, fingers on trigger. First puff, and with it, the good feel of the medication spray on the back of her throat. Wait; count. Breathe out hard again. Second puff. Normally she'd stop there—but now, a third puff.

Phoebe clutched her arms around her knees and put her head down on them, closing her eyes. She felt the smallest tear trickle out of one eye and moved her shoulder slightly to wipe it away. Mrs. Tolliver hadn't even stirred off her sofa to see what was wrong with Phoebe; maybe she was asleep. It didn't matter. Phoebe could take care of herself and she would. She had. She would take another couple of puffs soon. She was already recovering too. The tight feeling in her chest was beginning to ease. Wasn't it?

She just needed to sit still now. Sit still and breathe. And be calm.

Phoebe did not remember the next few minutes. It was as if she were a black dot in the center of an entirely white, entirely empty dream landscape. She focused only on her tight chest and her breathing, hearing nothing, not even thinking.

Then suddenly noise impinged on her—a door opening and closing, the stamp of feet, the rumble of voices saying words she couldn't make out. It was almost, Phoebe thought fuzzily, as if the voices were speaking some lilting, foreign language. But of course this was only because she was still so out of it. She knew, a moment later, that it was Mallory and Ryland who were speaking. Relief filled her.

Mallory was there. It was all right now, because her friend Mallory—Mallory the calm, Mallory the cool, Mallory who loved her—was there.

And yes, Mallory was kneeling beside her, arm around her shoulders, saying her name, grabbing her hand that was still clutching the inhaler.

"Oh my God, Phoebe. Are you okay?"

Phoebe tried to look up but could only manage to turn her head a little.

"She's bad, Ryland," Mallory said. "Out of it. I'm calling 911."

Phoebe couldn't understand the words Ryland said in reply. A spurt of alarm filled her, because this must mean she was sicker than she'd thought. She managed to get her head up so she could look at Mallory. Mallory was looking at her brother. "No," she said to him distinctly. "We have to take care of Phoebe. She needs human medicine." Then Mallory's eyes went back to Phoebe's face.

"I. Understand. You," Phoebe told her.

"Of course you do. Don't talk, Phoebe. You're all sweaty. Your breathing sounds awful." Mallory had her phone out and was pressing numbers. Phoebe relaxed as she listened to Mallory giving crisp, accurate information to the emergency operator, even taking hold of Phoebe's inhaler and spelling the name of the medication Phoebe had taken.

"I'm. Okay," Phoebe got out, when Mallory hung up.

“Shut up. Yes, you will be okay. At the hospital. Now I’m calling your dad.” Two seconds later, Mallory was speaking into her phone again. “Mr. Vale, Phoebe had an attack at my house. She’ll be fine. I’ve called for help.”

Phoebe tuned out and closed her eyes. She didn’t have to listen or worry anymore. Mallory would do everything perfectly. Her dad wouldn’t even be panicked because he knew Mallory had dealt with Phoebe’s attacks twice before. He would trust her, just like Phoebe did.

The ambulance would come. The medics would give her oxygen. They’d probably make her go on a stretcher even if she thought she could walk. At the hospital, they’d give her medication, keep watch, and in the end she’d get to go home to her own bed by tonight. Because she was fine. She was going to be fine.

She could feel Mallory’s hand on her forehead.

“Your dad will meet us at the hospital, Phoebe,” Mallory said. “Everything is under control.” Her voice was gentle and almost chatty. “You know, you were a fool not to call 911 yourself. I hope you weren’t thinking my mother would have the sense to do it.” A slight pause, after which Mallory made a little impatient, resigned noise. “Okay. I’m just going to make sure she’s breathing too, which I’m sure she is. Oh, wait.” She pressed Phoebe’s arm. “Hear the sirens? That’s your ambulance. I’ll get the door.” Phoebe felt her move away.

The sound of the sirens got louder, nearer.

"Phoebe." It was a soft breath of air on her left ear.

Turning toward it, Phoebe opened her eyes. She knew before she did so, though, that it was Ryland.

What she hadn't expected was that he would be so close. He was sitting cross-legged on the floor mere inches in front of her. How long had he been there? Phoebe's startled—and then guilty—eyes met his. She saw his thin, mobile lips moving in a smile, even though the expression in his green eyes was indecipherable.

As if it were entirely natural, Ryland took Phoebe's hand. His palm was hard, and his hand was large enough to swallow hers up.

Then, with his other hand, Ryland reached forward to run his fingers through Phoebe's flyaway, russet hair. She felt a tug as he detangled something and pulled it out. Then he held it up before her eyes.

It was a delicate new leaf of green ivy, the same ivy that had been entwined over the stone walls and archway in the secret, magical garden she had entered through Ryland's bedroom.

Ryland's gaze held Phoebe's. She would have looked away in shame if she could have, but she could not.

"Poor little Phoebe-bird," Ryland whispered. His hand tightened on hers. "You can't even sing. What spring woodland were you wandering in?"

Conversation with the Faerie Queen, 7

"Yes, it could have been a disaster, my queen. But it won't be. In fact, I believe it will end up an advantage, that the girl entered Faerie for a few minutes."

"I was interested to see her. She is not at all like my Mayer. She's dull-witted and fearful. I am glad. It is—easier when one is not fond."

"Yes, my queen. She is exactly what we need. I don't know how my sister could have failed to guide her properly. But I won't fail. She'll come to me now, and soon. Whatever the price, I will induce her to say the words we need."

"And your sister?"

"I will still need her help for a time with the girl, but also with the woman. Then I will ease her out. Her return to the court will restore some share of energy and balance to you. I regret it cannot be more."

"Any measure will stretch what time we have. None of this will take much longer, I hope."

"No, my queen. A month, perhaps two. You will be as beautiful as ever you were."

"I no longer care about beauty, Ryland. I have been thinking, however. I now understand what my Mayer did, and why. Before, I did not. My own situation is similar now in some ways to his."

"He imperiled us for his own survival."

"He did not know that he did so."

"No."

"I was the one who misjudged the situation, Ryland. I was the one who offered him the bargain, and I was the one who accepted his adjustments to it."

"You were not alone. For many years, we all misjudged the cost of our end of the bargain. Any year now, we thought, balance would be restored."

"And we behave now as my Mayer did then, taking from others because it is the only way to save ourselves. But we know fully what we do, which he did not. And we use guile, which he also did not."

"Yes, my queen. It is ironic, but necessary, and not even worth thinking or talking about now. We must do what we must do."

chapter 14

It was a blessedly quiet weekend. Phoebe was forbidden by her parents to go anywhere or do anything but rest at home. Even though she had recovered from her asthma attack and would normally have protested her confinement, or at least insisted that Mallory come visit, this time Phoebe did neither. And although she did not bother to put her feelings into words, they showed in her actions. Basically, wherever Catherine was, Phoebe wanted to be there as well.

Luckily, it was not one of the times when Catherine was away, something that tended to happen nowadays about one week in four. In between, she worked at home or in her Boston office, or used quick day trips to New York City and Washington, D.C., for meetings that, for reasons having to do with confidentiality and security, needed to be taken face-to-face.

It still sometimes felt strange to Phoebe when Catherine was gone, because, for the first twelve years of Phoebe's life,

Catherine had rarely been away from her. Anybody who absolutely needed to speak with her in person had simply been forced to travel to Boston.

This weekend, after the asthma attack—and really, after what had happened with Ryland, though she wasn't quite ready to think about that, and her heart beat a little too fast when by accident her mind drifted that way—Phoebe wanted that feeling again. She wanted, though she couldn't express it, to feel like a child; an important, even spoiled child for whose happiness and convenience the adults made automatic, massive adjustments, and who never, ever, not even for a moment, would not be safe. So she followed her mother from room to room at home, and when, on Sunday afternoon, Catherine mentioned planning to go into her office in Boston to work, Phoebe blurted, "Can I come too? I'll bring my laptop and do homework. I won't bother you."

"All right," Catherine said, after a moment of consideration. "And we can have dinner out afterward in Boston, if you'd like. Just us."

Phoebe's face lit up. "But will Dad feel hurt?"

"I wouldn't think so. We'll just tell him we want some mother-daughter time."

"Okay," said Phoebe happily. "Can we go to the North End?"

"Sure."

Phoebe hadn't been to Catherine's office on Rowes Wharf for a while, and enjoyed being there again. The office building was attached to a big hotel on the waterfront. Catherine's suite held a reception area with sofas and a desk for Catherine's assistant, a meeting room with a big oval table and high-backed, softly padded chairs on wheels, and a small kitchen and bathroom, along with Catherine's actual office, which had been deliberately designed to impress and also to intimidate. All of the rooms except the kitchen and bath had windows that overlooked Boston Harbor.

Phoebe went into the meeting room and stood watching the boats and activity in the harbor below. The water taxi arrived at the hotel marina and unloaded passengers who had just come from the airport. As Phoebe observed one man talking on his phone, she realized that she had taken her own phone out and was clutching it. Again.

She sighed as she tucked it back in her jeans pocket.

None of the photos that she had taken of Ryland's garden were any good. Oh, the pictures were there. It was simply that they showed only gray lumps and gray shadows against a gray background.

There was no evidence. Phoebe had not even so much as a leaf in her hair anymore for proof that the garden had been real.

But she knew it was real. In a way, the fact that the photos were useless was evidence. It was real enough to need to be concealed. Magically concealed, perhaps. It was evidence, at least, to Phoebe herself.

Her stomach churned a little with a feeling that was part excitement, part fear, and part something secret that she didn't yet feel able to examine closely. When she let herself think, questions came to her, questions that were, like the water-needles from an expensive shower, sharp and stimulating. Who was Ryland? What was going on? What did Mallory know? And what was she, Phoebe, to do? Should she talk to Mallory, ask questions, confide? Or should she go directly to Ryland?

No. Not Ryland. Phoebe couldn't. She felt hot with embarrassment and . . . something . . . even thinking of that. When she couldn't stutter out a normal conversation with Ryland before all this, how would she talk to him now?

Poor little Phoebe-bird, can't even sing.

His hand on hers.

God. Was she blushing?

"Darling? I thought you were going to do some homework." It was Catherine, in the doorway. Her voice was mild, inquiring.

Phoebe spun away from the window, not entirely unhappy to be interrupted. "I am. In a minute. It's just that the water taxi came and I kind of got mesmerized, looking at the people."

"I know." Catherine came up beside her daughter and they looked out together. "Sometimes I think I would do better in an office with no windows," Catherine said. "But other times, I love it here." Together, they watched the water taxi load more passengers. It seemed mostly to be businesspeople, in suits even on the weekend, who were taking the water route to the airport. There was not one child or teenager among them.

Phoebe leaned against her mother's shoulder and breathed in the comforting scent of her perfume. Catherine was a pragmatic woman without much in the way of personal vanity, but she had a signature French perfume. Its scent was light and barely perceptible, and yet once you had noticed it, it was wonderful. Phoebe was allergic to so many things, but she had never so much as sneezed at her mother's perfume.

She leaned into her mother and put her arm around her waist, and felt Catherine do the same, hugging her close. And then Catherine said, "Phoebe? I was wondering if there was anything in particular you wanted to talk to me about?"

Yes! Phoebe thought. And then: No! No, I can't.

Poor little Phoebe-bird, can't even sing.

"No," she said to her mother. She turned her gaze to the scene out the window.

"Are you sure? You know that sometimes when you have an attack, it's because you're worried about something. You might not even be aware you're worried, but your body knows."

What spring woodland were you wandering in?

"I don't think I'm worried about anything," Phoebe said. "I think the attack just happened because, well, it's spring now.

Allergens everywhere. What I need is to be more careful."

"Well, but nothing is blooming yet. There was even snow on the day you had the attack, and—"

"Yes, but I've remembered now that I forgot to take my pill that morning. I might have forgotten to use my morning inhaler too. I'm not sure about that part." The lie came out of Phoebe so smoothly, so easily, and so entirely without premeditation that she was shocked. "That's what I meant about being more careful," she said. "I'm so sorry."

"Phoebe—"

"I didn't want to worry you, Mom. I promise, though, I won't forget again."

"Phoebe." Catherine gathered her daughter in her arms. "Don't you *dare* forget your pill again."

"I won't." Phoebe hugged her mother back. How could she have told the truth, anyway? Maybe if she'd had the photos, she could have shown them to Catherine and said, *I think I must have been allergic to something in this magical garden that was behind the door of Ryland's bedroom.*

Except she knew there was no possibility of her saying anything about the garden to either of her parents, and there never had been, photos or not. The garden—the garden—what had happened belonged to her and her alone. Even if she didn't know what to do about it; even if it had caused one of the worst asthma attacks she'd had in years; even if she should never have gone into it—it was still hers.

Suppose she hadn't gone in? Suppose she had seen that Mallory wasn't home and had then simply said good-bye to Mrs. Tolliver and gone home? Then she wouldn't know now that Ryland . . . thought about her. Her, or her family. It was the same thing, wasn't it? Those books.

His eyes on hers.

The feel of his hand.

Suddenly, uncontrollably, Phoebe's whole body quivered. She pushed herself away from her mother, ducked her head down, and picked up her backpack. "Well," she said. "I suppose we both had better do work now."

"I suppose so," said Catherine. "We can talk later, over dinner. Just in case there is something bothering you."

"Sure," said Phoebe. "But there isn't. I promise."

chapter 15

Phoebe sent a text message to Ryland once she was home again that night. After considerable agonizing, she had decided on a simple invitation: "Coffee and a talk sometime soon? Just me. No Mallory." She stared at the message for a long time—changed "me" to "us" and then back again—before she finally sent it. The next moment, she wished she could recall it.

But she couldn't. It was sent. He would read it. He would know that she—that she—

She almost hoped he would wait for a day or two before getting back to her. But—as had happened the first time she texted him—her phone trilled the music for a message less than two minutes later.

Phoebe's fingers were clumsy as she accessed it.

"Tomorrow at 3 at Natalie's."

Natalie's, Phoebe thought. Brilliant.

Brilliant because—she suddenly realized, and it made her anxiety level skyrocket—she'd have to somehow ditch Mallory after school, and at least she could be sure that Mallory would not go to Natalie's.

Natalie's Café was not far from the high school. It was a small, colorful place with original—and usually bad—art for sale on the walls and casual food that cost a little more than it should. On weekday afternoons, the café attracted mothers with their babies in strollers instead of teens from the high school, and, to Phoebe's mind, this was a good thing because you could usually get a table.

Mallory hated Natalie's, however, because she had once almost crushed a live spider in her fruit salad. She had offered the spider a gentle finger and it had waved one leg delicately, as if in acceptance, before walking regally onto her hand for transport outside. Mallory had steadfastly refused to return to Natalie's after that, even though Phoebe had pointed out that it wasn't as if the spider had been found dead. This left Phoebe to sneak in alone sometimes in pursuit of a certain panini-style grilled cheese sandwich. The sandwich had both cheddar and Swiss between thick slices of farmhouse bread, and the butter it had been grilled in came off on your fingers when you picked it up. Phoebe suspected it contained an entire day's worth of calories, and it was, in her opinion, worth every last one.

Suddenly, painfully, Phoebe wished she were tall and willowy, like Mallory. If only she could lose ten pounds overnight. If only she routinely wanted the fruit salad, not the grilled cheese.

But still, Ryland had texted her back immediately. He wanted to see her. He could have blown her off, and he hadn't. Unless he was just indulging her, being nice to his sister's friend. No, no. That couldn't be. She had the evidence of the books.

Of his hand in her hair.

Little Phoebe-bird.

Thank God for text messages. Thank God she didn't have to speak to him.

"OK," Phoebe texted back.

By tomorrow, she would have herself in hand. She would use the social graces she had learned. She would sound sensible and sane and cool and sophisticated and only a little curious, in a mature way. She would not sound like a stupid little teenage girl who was—because she had to admit it, if only to herself—

In love.

Obsessively, crazily in love with her best friend's mysterious, fascinating—and magical?—older brother.

The next day, Phoebe arrived at Natalie's Café fifteen minutes before three o'clock, and was almost blown inside by a strong spring wind that caught the restaurant's storm door and threw it wide, while the string of bells on the inner door chimed out in tinny cacophony. She had to take a step back outside to grab the storm door in order to try to pull it closed. But as she was struggling, she felt Ryland come up behind her from inside the café. She knew it was him without even looking. Then Phoebe was inside the café and he had shut both the storm and regular doors behind her. He was standing two inches away from her.

The door bells were still clanking.

He had gotten to the café before her. She hadn't expected that, and it rattled her. Still, Phoebe looked up at him straightforwardly. She was not going to behave like an idiot. But the impact of meeting Ryland's gaze, green and cool and a little quizzical, dissolved her confidence. Though she finally managed to get the "hello" out, it sounded feeble and uncertain.

Her meticulous plans for what she was going to say to Ryland—how she would challenge him about the magic garden and about those Rothschild books—melted away to emptiness.

The problem was that Ryland just looked normal, in his jeans and a black-and-white long-sleeved henley shirt. Handsome, yes, and intriguing (Phoebe couldn't help noticing that the girl behind the café's counter was checking him out too), but not one single bit magical. He had even missed buttoning a button on his henley. Her fingers itched to fix it.

She tightened her hand on her bag.

All right. The wild thoughts she'd been thinking about the

garden and what it might mean—thoughts fueled by the kind of romantic reading Mallory laughed at but Phoebe loved, about faeries and danger and magic and forbidden love—they were silly. And she was silly, and also pathetic, for having delusional adolescent fantasies about her friend's older brother. He was just an ordinary, gorgeous, older man whose shirt buttons she desperately and inappropriately wanted to do. And undo.

She ought to leave. Make some excuse and leave.

"I've chosen a table toward the back," Ryland said. "There's more privacy there."

Phoebe glanced around. Right now, along with the single employee behind the counter to take orders and prepare them, there were only two other customers in the café, women at a small table at the front who had tea and scones before them and were talking intensely, oblivious to the rest of the world. The table Ryland was nodding toward was farther back, in a nook just beyond the pastry case. Phoebe could see Ryland's khaki-colored down vest slung over the back of one of the chairs.

Phoebe's pulse sped up. She knew she was not leaving. She walked toward the table, aware of him behind her. She wondered how messy her hair was, but didn't let herself put up a hand to smooth it.

Oh, God. She couldn't even remember what normal behavior would be so that she could simulate it. Should she talk about Mallory? That was what they had in common. That was *all* they had in common.

"I told your sister I was coming here," Phoebe blurted the second they were seated. She knew she was talking too fast. "I mean, I didn't say anything about meeting you, but I told her I was going to Natalie's. She's staying over tonight and ordinarily we'd just have gone home after school and so I told her that I was craving this special thing they make here and that I'd just run over after school and have it and then go back and get her at the library later. She hates it here—I was thinking you must have known that? She mentioned it sometime? The spider incident? I'm a little concerned she'll finish her homework at the library early and come here anyway to meet me, even though she does hate it." Phoebe stopped talking only because she forced herself to. She was pretty sure she hadn't even made any sense. She chewed on the inside of her cheek.

Ryland shrugged. "Mallory can come if she wants. I was just respecting your wishes for a private talk." His emphasis on *your wishes* was subtle but definite. She felt even more like a stupid girl with an inappropriate crush on a man who was being kind about it.

"Oh," she said. "I guess there's no problem then."

There had to be a way to leave now, quickly, before she died of mortification.

Except she still didn't want to go.

"Let me get you something." Ryland stood up. "Coffee, of course. And what was that special thing you just mentioned that you wanted here?"

"Um." Phoebe did not actually like coffee, but it felt immature to say so. "The panini grilled cheese. But I was just saying that. To, you know, to have an excuse for Mallory."

"So it's not good?" There was something about those green eyes and the way they fixed on her. He was laughing at her inside, the way he'd laugh at a child. She knew it.

Phoebe said miserably, "Well, you know. It's got like a million calories."

"I think you should have one. That way you won't have lied to my sister about what you were doing here." He paused, and then said: "Truth-telling is a science. There are . . . nuances."

He smiled kindly. And then he was gone before Phoebe could react either to the smile or to what he'd said. She was left to stare at his back as he ordered at the counter.

Nuances? That was a creepy way to look at truth, surely. The plain fact was, she was lying to Mallory, because a lie by omission was still a lie, not a nuance. She was choosing to lie and ought to at least own it to herself.

But this was only a little lie, and one that she didn't intend in any way to hurt Mallory. It was just that Phoebe's business with Mallory's brother was private . . . maybe especially from his sister.

Was that a nuance?

Phoebe watched Ryland as he talked with the girl behind the counter, watched that girl smile at him and be flirty, even though he was clearly with Phoebe. Maybe, Phoebe thought, it's obvious that he's older. She tried to estimate the age of the pretty girl behind the counter. Twenty-two, twenty-three? A more appropriate age for Ryland than Phoebe. She wondered if he liked the look of her. Was he flirting back?

Not that Phoebe was in a position to resent it.

Ryland returned with two coffees. Phoebe took a sip and found it hot and bitter. She wrapped her hands around the mug, which was warm. The gesture at least gave her something to do with her hands.

"Sugar?" said Ryland as he sat down across from her.

"No, thanks. I'll just let it cool a little." And there's another lie for you, Phoebe thought. She sneaked a quick look at Ryland.

He reached and put his hands over Phoebe's on the coffee mug. His touch was cool. He said quietly, "You went into my room the other day. That's what you wanted to talk to me about. Yes?"

She'd have looked away if she could have, but there was no possibility of it. "I—I—yes." Then, feebly, staring into his unreadable eyes: "I'm sorry."

Ryland didn't say anything, but he looked at her. And looked at her. She had no idea what he was thinking.

She was very conscious too that they were in a public place. She kept her voice low as she stumbled on. "I tried to tell myself I was imagining what I saw. Or having a hallucination—maybe because I was oxygen-deprived. But I don't think I was. Was I?"

"What did you see?" He was still covering her hands, entrapping them, actually. Suddenly she wasn't sure that hand-holding was always romantic.

"A garden," she blurted. "I know it was real. Please don't play games—" His hands tightened over hers. Somehow she knew it was a warning to stop talking, to be careful. And in the next moment the pretty counter-girl was standing beside the table.

"One grilled cheese panini." She put it down on their table. Phoebe felt rather than saw her notice that Ryland's hands were over hers, and in a dim place inside her, Phoebe felt a primal satisfaction, as if she had won a fight. The girl turned and walked away.

And by the next second, Phoebe had forgotten her. She made a motion to pull her hands away from Ryland's. But he didn't let her go.

"I know what I saw." She stared straight at him.

Without rushing, in his own time, Ryland released her hands. "Drink your coffee, Phoebe." He smiled, a crooked smile.

Phoebe still did not want the coffee, but she raised the mug to her lips and sipped at it anyway. It was as bitter as before. She said, her voice still very low, "Tell me I saw what I saw. Please don't play games. Please." Then she wished she had left off that last "please."

Ryland pulled the plate with the grilled cheese on it toward him. It looked wonderfully cheesy and buttery and delicious, but Phoebe no longer felt any interest in it.

"I like games," Ryland said mildly. "Just so you know."

"But I—I need—"

"Shut up, Phoebe," said Ryland. But he said it in a tone that seemed instead to say, *You're delightful.* The contrast between words and tone was both confusing and weirdly reassuring. Then he picked up the sandwich. It had been sliced into two. The insides oozed cheese in long reluctant strands as he pulled the two halves apart. He held one half out to Phoebe.

"For you, little Phoebe-bird," he said.

And it was like the first time she'd seen him, that same feeling, like she'd been hit by a brick, like she was almost about to lose consciousness, like there was nothing else in the world anymore—

His voice was silky and caressing. "When you've finished your half, I'll take you home with me for a little while. I'll show you my room, since you're asking about it. After that, you can go be with my sweet little sister. Who, by the way, thinks she owns you. But she doesn't. Does she?"

"No," said Phoebe, who hardly knew what she was saying. "We're best friends. But that's all."

"I thought so," said Ryland. "Now, eat up. Good girl."

chapter 16

It was a very quiet Phoebe who picked up Mallory later that afternoon. She wanted to act normal in front of Mallory, but in the moments when she was able to wrench her mind back from thinking about Ryland, she couldn't recall exactly what acting normal meant.

Who was Phoebe Rothschild? Was she usually chatty? Would she talk about school stuff? Was there anything she had meant to tell Mallory, or ask her? What had happened at school today, anyway? Phoebe couldn't remember anything from before she had met Ryland at Natalie's today.

And she couldn't think about much besides what had happened after that.

Phoebe had gone home with Ryland for one stolen half hour. With her hand in Ryland's as he pulled her along, she had tiptoed past Mrs. Tolliver, who was sleeping on the sofa with her afghan flung over her face. Phoebe had gone down the hall with

Ryland, and—heart pounding—entered his bedroom with him.

Where there was of course no enchanted garden.

It was a regular bedroom, as bland as Mallory's, with white walls, two windows with roller shades, a nightstand, and a small desk heaped with papers. And also, naturally, a bed—unmade, with tumbled sheets and a comforter slipping off one side. Phoebe glanced at it only briefly before looking down, away, anywhere else but at it or at Ryland.

He stood a scant inch behind her, so close that she could feel heat radiating from his body. His hands came down suddenly, heavily, to curve over on her shoulders and gently but forcibly position her in the middle of the room. His breath stirred the hair on top of her head. His voice was low, amused, narcotic. "Do you see anything unusual here?"

"I—no." Phoebe's answer whispered out of her throat.

Only when she felt his breath against the back of her bare, suddenly dampened neck did Phoebe realize Ryland had gathered her hair and moved it aside. "What do you see?"

"Uh—furniture."

She felt his mocking smile against her skin. "I see my bed. Do you see it too, or do you see that garden bower you mentioned? Or maybe, hmm, both?" His breath moved to her ear.

Now Phoebe literally could not reply. She had no breath, no thoughts, no words. But it wasn't asthma—

"Poor little Phoebe-bird."

His body brushed heavily against her back as he moved around her, stood in front of her.

Phoebe felt heated and ashamed, frightened and excited. Somehow she found the courage to look at him.

Holding Phoebe's eyes, he moved deliberately backward a few steps. He sat down on the edge of his bed. He was no longer the slightest bit amused, there was something else in him now, an emotion just for her; an unmistakable desire. It pulled at her. It felt perilous, exciting, and more than anything, disarmingly honest in its longing. Phoebe chewed the inside of her cheek and tasted blood. Reality was a regular bedroom that only felt enchanted, and that was enough.

He opened his arms.

She never remembered going to him. She was simply there, standing before him, reaching out her own arms, moving—awkward, untried—onto his lap. His arms wrapped around her, a dragon whipping its muscular tail around a small prey—no, what a weird vision! Another stupid hallucination. Phoebe closed her eyes—

Ryland's hands settled on either side of her head. They turned her mouth to his, gently, gently. His lips teased hers; warm, soft. His body, his arms, his hands, his lips on hers, his mouth opening hers.

She'd never been held like this. It was astonishing; she felt secure and at the same time, deliciously, dangerously, *wanted.*

Then the salt taste of her blood filled both their mouths. It sickened Phoebe, but Ryland murmured something, and she didn't pull away after all, but instead moved closer and—

Mallory's scream broke through Phoebe's fog.

"Phoebe—red light!"

Belatedly, Phoebe stepped on the car brakes. A horn blared ferociously from somewhere, while ahead of her a white Subaru wagon swerved, just missing Phoebe's car. She caught a glimpse of the driver's angry face and of his mouth moving, his middle finger flashing, before he was through the intersection and away.

Two other cars were now blowing their horns at her as well.

Phoebe exhaled. "Sorry," she said to Mallory. "Sorry, sorry!"

With the car at a standstill, Phoebe leaned her head momentarily on the steering wheel.

It had just been a kiss. True, a kiss on a bed, with arms wrapped around each other, bodies pressed against each other, but still only a kiss, no more than a kiss, she was eighteen, why couldn't she be kissed, what could be wrong with a kiss, even a blood-filled kiss—the blood was Phoebe's own fault, of course, for chewing her own cheek, a terrible habit, she had to stop it. There'd been no time for more than a kiss . . . which was good, wasn't it? Or was it?

"Phoebe? Would you drive on now?" Mallory sounded panicked, but not as panicked as Phoebe felt. "You can't park here in the middle of the intersection. Go a little farther and then pull over. Can you do that? Phoebe?"

Phoebe gathered herself. "Right. Sorry." She lifted her head, and then, after another second, moved her foot off the brake and got the car moving forward again. She drove gingerly through the intersection and, when it was safe, pulled over to the side of the road and parked. "Sorry," she said again. She glanced helplessly at Mallory. "I was thinking about—about—um, maybe it would be better if you drove?"

Mallory exploded. "What's wrong with you, Phoebe? Have you gone crazy suddenly? I don't know how to drive!"

"Oh," said Phoebe. "I knew that. Bad joke. You could hardly do worse than me." She tried a smile.

Her lips felt strange. Of course they did. She ran her tongue nervously over the wound on the inside of her cheek. His tongue had caressed that too—

"What's wrong with you, Phoebe?" Mallory's eyes were narrow.

"Noth—"

"Don't you dare say nothing's wrong. This is me. What's going on?"

Phoebe averted her eyes, but she could feel Mallory's gaze boring into her like a laser.

The desire to tell her everything was strong. She could almost feel the words pressing against her throat, clamoring to come out.

Mallory, I've had such a crush on your brother since I met him, and I found out today he's interested in me too, and so we're going to just try and see where it goes. Don't worry; I won't neglect you and neither will he. We talked about that already. Actually, I think it will be great! I already love you, so it just makes sense, doesn't it, that I'd love your brother too? And even the other way around? And imagine—and I know this is way too soon, years too soon, to think about—but imagine, what if Ryland and I ended up married one day? We would be sisters! And you're the exact sister I would have picked if I could. How great would that be?

The rush of words in her head sounded hysterical even to Phoebe. She was glad she wasn't going to say them. Ryland had said not to confide in anybody, not yet. He had said they needed to keep this a secret, at least for now, from everybody.

At first Phoebe thought he meant that they should keep the secret only from her parents. She had not needed that warning; she knew that would be a bad idea right now. Her parents would worry about the age difference between her and Ryland—silly, given that the age difference between Phoebe's parents was even wider.

But Ryland had meant Mallory too.

He said, "You don't know Mallory as well as I do. I know you think you do, and it's sweet that you care so much about her. I like that. But there're some family things that go into Mallory's makeup, and I know them and you don't, and so

I'm a better judge. She's a complicated girl. She's going to be jealous of you and me. She might even warn you away from me. So we'll have to handle her carefully, and we really don't need the stress of that just yet. We have other things to focus on. More important things." He'd paused. Smiled. "Personal things. You understand?"

She'd blushed. "Yes."

"Also, I don't really like the thought of you confiding, uh, private things to my sister. You know what I mean?"

She did.

She had said she would not.

"So you won't talk about me with my sister? You promise? And if she tries, you'll refuse to listen? You'll leave her?"

"Okay. Yes."

"Phoebe?" Mallory's voice had risen. "You look so strange. Is everything all right with your parents? You didn't just get bad news—an accident, or—Catherine was traveling today, wasn't she? She's okay? Phoebe? Your mother is okay, right?"

This shocked Phoebe out of her unwitting haze. Why in the world would Mallory suddenly be worrying about Catherine having an accident?

"Yes, of course my mother is okay." She turned fully toward Mallory. "She's fine. It's nothing like that." She found herself laughing, ironically glad of the change of subject. "God, Mallory! Believe me, something like that, I'd tell you right away! I'd be crying in your arms, I'd be—and you'd better believe I wouldn't be driving! Licensed or not, I'd make you do it. I'm sure you could figure it out."

In that moment all the tense, strained feeling between the girls disappeared. Mallory laughed too, and Phoebe grinned back. "What I'd do," said Mallory, her calm self again, "is call Jay-Jay. Or a cab. I'd take care of everything, though, because you'd be a wreck. You're right about that."

Phoebe shuddered. "No kidding. I don't even want to think about it." Then she thought of something she *could* tell Mallory. "It actually is a little bit about my parents, just not in the way you mean. It's my SAT scores. I was trying to figure out a way to break it to them that I didn't do well. I was rehearsing what I might say."

Mallory leaned in, frowning. "Wait, you got your scores? How come you got them and nobody else did?"

"No, I didn't hear about them yet. But any day now, and since I already know how I'm going to do, I just want to be ready. My mother is going to be disappointed."

Mallory sighed. "One, you don't know how you're going to do. You're just guessing. And two, you're wasting time and energy on stuff you have no control over."

"I know, but—"

"Listen, do you feel safe to drive again? You can pull out now; there isn't anybody coming."

Phoebe pulled out again onto the road. It was only a few

more blocks to her house, and she managed to stay carefully focused both on her driving and on the lecture Mallory was delivering. "I'm sure you did better on the SATs than you think, but even if not, you can study this summer and take them again in the fall. Plus . . ." Mallory fell silent as Phoebe drove into the garage and turned off the car. They got out and headed inside.

"Plus what?" Phoebe prompted, more to show that she was paying attention than because she really wondered what Mallory was going to say.

"Plus, you don't even know that Catherine would be disappointed."

"We'll see." This was comfortable, familiar territory to be on with Mallory. Mallory insisting that Phoebe was better than Phoebe herself thought. The dangerous moment—the desire to confess—had safely passed and she could breathe easy. For now, anyway.

So there was only the evening of acting normal to be gotten through—dinner, homework, chat—before she could be alone in her room and call Ryland.

Only a few more hours and then she would hear his voice again, and be reassured that what had happened with him today was real, not a dream or another stupid hallucination.

It was actually worth knowing she might be a little bit unstable, a little bit crazy, if, in exchange, Ryland wanted her.

Conversation with the Faerie Queen, 8

"Your Majesty, please listen to me. I know Phoebe better than my brother does. It's true that I failed with her so far. But he's going about this the wrong way. Seducing her—playing with her mind—please—"

"He has told me his plan and it has met with my approval. Child, listen to me. I understand what you are feeling. But we have already tried it your way. We do not have much time. And you now have one last important part to play in your brother's plan."

"What's that?"

"You will now quarrel with the girl. It will be simple enough. He has told her that she is to conceal from you that she is involved with him. When she has done this long enough to feel guilty, then you will act. You will reveal to her that you know. You will be very angry at her for her deceit. You will hurt her with your words, as deeply as possible, and thereafter you will no longer be her friend. This will isolate her so that she depends entirely on your brother. Do you understand?"

"I—yes. I understand."

"There will be no changes or plans of your own. That time is past."

"Yes, Your Majesty."

"You will do exactly as you are instructed. I must have your promise on this, child. No improvisations; no better ideas."

"I promise. I know we're out of time. I won't fail now. I'll push Phoebe away and—and hurt her."

"As badly as you can, child. Undermine her sense of herself to prepare the way for the work your brother has yet to do on her. This is where her trust in you will be of good effect. If she believes you think poorly of her, she will think the worse of herself."

"Yes, Your Majesty. It's true. I can make her bleed inside. It's only that—"

"What?"

"I'll bleed inside too."

"I have read your heart, child, and I understand. You may indulge in sadness about it later on."

"I understand. I—I know that you're right. I'll do it. I'll obey."

"In every particular, you will do as your brother has decreed."

"Yes. I will. There's no other way for us."

"And, child? I remind you: In any sacrifice, blood is always involved."

"I just didn't think that it would be like this. For me."

"You made that choice, child."

chapter 17

The next couple of weeks were both exciting and troubling. Phoebe felt as if she were a spy, figuring out with Ryland safe times and places to meet in secret. It was difficult, which in practice meant they could meet only briefly, frustratingly.

Once, Mallory was also there. That was nerve-racking, but Phoebe discovered that part of her almost enjoyed the need to pretend in front of Mallory that she and Ryland hardly knew each other. The secrecy—paired with a few taut, clandestine seconds when Ryland laid his warm hand at the base of Phoebe's spine, while Mallory was only inches away but turned in another direction—was—it was—well. It was dangerously, shamefully, wonderfully erotic.

A split second after this incident, when Mallory turned back to face Phoebe and Ryland, Phoebe observed a sharp glance dart from Mallory to her brother. For one flash of a moment she thought Mallory knew, but then Mallory had smiled and laughed as if she didn't have a care in the world. Then Ryland laughed as well, and Phoebe knew she and Ryland had fooled Mallory. She was so relieved; she didn't want to disappoint Ryland.

There were other ways in which the secrecy felt right too, and Phoebe decided this was because her feelings for Ryland were like a tender new plant that needed a protected environment in order to grow. She would probably not have confided in her parents at this stage, she told herself, if it had been some boy at school or even her friend Benjamin on Nantucket, who her parents liked. So why should this be different? Why should she feel guilty about not telling her parents about Ryland yet? She would not.

On the other hand—with another boy, she'd certainly have told Mallory. It would have been a delicious part of the whole experience; sharing with Mallory, laughing with Mallory, getting advice and opinions from Mallory. Phoebe felt so sad about missing this, and at first she couldn't figure out why. She had never heard anyone, anywhere, claim that part of love was talking to your best friend about it. Heroines in romance novels weren't calling their friends every day and reporting in, were they? Jane Eyre, for example, loved Mr. Rochester in tortured silence.

Jane Eyre had no best friend, however. A better example was *Pride and Prejudice*. Mr. Bingley and Mr. Darcy couldn't blink without Jane and Elizabeth Bennet discussing what it might mean. Phoebe longed to talk to Mallory like that, but she couldn't. Apart from the uncertainty about how Mallory would react, Ryland had forbidden it.

So maybe it was Phoebe's consciousness of this missing piece that caused the new, uncomfortable constraint between her and Mallory. Maybe this was why Phoebe found that she was suddenly unable to talk normally to Mallory anymore, even about things like school that had nothing remotely to do with Ryland.

But Mallory was acting odd too. She was jumpy, brooding, quick-tempered, and impossible to understand. Her behavior had changed in general, not only toward Phoebe. One day in school, given a surprise math quiz, Mallory simply curled her lip in scorn and crumpled the paper. Phoebe could almost see the black storm cloud over her head, and she had a sudden flashback to the Mallory of seventh grade, with the tawdry fairy wings hanging off her back, the Mallory who had seemed so ferocious, so needy, and yet so completely incomprehensible.

Phoebe didn't say a word about the quiz. She didn't even dare ask what the math teacher said to Mallory after class. She was too afraid that Mallory would whirl on her, scream at her publicly. She could almost feel that Mallory longed to do just that. And Phoebe's guilt about Ryland made her feel that she deserved it. But that didn't mean she wanted it.

It was in fact amazing how quickly the mood between the

two girls ripened toward an explosion. Phoebe could almost feel it coming . . .

And it happened on a Friday night; the same Friday on which Mallory had spurned the math quiz. Mallory had that afternoon abruptly announced that she was staying over at Phoebe's.

There was nothing unusual about Mallory inviting herself; she had done it all the time in the past. Her room at the Rothschilds' was truly hers, after all. But Phoebe could feel how different this was. Every minute of silence or forced conversation weighed heavily on her. She wondered how her parents could miss the strained atmosphere, but they chatted at dinner in the usual way.

By eight o'clock, the girls were alone in Mallory's turquoise room. Mallory sat on her bed, her back propped with pillows, tapping on her laptop, while Phoebe rocked, uneasily, in the little Shaker chair by the gas fire and pretended to read. She was supposed to call Ryland soon. How would she do that, knowing that Mallory was just across the hall? Should she go downstairs and call from the library? Slip out into the garage and call from her car? Should she text instead? But Ryland hated texting. He had told her that it was important to hear each other's voices, if they couldn't see each other.

She was just trying to find the words to tell Mallory she was tired and was going to bed—even though it was barely past eight—when her dad showed up at Mallory's open bedroom door.

"This came in today's mail for you, Phoebe." Drew Vale handed over a college brochure. "It got mixed in with my mail. Huh. Oregon. Are you thinking of going west?"

"No. There are plenty of good schools here in Boston," said Phoebe. "Why go far?"

"It's up to you, of course." Drew smiled at his daughter and at Mallory before he left.

Mallory looked up from her laptop, her fingers stilled. "So. Suddenly you want to stay in Boston for college?"

"It's just an idea." Phoebe had made the comment about Boston without really thinking, but now she realized that it was because of Ryland. If he stayed in Boston, she'd want to also.

"But you used to talk about wanting to go to England," Mallory said. Her voice made Phoebe squirm; it was accusing and hard. "Last fall, you spent hours and hours looking at Oxford's website. You were talking about how great it would be to be near your cousins, and that you'd be able to go to London and stuff like that. You were trying to talk me into coming too."

"Oh. Well," said Phoebe weakly. "That was just talk. It doesn't matter where I go."

Mallory snapped her laptop shut and put it aside. "Really? Why doesn't it? What's changed?"

"I don't know. I'm just going to be an English major. Everybody has good programs in English literature."

"That is just so not what you were saying before."

"I guess I changed my mind. Can we not talk about it now?"

Silence fell in the room; heavy, loaded silence. Phoebe thought again about excusing herself.

"Phoebe?" Mallory's voice was quieter now, less accusing. But something about it made the flesh on Phoebe's arms crawl.

"What?"

"It's about my brother."

Phoebe's whole body went on alert. Ryland had told her not to talk to his sister about him—about them. If she did, he would be angry. She didn't know why that was so very bad, but it was. *It was.*

Phoebe leaped to her feet and headed for the bedroom door.

But almost as if she'd teleported there, Mallory was suddenly in front of Phoebe, slamming the door shut in Phoebe's face, and then backing up against the door to block it.

"I have to go," Phoebe said. Her pulse drummed in her throat. "Excuse me."

"You're not going anywhere until I've said what I have to say."

Mallory's face looked like it was carved from ice, and Phoebe knew then, not exactly what was coming, but that it would be terrible. Maybe even worse than Ryland's anger.

But she also thought that she deserved it. She straightened her shoulders and met Mallory's eyes. "All right," she said evenly. "Go ahead."

There was one strange moment in which Mallory said Phoebe's name. Her name only, and as she said it, a wistful note in her voice seemed at odds with the rage that radiated from her. But in the next second Mallory grabbed Phoebe by both shoulders, and there could be no doubt of her complete wrath. "I know about you and my brother," Mallory said. "You lying little sneak."

Phoebe swallowed. But it was true; she had lied and she had sneaked. "I'm sorry. I—when did you—I'm so sorry. I wanted to tell you, Mallory, but—but Ryland said—and of course he's right—it's private. I thought later—I—he—we would tell you later—"

"You're just up to your old tricks, aren't you, Phoebe?"

"I—what?"

"You don't know yourself at all, do you, Phoebe?" Now Mallory sounded almost casual. She released Phoebe's shoulders, but stayed close. "You dumped Colette for me. Now you're dumping me for my brother. You don't care who you hurt, just so long as you get what you want when you want it. You're like a bratty toddler. And if you can't get what you want in a straightforward way, then you try to buy it."

Phoebe gasped.

Mallory continued, "You've been treating me like a piece of trash for over two weeks, and now I know why."

Phoebe managed to say, "No—I mean, Mallory, I never meant—"

"Don't even try to deny it. You've been lying to me and avoiding me. And you talk to me in that fake nicey-nice voice, like I'm someone you hardly know. I had to invite myself over tonight. You didn't ask me."

Everything that Mallory had just said was also true. Sort of. Phoebe tried to think of how she could explain. "You've got things all twisted—"

"Twisted? Me? Funny. I'd say you're the one who's all twisted." Mallory's eyes glittered as she leaned closer. "And you don't even have the brains to see it for yourself. You have this totally delusional la-la-la picture of who you are. Sweet little Phoebe, helping others! Yeah, right. Twisted is the word for it. It's really so you can show off. Feed your own little ego."

"Mallory—"

"And your ego desperately needs feeding. You want to know why? It's because deep down, you're nothing. And you know it too. All those talks we had about your fantastic mother and your extraordinary family? The ones where I tried to reassure you? But you weren't really reassured, were you, because you already know the truth. You've said it yourself sometimes. You don't belong in your family. You're actually so dull, it's unbelievable. If you weren't your mother's daughter, she'd be so completely bored talking to you, she wouldn't even be able to remember your name. You've never had an original thought in your life."

It was like being stabbed, Phoebe thought. Mallory's face so close to hers, her low, mean voice going on and on—stabbed and stabbed and stabbed—

And she couldn't even move, as Mallory went on—

"When I met you, you'd sold your very soul just to belong to Colette's little group. Don't deny it. Then you sold it again to be my friend. You begged me, remember? And now you're doing the very same thing with my brother. Just now, Phoebe?" She mimicked viciously. "*Oh, I'm going to be a little English major! I can study anywhere.* Right? You're all set to throw out your own ideas about college because you wonder where your boyfriend might be. It's true, isn't it? That's exactly what was going through your mind, five minutes ago. *Isn't it?*"

Finally Mallory stopped. Finally. But she was still in Phoebe's face and her question rang in the air, and Phoebe knew the answer.

"Yes," she whispered.

She closed her eyes, briefly, against the scorn and disgust that flooded Mallory's face. When she opened them, Mallory had cocked her head to the side and appeared to be waiting for Phoebe to say more. But Phoebe had nothing else she could say, and it wasn't only because her mind was empty with shock and hurt and defeat and shame.

"I'm going to go get your inhaler," said Mallory crisply. "You'll be fine after a couple of quick puffs. And by the way, Phoebe? Your asthma is just another one of your selfish, stupid manipulative techniques." She opened the door and within a few seconds was back again from Phoebe's room across the hallway, with Phoebe's inhaler.

Hand shaking, Phoebe snatched it. She felt Mallory watching her while she worked the mechanism.

After a few minutes she looked up. She still couldn't believe that she had heard what she had heard. "Mallory," she began. "You can't have meant it—"

Mallory interrupted. "Yes, I did. I meant every word. You are nobody. You're an empty name, Phoebe Rothschild. Go and be with my brother if you want. It won't help you. Nobody can help you."

Phoebe lingered for one more moment, looking at her ex-best friend, unable to believe what had just happened. Thinking that surely, surely, Mallory would take it back.

Though even if she did, Phoebe knew she'd still never forget a word Mallory had said.

You're a bratty toddler.

Never had an original thought in your life.

Sold your soul to belong to a group, and then to be my friend, and now for a boyfriend.

Selfish.

Stupid.

Manipulative.

An empty name.

Mallory held the door. She said pointedly, "Good night, Phoebe."

Phoebe stumbled from the room.

Conversation with the Faerie Queen, 9

"So, the great friendship is over."

"My sister was masterly. I thought the girl would never stop crying when she came to me. She said that she now believes that all these years, my sister secretly thought she was an empty little rich girl with no special personal qualities and that she only pretended to value her. Given the high esteem in which the girl previously held my sister's opinion, she can't help wondering if it could be true that she is nothing. It reinforces her worst fears and will continue to eat away at her."

"It sounds as if the girl will be ready for us very soon."

"Soon, but not immediately. My sister was right that the girl is stronger than she looks. More work must be done to destroy her fully."

"You sound so hard, Ryland."

"Is it not best?"

"Yes. Of course. It is only that I have had too much time to think these days. Empty time breeds useless regret for what cannot be helped. But let that go. Ryland? It is now time for your sister to return to court."

"If you can manage without her, I ask that this not occur yet. My sister is still useful in taking care of the woman and I have not the energy for that myself. I need all that I have to manage the girl and complete what my sister has begun."

chapter 18

Ryland had rented an apartment, a little studio in a brick building about five miles away from Phoebe's school. A week after the horrible scene with Mallory, Phoebe went to meet him there.

It was after school on the last day before spring break. Phoebe had been feeling so sad and depressed about Mallory. Mallory's bedroom across the hall from hers, with Mallory's stuff still in there, was a constant reminder. Phoebe had taken to keeping its door shut.

The end of their friendship was now a second secret to be kept from her parents. She knew at some point it would have to be confessed, but it was too enormous and painful to tell them right away. She would also have to come up with a lie about what exactly had happened, because she couldn't imagine telling her parents what Mallory had said to her. Even if she omitted the information about Ryland, she hated the thought of repeating to her parents what Mallory had said about her.

She had run to Ryland, though. That very night, she had called him and told him what had happened, and they had met the next day at Natalie's. She'd cried buckets, sitting across the table from him, and he had been amazing. She needn't have worried that he would take Mallory's side. He had said too that Mallory had always had a hard, mean streak, even when she was little, and that the only surprising thing was that Phoebe hadn't seen it before. "She has a very jealous personality," Ryland said. "It's one of the reasons I thought we shouldn't tell her about us. You'll be lucky now if she doesn't make a scene about it at school. You'd never be able to cope with something like that."

Phoebe hadn't even thought of that possibility. Ryland was just so smart and considerate and insightful. She was so lucky to have him.

She hoped he would eventually tell Mallory he loved Phoebe, though. Then Mallory would realize that a relationship took two people; that Phoebe actually hadn't chased Ryland the way she—for the first time she was ashamed of it—the way she had chased Mallory. Or *had* she chased Ryland in the exact same way? She wondered. She'd called him and invited him to meet her that first time. She had thought she was being honest and up-front. Also, it had really been to talk with Ryland about the garden—the weird, imaginary garden—

She winced away from examining the sequence of events too closely. She pushed the emotions, the doubts, and the confusion down and away and out of sight.

Bottom line: She hoped Ryland would tell Mallory that he found Phoebe to be smart and lovely and incredibly special. She hoped it would hurt Mallory to her core to discover that her brother and her friend had truly fallen in love. She hoped it would make Mallory feel even half as isolated and betrayed as Phoebe felt now. Even if Mallory did make a big scene at school—which was something Phoebe actually couldn't imagine her doing, but Ryland said he knew his sister better than she did—it would be worth it to Phoebe, if she was really loved.

Phoebe found Ryland's new apartment building in West Newton easily, but then had the thought that she needed to buy him a house-warming gift. The only shop nearby was a supermarket, though, and ten minutes later, she was still wandering its aisles. They had a flower shop, but the flowers all looked a little sad and wilted and picked-over. A cake? Too birthday. She thought longingly of the extravagant, perfect presents she could have gotten if she'd had the brains to think of this earlier—and then she remembered one of Mallory's comments about Phoebe trying to "buy" what she wanted. Finally she grabbed some chocolate-dipped cookies. In the end, by the time Phoebe actually rang Ryland's bell, she was three-quarters of an hour late.

He buzzed her in immediately and she felt her heart start

pounding. Three flights of stairs and then she stood, finally, before Ryland's door.

This was the first time they would really be alone together, safely private. Suddenly, Phoebe realized that she was nervous. This was why she'd gone to the grocery store and wasted so much time there.

Oh.

She knocked once, tentatively. Twice. Then a third time. He was there—he had buzzed her in. Was he angry that she was late? Phoebe felt strange and illicit, standing in the hallway of an apartment building, more dressed up than she usually was, knocking on the door of a place she'd never been before, nobody knowing where she was or what she was about to do. It was exciting. But . . .

But she could also just leave. Part of her wanted to.

No! She straightened her shoulders and stayed where she was. She lifted her hand to knock again.

The door swung open and there he was. Ryland.

He seemed even taller than Phoebe remembered, and more handsome. He didn't say anything, merely nodded and stood back so that Phoebe could enter. His face was unreadable—not welcoming, not anything, almost empty—and, seeing it, Phoebe understood that she had expected an expression of happiness at seeing her. A kiss. An embrace. Something that would enfold her and reassure her and drown the anxiety inside her.

“Hi. I’m late. Sorry.” She held out the cookies. “I realized I should bring something. So. Um. I got this.”

“Thank you,” Ryland said. At least he was looking at her. He took the cookies, but didn’t so much as brush her hand in the process. He closed the door, but still made no move toward Phoebe. She shifted awkwardly from one foot to the other, and Ryland looked down at her shoes and said, as if he were a stranger, “Those look painful.”

She had hoped he would think the deep blue three-inch heels were sexy, with their lacy ties that wrapped in a crisscross pattern around her ankles. At school today, Colette Williams-White, queen of high-fashion shoes, had even paused to gush at Phoebe about them, seemingly quite sincere.

“I like these shoes,” Phoebe said. Her voice quavered.

“You don’t really have the legs for them. Take them off.” Ryland turned his back on Phoebe, but threw over his shoulder, “Come in the kitchen. We can have tea.”

Phoebe was still wincing inside over the legs comment as she bent clumsily to undo the tiny, tricky laces of her shoes. Tea? That didn’t sound very romantic.

What was going on? Had Mallory said something directly to Ryland about Phoebe, something ugly and bad? Did he no longer want her? With her shoes finally off, she straightened and looked around, trying to take her mind off the feeling of being pushed coolly away.

The apartment was a single room, with a kitchen area at one end that was separated from the rest of the space by a counter with high wooden stools. A desk sat in the middle of the floor, with a laptop computer open on it and an office chair behind it. The rest of the furniture was sparse; a couple of straight chairs, a bookcase, a futon sofa, a rag rug in shades of green and yellow and white, a lamp.

It wasn't exactly a love nest, not with the desk dominating the space. Covertly, Phoebe smoothed her hair. Then she put her shoes by the door, along with her backpack, and padded in her stocking feet on the wooden floor to the kitchen counter. She'd reached it just as the kettle began to steam.

"Is Earl Grey tea all right with you?" Ryland still had his back to her, and seemed quite busy with the tea bags. "And you don't actually need the cookies, do you? They're high calorie."

"Okay," said Phoebe feebly. "I mean, that's fine. I mean, yes. All right."

"How was school today?"

Phoebe clambered up onto one of the stools. "Fine. I guess." Her legs dangled; there was no crossbar on the stool on which she could hook her feet. It was true what he had said; she didn't have long, elegant legs. And she did need to lose weight. And—

"How was *your* day?" she said. Then, rebelliously, she replied for him: *"Fine."* It came out in the most sarcastic tone that had ever emerged from her throat when talking to him. She was shocked at herself. And then defiant.

At least it made him turn and look at her. Then, and at last, he smiled, but the expression didn't reach his eyes.

Phoebe's last defense, the sarcasm, drained out of her completely. "What's wrong?" she blurted.

Ryland put a cup of tea down in front of her, and then moved to bring the second stool around to the other side of the counter. "Don't be stupid, Phoebe," he said gently as he sat down across from her. "What do you think is wrong?"

"I don't know! You're acting like you don't even know me. And also—" She made a motion with her hand toward the rest of the apartment. "This doesn't look like you're planning to live here."

"I'll be here sometimes," Ryland said. "But as far as my mother and sister know, it's just my office. Think for a minute, Phoebe. It wouldn't be fair to Mallory if I moved out. She's very comforted by knowing I'm living with our mother too, and that she's not alone. You don't have an issue with that, I'm sure. After all, you and I talked about it."

They'd talked about it? Phoebe didn't remember that. She could swear Ryland had told her he had found an apartment and was going to live there; that it would be his own space, a place where Phoebe could come. But if he said otherwise . . . she'd been so upset about Mallory. Ryland might have said stuff that she just hadn't taken in.

"No. I don't have an issue with it," Phoebe said. Because of course he couldn't abandon Mallory and their mother. She had never meant that. "Office, apartment, whatever. I don't care. Just tell me what's wrong. Something is." She ducked her head, her nose almost in her teacup. "Have you changed your mind about me? I mean, well, about us? Also," she finished, "I'm not stupid. Okay? Don't call me that."

She waited, her head down.

"Are you crying, Phoebe?" Ryland sounded affectionate. At last. But was it the wrong kind of affection? Was she losing him too?

"No."

She wasn't. She would not cry.

Suddenly Ryland was holding her hands again, as he had at Natalie's Café. "Phoebe, look at me."

After a few seconds, she did.

He said, "I won't lie to you. I'm having second thoughts. I've been selfish. I'm attracted to you—of course I am. You're so sweet." Ryland's hands squeezed hers, and unconsciously, Phoebe squeezed back. "But this can't be about what I want. I'm too much older than you for that. It has to be about what you want. And I don't believe you really know. You're uncertain, aren't you? Admit it. You go back and forth in your mind."

She could look at him again now. It was easy to look at him. Oh, he was beautiful. "No, no—"

"Phoebe. Be honest. Maybe you want to be here with me, but also, you don't. Not completely. You have doubts."

For a moment, Phoebe sat frozen. He knew! How could he know? But he did.

A breath later, she knew why he knew. It was because he understood her. He truly did. Fully and completely, he understood her.

Later, she would think that this was the moment she came completely to believe that Ryland did really care about her. Because how could he be so sensitive to her ambivalence if he didn't? He really must love her, because he had hesitated. Because, in the end, he had waited for her to be the one to reach out to him. For her to make the decisive move. For her to make the invitation.

Which, in the next moment, she did, all her doubts and fears falling away like leaves detaching from a tree as it succumbed to autumn. She opened her arms so he could come into them.

"I love you, Ryland," she said.

"And I love you, Phoebe," he said. "I only want what's good for you."

"That's you," she said, sure now. "You're what's good for me."

And then he kissed her, and it was just like the first time, only more. Much more.

chapter 19

"What do you mean, Phoebe? You have to come to Nantucket with us tomorrow."

It was later that same night, and Phoebe's parents were staring at her as if she had sprouted wings before their eyes and was flapping them madly.

Phoebe avoided their gaze and instead addressed herself to her dinner plate, where she was using her fork to sculpt a little mountain out of buttermilk-mashed potatoes. Jay-Jay had given her too much. She needed to lose weight; Ryland had said so again that afternoon, very gently, very kindly and lovingly.

"I'd just rather stay here during spring break. I have a couple of papers to write and I'd focus better here at home. You guys should still go, though. Actually, I was thinking you'd probably really like some time alone, without me. And it's not like I'd be here all by myself or anything like that. There's Jay-Jay."

Phoebe knew she was talking too much, and also that she was doing a bad job of making her case. The problem was that Phoebe loved the Rothschilds' home on Nantucket, adored everything about the island, looked forward to each and every vacation there. In fact, Phoebe had used to say that one day she was going to move permanently to Nantucket. So there was no way on earth that the Phoebe her parents knew would have decided to do schoolwork instead of going there.

But of course, as of today, Phoebe had become someone who was not quite her parents' Phoebe any longer. Today Phoebe had become a woman in love. Ryland's Phoebe. And if she stayed home, she would have one glorious week in which she could see Ryland alone, for hours and hours, every single day. Time in which things could develop the way they should, slowly and surely and naturally. He had told her there was no rush. But somehow the very fact of his saying that, and even the way he had said it, had made her feel like there ought to be a rush—a sort-of rush, anyway—that he would be disappointed if Phoebe delayed *too* much—

Her heart sped up to think about it. All she would have to do, in order to spend all that time every day with Ryland, was tell Jay-Jay she was working at the library.

She waited tensely. Her parents were looking at each other. Then Catherine spoke.

"We don't need time without you right at this moment. You can bring your homework and do it there. Phoebe, really. You can't impose on Jay-Jay. You know that. Next week is his vacation time too."

"I *do* know that." Had her parents always treated her like such a child? Phoebe tried to speak calmly and reasonably. "I'm eighteen. I don't need a babysitter. And I didn't mean that I expected Jay-Jay to cook for me or anything. I just meant that he lives here too, so I won't be alone in the house. I know you'd worry about that, even though there's no reason to." Having fluffed her potato mountain up, Phoebe now flattened the top of it. "I'm just suddenly not in the mood to go to Nantucket, okay? What's the big deal?"

"But yesterday you said that you and Benjamin were going birding on Sunday," said Drew. "There was some rarity he wanted to show you."

"A painted bunting." Phoebe grabbed at the opportunity to change the subject even temporarily. "It's not rare-rare, exactly, but they're not usually seen this far north. They're really colorful. I like the showy birds." She was babbling again and not helping her cause, but she couldn't stop. "Benjamin thought it might hang around a couple more days. But, you know, it's not like I *need* to see it. He's the real birder. For me, it's just something I do when I'm there. And today I realized I don't want to go to Nantucket right now."

"Why?" asked Drew simply.

Phoebe found she had nothing to say. She met her father's mild brown eyes. Finally, she muttered, "I just want to stay home."

Catherine had her elbows on the table and her chin cupped in her hands. "I have an idea. Why don't you invite Mallory?"

Phoebe blinked.

"I know, you've always said you like to have time alone with Benjamin on Nantucket, but maybe it's time for a change. Invite her."

"Mallory's not interested in coming." Phoebe ducked her head again and smashed the potato mountain with her fork. "She never has been. She likes to stay with her mother."

"Why not try again? She might have changed her mind. Her brother's here now."

Phoebe compressed her lips. She didn't want Mallory with her on Nantucket. She wanted Ryland. She could just imagine them, hand in hand on the beach, in the evening, with the sun sinking below the horizon and a giant flock of tiny sandpipers sweeping along the surf in their magical, synchronized formation.

Instead of her sneaking up to his apartment, she could be showing him all the places and things she loved. Benjamin could take them out on his little sailboat. Or, better, she could borrow Benjamin's boat and take Ryland out herself. And he could have the room next to hers, and even though they would have to behave themselves—actually, she would want them to behave themselves—

"No," Phoebe said. "I'm sure Mallory can't come."

"Ask her," Catherine said pleasantly. Firmly.

Phoebe was suddenly furious. Why wouldn't they just take her word for this? She looked straight into her mother's eyes, and spat: "Are you going to make me?"

Then she was shocked at herself.

But she didn't take it back. She didn't apologize. She couldn't! It was time they understood she was a grown-up. Wasn't it? And so, heart in her mouth, she stared defiantly at her mother while her mother stared back, obviously stunned. Stunned and hurt at the vicious expression she'd just seen in Phoebe's eyes.

Phoebe braced for what would happen next. But it wasn't what she expected.

Catherine's face transformed. Between one second and the next, she looked her age and more; her skin all at once seeming paler and more crinkly than it had been; and with more and deeper lines graven between her mouth and nose and around her eyes.

Phoebe was going to win. She recognized it in that moment. She was going to win by having hurt Catherine, by having stabbed her mother in a way her mother had never expected. And so, in this moment of shock, Catherine was going to back down and let Phoebe do as Phoebe wanted. And Phoebe would not only escape having to ask Mallory to Nantucket, but she'd even be allowed to stay home.

And this knowledge was like a blow. Phoebe could not in that moment have articulated the reason for her dismay, could not have expressed why it was that she simply could not bear to see her indomitable mother defeated, to realize that she had been the one to defeat her.

She only knew that she would do anything—anything at all—to take that look of betrayal from Catherine's face.

So before Catherine could say a word, Phoebe scrabbled in her pocket for her phone. "All right," she said, and her voice cracked. "All right, yes, I do want to go to Nantucket. I'm sorry, Mom. I'm sorry I said that. I didn't mean it."

"And Mallory?" Catherine still looked old. So old and vulnerable. And so worried.

"I'll invite her," Phoebe babbled. "I don't know if she'll come, though."

Now Catherine looked like she was recovering. "I'll be the one to ask her. Okay? So she'll know she's really wanted." She pulled out her own phone.

Now all that Phoebe could do was pray Mallory would say no.

But, incredibly, she didn't.

Conversation with the Faerie Queen, 10

"Ryland, you say there is some emergency?"

"I am sorry, my queen. I require your help."

"What has happened?"

"Despite the ending of her friendship with the girl, my sister has gone with her to an island."

"What? But she was finished with her! What is she thinking?"

"My sister has been too long in the human realm and in human guise. I fear she has become confused about her loyalties. I fear she thinks to warn the girl and stop her from giving us what we need."

"She would destroy us all? Just when we are getting so close?"

"I don't know. Not for sure. But I fear so. My queen, she loves the girl. She aches at being separated from her. And she is so much younger and less experienced than all of us. She is not much older than the girl herself. And despite her training and her heritage—

forgive me, my queen—my sister is selfish."

"But the girl has chosen *you* of late over your sister. She has even claimed to love you. Cannot you command her loyalty? Take her from your sister?"

"I am trying! But I need your help. We must open another portal, on this island."

chapter 20

Nantucket Island, located off the coast of Massachusetts below the arm of land called Cape Cod, was a place whose beauty stirred Phoebe to her soul. On the next day, as she stood on the outside passenger deck of the ferry, she couldn't help feeling some of her usual joy at returning, even though the past few hours of travel had been a polite nightmare of superficiality between her and Mallory, and she had zero hope of things improving.

Mallory was by her side now, silent as stone. She was wearing an enormous down-filled coat and had her gloved hands tucked into her armpits; for though it was a balmy April day on land, here on the ocean, the air was frigid. They had had nothing to say to each other during the trip, even though they stood together the entire time, neither making the move to join Phoebe's parents in the cabin. Phoebe supposed that Mallory was no more eager to pretend to be friendly in front of

Catherine and Drew than she was. They'd have plenty of time ahead of them this week to do that anyway.

Why on earth had Mallory said yes? Phoebe couldn't imagine how she was going to handle being with her this coming week. Though maybe Benjamin's presence would help things. Benjamin with his goofy grin and his surprising ability to be still and quiet. She would invite him to be around as much as possible.

It would also be a way to stab Mallory covertly. She'd see that she had never been Phoebe's only good friend. She would see that Phoebe and Benjamin were also almost like siblings.

Nantucket loomed bigger and bigger as the ferry approached it.

"We'll be docking soon," said Phoebe.

Mallory made a little jerking movement with her head that probably meant: *Yes, I have eyes.*

"I'm glad you were able to come." Phoebe tried to sound warm. "I hope we'll have a nice week."

Mallory gave Phoebe a look. The ferry whistle sounded.

"Can't we try to be polite?" said Phoebe. "I mean, we can at least manage that, right?"

"I don't know."

Phoebe couldn't stand it. She demanded, "Then why did you come, if not to try to make up?"

Mallory grabbed Phoebe's arm and pulled her around so that they faced each other. "Because I wanted to. I've always been curious to meet your friend Benjamin, for one thing."

Phoebe shook herself free. It wasn't hard, as Mallory's grip had slackened. She turned her back and started walking. It was time, anyway, to get in the car and drive off the ferry onto the island.

Catherine and Drew's place on Nantucket was often a surprise to their guests, who came expecting something much grander. After all, there were homes on Nantucket that cost twenty million dollars, homes that overlooked beaches and conservation land, homes with separate guest cottages and every amenity you could imagine.

But the Rothschilds' house was not like that. It was a three-bedroom cottage with weathered clapboard shingles and a detached single-car garage. Drew had bought the house as a single man at the age of twenty-two, using his graduate school tuition money as a down payment.

"What can I say? I fell in love with the island. Living here felt more important than school." He told Mallory the story over dinner. "So, I was working as a waiter at three different restaurants during the tourist season to afford the mortgage payments. Then Catherine came to Nantucket to visit friends. We met. One thing led to another, and I told her the house was my dowry. She told me it needed a new roof, a remodeled kitchen, and an extra bathroom. And here we are."

They were at the round table in the kitchen while Phoebe cooked omelets for them one at a time. She had volunteered for this because it would keep her busy at the stove and she wouldn't have to talk. And it worked perfectly, until the doorbell rang and she heard a voice call, "Hi, it's Benjamin. I saw your car."

Benjamin Michaud came into the kitchen as though he were a member of the family. And all at once the room felt lighter to Phoebe, easier, and she thought she might just get through the evening after all.

"Hey, Pheeb." Benjamin smiled his sweet goofy Benjamin smile, and made a little motion with his arms like he wanted to hug her but wasn't sure he ought to.

"Hey, Benjamin," she said, and put out her arms. He hugged her shyly.

Nobody could have been more different from Ryland. She couldn't help thinking this. Benjamin was still teetering between boy- and manhood; with brown, long-lashed eyes and a gangly, skinny body, and enormous ears sticking out beneath his ratty old Red Sox baseball cap. Looking at him, Phoebe had an impulse to hug him again, but didn't. He was always hungry, though, so she said, "I'm making omelets, want one?"

"Yes. Sure. Thanks." He went to shake hands with Drew and—with no shred of shyness this time—to hug Catherine.

And then all Phoebe's plans of making Mallory jealous of Benjamin came crashing down. It was because of how Benjamin was looking at Mallory. Mallory with her silky hair, her deep-set eyes, her faultless skin; her slender curves; her willowy grace.

Benjamin had grown to nearly Mallory's height, Phoebe realized, as Mallory unfolded her long legs and stood up to shake hands with him. It made Phoebe feel positively squat.

Unbelievably, Mallory was checking Benjamin out too, and not subtly, either. She actually smiled, for the first time all day, while Benjamin hunched his shoulders as they shook hands and said hello.

Phoebe set her teeth. If Mallory messed with Benjamin, it would be to play with Phoebe's mind. And it would mean Mallory *was* what Ryland had said she was—hard, mean, and jealous. Not that Phoebe had doubted it!

Fuming, she turned back to the kitchen counter and reached for the egg carton to start Benjamin's omelet.

Things didn't get much better. After dinner, in the living room, all the talk was about the bird that Benjamin had spotted and wanted to show Phoebe.

"Do you want to go look at him with us tomorrow too?" Benjamin asked Mallory.

"You can borrow my bike if you want to go, Mallory," said Catherine.

Phoebe sat tensely. She had never known Mallory to express any interest in birds.

"Sure," said Mallory, and smiled lazily at Benjamin.

In her head, Phoebe counted slowly to ten. Then she jumped up. “Well, I should go check on the bikes and make sure they’re set for tomorrow. Benjamin, you want to help?”

Benjamin didn’t move. “No, but you can come get me if you need me to pump up a tire or something.”

“Right,” said Phoebe. She went outside to the garage by herself.

The bikes were fine. Phoebe thought for a second about slashing the tires on both of her parents’ bikes so there’d be nothing for Mallory to ride. Then she was shocked at herself. Had she gone completely around the bend? No, she hadn’t, and she wasn’t going to start in slashing bicycle tires or anything else.

How had this happened? How in the world had this happened? She had loved Mallory so much, so recently. Mallory had loved her. No, no, that wasn’t true. Mallory had only pretended.

Phoebe left the garage, but couldn’t bear to go back into the house yet. She stood on the stoop and breathed in the crisp Nantucket air and closed her eyes.

What if she didn’t give Mallory up? They had this week together. What if she told her about Ryland, not in a mean way, but explained everything openly? What if she told Mallory how hurt she’d been by her last week? What if they tried, really tried, to talk things out, to repair their friendship?

Phoebe nibbled on the inside of her cheek. Could that possibly work? Maybe. Maybe Mallory had even come because she too hoped they could salvage things.

Suddenly Phoebe felt a strange alertness on her skin. And she thought: Ryland. He's here.

Which couldn't be.

Still, Phoebe's throat went dry. She took a step forward, down, so that she was standing on the ground before the two steps of the cottage stoop. With her eyes closed, she felt herself slip helplessly into a weird waking dream state. And in it, she could sense Ryland; it was as if he had just come up behind her, on the step above, and was standing so close that she could feel the heat off his body through his clothes and hers, even though he was not actually touching her.

This had to be another hallucination. What was wrong with her?

"Hello." It was a whisper in her ear.

It was Ryland's voice.

Phoebe couldn't stop herself from responding, from acting as if this were real. "Hi," she said, and it came out like a croak.

And now she actually felt his hands, both hands, solidly on her shoulders, cupping and kneading them deftly, warmly. It felt real. But it couldn't be. She thought of wrenching herself forward, of whipping around to look, but she didn't. She wanted this to be real. She kept her eyes closed. Her mouth opened to say something—anything—but what came out was a sigh.

Unconsciously, she stepped backward and sank against Ryland; felt his body all along her back. It was solid; he was solid. Then he put his arms around her—touched her—held her—yes, oh—like that—

Then his hands and arms tightened, hurting, and Phoebe heard, like an echo, a sound that had actually happened a full second earlier in the quiet night. It was footsteps just behind her, on the wooden floor inside the cottage.

Then the small sound of a sharply indrawn breath.

"That was my sister," said Ryland's voice. His arms around her had relaxed. "She just peeked out at you. She's gone now."

"Could she—"

"See me? Now, how could she? You're imagining me. Aren't you, sweet Phoebe-bird? You're an imaginative girl. You imagine many things."

This time it was a soft kiss on the base of her neck that stopped Phoebe from talking.

"Shh," said Ryland. "Shh. Forget Mallory. She doesn't care about you. I do. You know that, don't you? Good girl. Such a good girl. So sweet. So mine. It will all be so good, Phoebe, so good, as long as you do just exactly what I tell you to do."

The words whispered in her ear somehow turned her knees to liquid. And then Ryland—his presence—was gone, and Phoebe was left shivering, hardly able to stand up, and filled with an indescribable longing and confusion.

But . . .

What—what—what . . . ?

It took her quite a few minutes before her legs were steady enough to let her go back into the house.

chapter 21

In the living room, Mallory had taken over a big overstuffed chair and sat curled up in it, with a mug of hot chocolate cradled in her hands. Phoebe's parents were on the sofa together, also with mugs. And Benjamin, who was still glancing at Mallory from time to time like he'd seen an angel, had settled on the rug before the fireplace.

Benjamin had the poker and was minding the fire. Its logs crackled softly and its light cast a soft glow on the room. Benjamin had already stayed far longer than he normally would have, especially on a night before getting up early to go birding. But as far as Phoebe could tell, he was showing no sign of going home.

She felt annoyed, but only dimly. She was so confused. Was she going crazy? But if only Ryland would hold her, like he just had, if he would only be with her, she wouldn't care. Why wasn't she with him now, the way she had intended to be? Why was she here instead? She couldn't remember how it had happened. She didn't belong here; she belonged with him. To him.

She could feel Mallory's gaze on her.

The others had been talking, but they stopped as Phoebe came in. They said something to her, but she wasn't sure what it was. She put one hand up to her neck and brushed her hair off it, aware only as she did this that she was perspiring as if it were summer. Her forehand was damp too.

"Are the bikes okay?" Benjamin asked.

"Oh," said Phoebe vaguely. "The bikes. Right."

"They're okay? The bikes?" said Benjamin.

"Yes." Phoebe's voice now sounded too loud even in her own ears. And also somehow uncertain.

"You checked the air level in the tires?"

"Yes." She gathered herself together. "The bikes are in good shape. We're all set to go after the bunting at six a.m."

Phoebe felt Mallory's very steady gaze on her still. In avoiding it, she found herself inadvertently catching her mother's worried eyes.

The sweet longing she'd been feeling faded, and the real world came into abrupt focus around her. She stumbled and sat down quickly on the rug near Benjamin.

There was a little silence. Then Mallory said crisply, "Phoebe, we've been talking about fairy tales. I want to tell one."

"What? You want to tell us a fairy tale?" This was strange, Phoebe thought.

"Yes."

"It will be fun, Phoebe," said Drew. "Mallory's already told us just enough to intrigue us. Do you want me to get you some hot chocolate first?"

"Oh. No. I don't want any."

Benjamin tossed a big seating pillow at Phoebe; she caught it and used it to lean more comfortably against the wall.

Maybe this was good news. If Mallory was going to tell a story, nobody would expect Phoebe to do more than sit and listen. Or pretend to listen.

"Are we ready?" said Mallory.

"Yes," said Benjamin. "Go ahead."

"Very well," said Mallory. "Listen.

"This is a story that takes place nearly two hundred and fifty years ago. It is the story of a man born poor." Mallory's voice suddenly had the cadence of a born storyteller, warm, low, inviting, and irresistible.

"But poverty was not his worst disadvantage. He was also born into a social caste scorned and despised by other people. People from this social caste could have every personal advantage, but none of it would do any good. At best, his people were ignored; at worst, they were persecuted and murdered.

"The most that this man could hope for was a life in which

he would be allowed to scrape a living at one of the few jobs he had access to, and that he would be lucky enough to marry and raise children in peace."

"Like the Untouchable caste in India," said Drew. "Hey, Mallory, does this story take place in India? Or Japan?"

"Drew." Catherine blinked owlishly over her half-glasses. "Let Mallory tell it. It doesn't matter where the story is set. It's a fairy tale."

"Actually, this is a story with a European setting," Mallory said. "And the setting does matter, because, well, as you'll see, the story is about European faeries." She spelled the word. "Phoebe? Are you listening?" she said sharply.

Phoebe's mind had been wandering to Ryland—his warm hands on the skin of her throat and shoulders—but Mallory's tone pulled her back to the room. "Yes."

"All right. Back to our hero, the young man of low caste. He was not only intelligent and ambitious, he was extraordinarily so. And those weren't the least of his talents. Although he would never have been permitted to join the military, let alone rise to an important rank in it, he had the kind of mind that excelled at tactics, at strategy, and at long-range planning. From when he was a very young child, he was unbeatable, for example, at chess.

"And of course he knew of his own intelligence. Now, because of his father's small business as a money lender—"

"A money lender?" interrupted Catherine.

"Yes. It was one of the few professions open to members of this caste. The actual handling of money was felt by the upper classes to be dirty, though having wealth was as important as ever to them."

A smile curved Catherine's lips. "Mallory, sweetheart, you interest me strangely."

"What am I missing?" said Drew. "Benjamin? Phoebe?"

"I don't know," said Benjamin, and Phoebe shrugged as well.

"You'll catch on soon, I think," said Catherine. "Go ahead, Mallory."

Mallory nodded.

"Because of his father's money-lending business, which he would one day take over, the young man met many people from outside of his caste. They lived in a large city in the middle of Europe, and the business had many customers. These people were often a little desperate, a little vulnerable, the way that one is when in need of money.

"But at the same time, though it might seem like a contradiction, the customers tended to be arrogant. Thus they were more revealing of themselves than they might otherwise have been. Our young man observed them, and assessed them—their natures, their capabilities. Especially he observed the people from the nobility and merchant classes. And by the time he was in his twenties, he believed, and in this he was quite correct, that he had never yet met a man who was his superior in mind.

"And yet he was nonetheless fated his whole life to be condescended to and scorned—and, worse, to live his life afraid of yet another time when his people would be senselessly murdered. His father, whom our hero loved, told him bluntly that this had to be accepted. That comfort could be found in prayer and in belief in God, and also in marriage and children. The father had in fact already picked out for his son a lively, intelligent young girl of their caste. This girl, the father felt, had a firm enough personality to cope with his extraordinary son. She would make him an excellent mate and provide for him children and a peaceful, happy home. Life would be good in many ways, he counseled his son, if he was careful and if God was kind."

"These people were religious?" asked Benjamin.

"Oh, yes. They placed their God at the center of their lives. In any event, our young man saw the wisdom of his father's advice. He discovered that his father had been right about the joys to be found in a good marriage. In fact, our young man fell in love with his wife, for his father had picked wisely. He was happy.

"And yet, he still could not help feeling frustrated. Sometimes he would slip away from the city—and this was not easy, for there were travel restrictions upon his caste—and take long walks in a large, ancient forest. He would stride along, scarcely seeing the trees around him, imagining how he might force change upon his world. But not even to his wife did he confess his burning longing. He chafed secretly. And secretly, though he knew it was useless, he planned what he might do, as if it were a game of chess.

"Then one day his wife came to him, took his hand, and put it on her stomach. 'This,' she said, 'is going to be our first son.'

"The words *our first son* reverberated inside the young man's mind and heart like the echo of an enormous bell. Until this moment, he had not known how the reality of children and family would make him feel, or how his ambition would suddenly find a new focus and direction.

"And he had two thoughts. The first was this: that he must find a way to make his family invulnerable. Nobody should be able to hurt them, ever. And the second was that, in his sons, he might have allies and partners for his plans. If his sons could only be safely raised to adulthood, they could join him in changing their world, their prospects.

"Our young man had a vision: that the sons that he and his wife would create together would be extraordinary. Like him.

"In fact, for his plans to work, he would *need* his sons to be extraordinary.

"Then despair filled our young man, because such a thing is up to God. No mere mortal can guarantee the character of children. So, as he clasped his wife in his arms and kissed her, all the young man could think was that he needed to go to the forest as soon as possible and be alone there. There, he would find a way to humble himself and give up the future to God. He would leave his fantasy in the forest, and would return to the city resigned.

"He knew he must do this, or the reality of his life, and of his family's life, would be poisoned by hopes that could never be realized.

"So, that night, as his wife slept, he slipped out from home and city and went to the forest. It was a night in June. It was, in fact, Midsummer Eve. Do you know anything about Midsummer Eve?"

Phoebe, who had to her own surprise become totally absorbed in Mallory's story, was startled at the direct question. And Mallory was looking straight at her.

"Yes," Phoebe said. "It's solstice."

"Right. But also, on Midsummer Eve, the faeries dance." Mallory's gaze paused on Phoebe, then Benjamin, then Drew, and then finally on Catherine.

"Faeries appear in the human world on Midsummer Eve, in certain sacred places, to perform their rituals. These are sacred rituals that renew the earth and all the nature it supports. On that night, and only on that night, humans may see the faeries in those places."

"Oh, don't tell me," said Drew. "The ancient forest of our young man—does he have a name?—this forest contained just such a sacred place."

Mallory nodded. "Yes, it did. And yes, our hero has a name. His name was Mayer."

Catherine laughed.

"Just a minute," said Drew. "Middle of Europe, two hundred-plus years ago, money lenders, ghetto. Mayer. And his wife's name is Gutle, right?"

"Exactly," said Catherine. She and Drew smiled at each other.

"What?" Benjamin said. "Phoebe? What are they getting that I'm not? Do you know?"

Phoebe didn't answer, though she could have. Anger had begun to brew in her as she understood what story Mallory was telling. She clenched her fists. But she contained herself because her parents were clearly not angry.

"You'll see in time, Benjamin," said Catherine. "Go on with the story, Mallory."

"I will," said Mallory. "So, soon our hero, Mayer, was walking deep into his forest. He saw little of what was around him, so filled was he with longing for his extraordinary sons, the sons who with his guidance would change everything and make all his dreams come true, and so hard was he struggling to give the vision up and accept instead whatever God brought him.

"He walked faster and faster. Eventually he ran, crushing tender new plants and shoots underfoot and kicking small stones out of his way and noticing none of it. At last, however, a sharp pain in his side caused him to stop. He leaned against a tree trunk, and slowly he realized that he had come to a part of the forest that was unfamiliar to him."

And now Phoebe couldn't help herself. She snorted. "Oh, please," she muttered.

Initially, despite herself, Phoebe had been irresistibly compelled by Mallory's story and by the way in which she told it. The world had dropped away around her as she listened. But now that she recognized it, she was no longer enchanted. In fact, she was beginning to boil.

The story was obviously a thinly veiled account of Catherine and Phoebe's famous ancestor Mayer Rothschild. Mayer had been born in the Jewish ghetto of Frankfurt am Main, Germany, in 1744. He had married Gutle. They had five sons: Amschel, Salomon, Nathan, Calmann, and Jakob. These sons were later represented on the family coat of arms by a clenched fist holding five arrows, because Mayer had eventually aimed his sons like weapons across Europe. And the word *extraordinary* did not even begin to describe Mayer, the five sons, and their effect on the world.

The family money-lending business became an international banking business that served kings and princes. Four of the sons were elevated to the nobility. The family and their business had been marked by wealth and power and privilege ever since. Even Hitler had been unable to hurt the Rothschilds; and their position, power, influence, and wealth had helped ensure the survival of many other Jews in that time of terror.

But it wasn't a *faerie* tale, Phoebe thought furiously. It was history! It was the very real history of a very real Jewish family. Her family.

And she thought she knew where Mallory was going with this, and if she was right, it was offensive!

But a glance at her parents' faces told Phoebe that they were still enchanted. Benjamin too. Everybody but Phoebe couldn't wait to hear more.

Mallory had already gone on, ignoring Phoebe. "Mayer was lost, but he would never have said so, or even have thought it. He knew how to orient himself using the sun and moon, so it didn't matter that he didn't recognize exactly where he was. I suppose you can guess what happened next?"

"Mayer saw the faeries?" Benjamin said.

This time, Phoebe really did roll her eyes, but nobody was looking at her. She looked again at her parents, but they didn't even notice. They were holding hands and grinning at Mallory.

"Yes," said Mallory. "The sacred place, a large and open glade in the heart of the forest, was right before Mayer's eyes. As he looked at it, holding his side and panting, the moon came out from behind the clouds. It illuminated the glade.

"And dozens of shadows that a moment before Mayer had assumed to be trees came alive. They gathered silently into a perfect circle around a female who was taller than any of them. She wore a crown of flowers on her long hair, hair composed of dozens of colors that were all to be found in nature and yet would never be found there together. The yellow of a bee's fur; the russet of a fox's pelt; the white of a dandelion gone to seed; the shiny black of a songbird's eye. Her unearthly hair fell in waves that looked alive against her skin; skin that glowed in the moonlight as green as the most tender leaf of early spring.

"And then Mayer saw that her skin was not simply the color of leaves, but was actually formed *from* leaves. And he saw that despite her womanly shape, the female was as much akin to trees and plants as she was to humankind. She was of the earth in a way that no human can ever be. And she was both frightening and glorious to behold."

"The queen of the faeries," Drew said.

"Yes." Mallory nodded. "Never before had Mayer seen anyone—anything—so terrible, and yet so beautiful, as the queen. If his shock had allowed him to move, he would have fallen to his knees before her and worshipped her."

Phoebe's jaw dropped. This had suddenly gotten even more offensive than she had thought it would. She wasn't even particularly religious and she found it insufferable. How dare Mallory? But her parents were still smiling, still leaning forward in fascination. Somehow, Phoebe managed to keep silent.

"Mayer saw that the other figures were, like the queen, only humanoid in the general shapes of their bodies—and not all of them, at that. Some, like the queen, seemed related to plants; others, to animals or birds. He saw hoofed feet, and feathered backs, and wing-like arms, and on one head, a set of powerful antlers. He saw skin like bark; wrists that blossomed with flowers. On one male, he saw the face of a ferret. They all swam before his eyes, a wealth of visual sensation and of life; the very pulse of the earth and of nature.

"Watching, Mayer felt as if his senses were coming fully alive for the first time. He heard music, the sweetest strumming of strings and the highest, most delicate piping of flutes. Initially the music was faint and far away, but then it increased in volume and tempo.

"The faeries began to dance, moving in complicated steps, twisting and twining around each other. Only the queen in the center did not move. She was the still center of the dance, and Mayer understood instinctively that the dance was in tribute to her and that it served a greater purpose.

"He had forgotten his own fear and rage; forgotten his personal desperate hopes and dreams; forgotten his despair and his determination. He slipped away even from a sense of self. The tempo of the music and the dance increased; its movements grew faster and more complex; the bodies before him seemed to blur into each other and into the earth and the glade around them as they moved, joining together in ways that spoke of the intricacy of nature. Faerie laughter rang out, wild and filled with joy. A drum-like beat began, underlying the music with its insistent rhythm.

"Mayer's skin came to tingling, excited life all over his body. His clothing was suddenly an intolerable burden to him, and he tore it off. He felt the sweet air of the night breeze on every inch of his skin and knew no shame. He breathed the air in and it nourished him.

"Without hesitation, Mayer stepped forward and entered the faerie dance. He entered the worship of the queen and of the earth."

And suddenly Phoebe could bear no more. "Oh, please!" She scrambled to her feet. "You can't seriously expect me to sit still for another second of this. I've heard enough! Mallory, I won't sit here while you insult our family with this. I'm leaving."

Conversation with the Faerie Queen, II

"What is happening, Ryland?"

"My sister is fighting me for the soul of the girl. Her weapon is truth. But do not fear, my queen. The girl will not listen to her. She does not wish to believe. I will win."

chapter 22

There was a moment of shocked silence. Then Catherine stood up too.

"Personally, Phoebe, I'm very entertained by Mallory's story. Where's the insult? It's creative and fascinating."

"I think so too," said Drew. Benjamin nodded.

But Phoebe looked only at her mother. "All that stuff about Mayer worshipping the faerie queen? Mayer was a good Jew. That's history. Also, can't you see where Mallory's going with this? It's like something from the worst kind of trashy novel!"

"You might know where Mallory is going," said Drew mildly, from his seat on the sofa. "Or think you do. But I don't, not for sure, anyway, and I'm dying to hear the rest. So don't spoil it." He smiled at Mallory. "I had no idea you were such a good storyteller."

His gaze went back to Phoebe and it was as stern as she

had ever seen it. "Sit down again, Phoebe. Personally, I'd like to hear more about Mayer dancing naked with the faeries on Midsummer Night."

"Midsummer Night 1772, to be precise." Mallory was still using her storytelling voice.

Catherine sat down.

Temptation shimmered before Phoebe. Why not sit down again, with her parents and her two best friends, and listen, listen . . .

A whisper in her inner ear. *She doesn't care about you. She's trying to trick you.*

Phoebe stamped her foot like a toddler. "No! How can you guys not get it?"

All four faces turned again toward her. The irritation on her parents' faces was plain, while Benjamin only looked a little embarrassed.

Mallory's expression was a flat unemotional mask.

"Then don't listen, Phoebe! Go to bed instead," Catherine snapped. "By morning, maybe you'll be acting your age. Mallory, ignore her. Continue."

Bratty toddler, whispered the voice in Phoebe's inner ear.

"Phoebe," said Mallory quietly. "Please stay."

The girls' eyes met. Phoebe felt a pull—a desire to sit down again—to listen to Mallory's voice—

But Phoebe, you know she despises you.

"No," said Phoebe rudely, and stomped off. She raced from

the cottage like Mayer himself running through the forest. She slammed the door behind her for good measure.

Once outside, however, she slowed down to a walk. Up and down the road. Up and down the road. It was almost completely dark outside now, and if not for the lights at a couple of the houses on the road, and one streetlamp, she wouldn't have been able to see anything.

Phoebe felt that she knew exactly where Mallory's story had been heading. Mallory was going to say that Mayer had had faerie assistance, magical assistance. That it was the faeries who gave him the extraordinary sons. Perhaps Mallory would even have implied that the faerie queen was responsible for the sons' success, rather than Mayer and the sons themselves. Would she then say that the sons were part faerie, even, rather than human? It was not only insulting, it was demeaning. How could Benjamin and her parents not see that?

Because, Phoebe thought with sudden clarity, they don't imagine for a second that it could be true. To them, it's only a story. Whereas to her—

Phoebe discovered that she was crying. And the moment of clarity was gone now, leaving confusion in its wake. Impatiently, she smeared the palms of both hands across her cheeks and sniffed. What was wrong with her? It *was* only a story.

Maybe it was some plot of Mallory's to drive Phoebe crazy.

Or maybe she already was crazy. Imagining Ryland was there, as she had earlier this evening. Imagining his voice in her ear. That was nuts, wasn't it? And the garden inside the Tollivers' house—no, no. She felt so confused . . .

After a while, she heard the soft sound of gravel on the road behind her, and turned. It was Benjamin, walking his bike. "Hi," he said. He came right up to her.

Phoebe was glad it was dark, so she wouldn't have to look in Benjamin's face and see what he was thinking of her. She was trying to figure out what to say when he spoke.

"Pheeb, I have to go home, but I wanted to talk to you first. Are you okay now?"

Phoebe felt tears threaten again. She didn't want to let them out; for one thing, she knew they would embarrass Benjamin. So she stood there, holding the tears back, but because of them unable to say another syllable.

"I guess not," Benjamin said.

Phoebe managed a hand motion meant to indicate apology.

"You still up for birding in the morning?"

She nodded.

"I'll be here at six. And listen, Pheeb? Don't bring Mallory."

Phoebe was so surprised that the lump in her throat receded and a few words made it out. "But you—and she—"

"What are you mumbling about? There's no me and her. There's you and me. And there's you and her." He was trying to tease her.

But this only made Phoebe's anger resurface. The good

news was that the anger made her able to talk again. "Benjamin, don't humor me because I had a tantrum! Okay? She's pretty and fascinating and you were staring at her like she was a model and you were listening to her like she was Scheherazade. You know you were. And you were dying for her to come with us tomorrow."

"Yeah, I was. But I'm not now."

A moment of silence.

"Benjamin," Phoebe blurted.

"What?"

"About Mallory."

"Yeah?"

"We haven't been getting along lately."

"You don't say."

Phoebe laughed. It was a little, choked laugh, but it was a laugh. And then somehow, even in the dark, she knew Benjamin was grinning at her too.

"Six a.m.," he said. "Painted bunting. You'll feel better when you see him, you really will."

"All right," said Phoebe. She knew the painted bunting wasn't going to help. But still she would go.

She watched Benjamin get on his bike, wave at her, and then she listened to the sound of his pedaling until he turned the corner.

Eventually, Phoebe walked home and saw that the lights in the living room had gone out. Her parents and Mallory must have gone upstairs to bed. She forced herself to go back in. She climbed the stairs and steeled herself to peek inside the half-open door of her bedroom.

Mallory was in the second twin bed in Phoebe's room. She was lying on her side curled up and facing the wall, with the covers pulled up around her. She had left the small nightstand light on for Phoebe, and it was clear from her rigid posture that she was wide awake.

Waiting? Was that why Mallory hadn't taken the guest room?

Phoebe turned away and crossed the hall to the bathroom. She had been in there for ten minutes and was brushing her teeth when she heard a knock. "It's just me," said Catherine. "May I come in?" Without waiting for an answer, she did. She came right up behind Phoebe at the sink and met her gaze in the mirror.

Phoebe continued brushing her teeth.

"Mallory didn't finish telling her story," Catherine said after a minute. "She said she was tired, but I think it was because of you. She wanted you to hear the story."

Phoebe indicated that she couldn't talk because of the toothbrush.

Her mother sighed. "Phoebe? There's something very wrong between you and Mallory. Right?"

There was no possibility of lying, not with Catherine looking directly into her eyes. Phoebe nodded reluctantly, but with the movement, relief unexpectedly began to course through her. Even if she could share just this one part of the tangled web she was in—

Catherine said, "Do you want to talk about it?"

Phoebe's mouth was still full of toothpaste. Carefully, she spit and began to clean up. Yes, she did. She wanted to talk. Desperately. But—

"No," Phoebe said. "It's just one of those things. I wish you could help, but Mallory and I will have to figure it out by ourselves. Or not."

Catherine put one hand to her temples and rubbed them. "You're sure? I could even talk to Mallory for you, if that would help. If you would tell me what needs saying?"

"Thanks, Mom. But I have to handle it myself." Phoebe felt as if her brain were entirely disengaged from that confident, sure voice coming from her throat. "I can't act like a baby with Mommy taking care of everything. And yes, I know I did act that way tonight, and I'm sorry. All the more reason for me to change, right?"

A moment of silence. "I don't know," said Catherine. "That's the kind of thing that sounds good, to take care of it yourself. But you have to be wary of making rules like that. Sometimes you need other people. You shouldn't scorn their help." Her eyes were sharp on Phoebe's face. "The thing is, too many girls lose good friends at your age." Another pause, and then, as if casually: "Often, it's about a boy."

Phoebe winced. But she said nothing.

Catherine sighed. She reached to hug Phoebe, and Phoebe was relieved to find that to this, at least, she could respond honestly. She hugged back, tight. She clung for another second even after her mother loosened her grip.

"Good night," said Phoebe. "Sleep well." She watched her mother leave the bathroom.

Once her mother left, she understood that really she had done the right thing. It was better that she hadn't said anything. There would have been no way to explain without telling too much, far too much, and maybe even sounding insane.

Also, she was drooping with weariness. She switched off the bathroom light and made her way to her own bed, across the room from Mallory, who now did seem—thankfully—to have fallen asleep. Her breath was even, like a metronome.

A minute later, Phoebe too had fallen into an exhausted sleep.

Conversation with the Faerie Queen, 12

"But Ryland, you won."

"Temporarily, yes. But now the girl has yet another friend for support. And she nearly talked to her mother about what she was experiencing. And then there is her father. There are too many people from whom she could potentially draw resolve, and since I can no longer rely upon my sister—in short, my queen, desperate measures are now necessary."

"It seems your sister was right when she said this girl was not quite what we were looking for."

"None of the Rothschild girls have been, my queen, these last two hundred years and more. Time runs short."

"I know."

"I will *make* this girl fit our needs. I can do it if she will cling to me alone. She must have no one else to turn to."

"What is your plan?"

"I will take her mother from her, which will also

effectively remove her father. With your permission, my queen. My queen? What is it? Please, take my arm."

"I shall be better soon. It is only—sometimes I wonder how it is that I have wandered so far down this road, and taken our people to such a desperate place, and you and your sister to such evil doings."

"Not evil, my queen. Necessary. My queen? May I do what must be done?"

"Yes. Of course."

"It will require even more energy."

"I know. Ryland?"

"Yes?"

"Be as merciful as you can."

"No. To leave the girl with any hope is dangerous."

"Indeed. You are right. What a terrible tangle. I sicken myself, Ryland. But we have no choice."

"No. None."

chapter 23

The early light filtered into Phoebe's bedroom and she awoke feeling hopeful. She slipped from bed, dressed hurriedly, and was out of the room within minutes, relieved that Mallory had not stirred, but also feeling a little more generous toward her.

Phoebe had to acknowledge that she had probably overreacted to Mallory's story last night. She had been too sensitive. Possibly, she thought, she'd been jealous of how effortlessly Mallory's storytelling had enchanted Catherine and Drew and Benjamin. Well, she would let it go now, and when she got back after birding, she'd apologize to everyone.

She grabbed some bananas from the kitchen, located her binoculars, and was ready with her bike when Benjamin arrived. Half a minute and they were on their way.

There was something miraculous about Nantucket on a beautiful morning. It promised to be a perfect island spring day, with the sun climbing up in a blue sky and the air just the right temperature for a light jacket. They had a mild wind at their backs as they pedaled east toward 'Sconset. Benjamin had bungee-corded his telescope and its tripod on the back of his bike and hung his binoculars around his neck so he could get to them fast, but Phoebe put her own binoculars in her front bike basket with the bananas and her other things. She found them too heavy to wear for long.

After about a mile of riding side by side, Phoebe asked Benjamin, "The bird's been hanging out by the pond, did you say? Or is he right in Hoicks Hollow?"

"By the pond. At least, I hope he's still there."

"How far is it again?"

"About nine miles. We can rest partway if you need to."

"No. I'd hate to miss him because of a rest."

"We won't miss him. Hey, you have your inhaler and stuff, right?"

"Yes. But I feel fine. I won't need a rest."

And she didn't. When they got to Sesachacha Pond, they left the bikes at a small parking lot and Phoebe let Benjamin go ahead as they tramped around the edge of the pond. Benjamin had his binoculars raised to scan the nearby grasses and trees. Ten minutes later, without needing to look at Phoebe, simply knowing exactly where she was, Benjamin spoke, using the soft voice he always used in the field.

"I've got him. Not too far from where he was yesterday. Polite of him, huh?"

Phoebe spoke just as quietly as she raised her binoculars. "Where?"

"See that tall marsh grass over to the left? The large tree branch just above? Follow it out to the fork. He's about an inch above the fork, just sitting on a branch, waiting to be admired."

"I'm not seeing—oh, yes! Wow. Wow!"

The male painted bunting was just gorgeous. He cocked his little blue head, fluffed out his green wings, and displayed his red breast.

"He's posing for us," she said to Benjamin.

"Full breeding plumage. He's looking to impress a female. Too bad."

"Yeah. Poor thing."

Involuntarily, Phoebe sighed. The bunting had wandered far from home and there was little likelihood of a mate for him here. He'd have to find his way back south, to his breeding grounds. Birds and their migrations were so mysterious, so miraculous, but sometimes it just didn't work out. A bad wind, the wrong direction—there were always birds that lost their way completely and never found home and the mate they sought. Still, Phoebe thought, it was clearly simpler for birds than it was for humans.

For close to three incredible minutes, the bunting preened and posed, and Phoebe and Benjamin watched. Then the bird flew into the marsh grass and disappeared from view.

"That was amazing," Phoebe said. "Thanks, Benjamin."

"I'm just glad he stayed. Do you want to hang out here a while and see what else shows up? And the bunting might come back out too."

"Sure. I was counting on it."

Benjamin lifted an eyebrow. "You don't need to get back?"

"Not in a real big rush to do that," said Phoebe honestly. As if to make her point, she settled herself down onto a rock.

"Yeah." Benjamin sat as well.

Phoebe took a deep breath. "Though—I should tell you—I'll apologize to everybody when I do get back. And if you want to come over tonight for supper, I'm also planning to ask Mallory to tell the rest of her story. I'll just suffer through it and behave myself. So, if you want to hear the end, you're welcome to come."

"I guess I do," said Benjamin. "It was pretty interesting. And she'd just gotten to the good part."

Phoebe felt his gaze on the side of her face. She turned to look directly at him, and then she smiled ruefully, because he looked so uncomfortable, but also determined, and she knew that look of his. She nibbled lightly on the inside of her cheek and then said, "Okay, go ahead. Give it to me straight. You know you want to."

Occasionally, in the course of their friendship, Benjamin had asked Phoebe a question or made a comment, and what he said had jogged Phoebe into an important new place in her mind. A place of truth. *You let her boss you around,* he had said once, about Colette Williams-White. He'd barely been eleven when he said it. A couple years later, he had said: *Your father doesn't care what anybody thinks of him. In a way, he's much more confident than your mother. It makes me wonder what she'd be like without him.*

It wasn't always easy to cope with these zingers; in fact, it usually took a while before Phoebe was glad of having heard one. Anxious now, she steeled herself.

Benjamin was looking at his feet. "Last night, you said I was staring at Mallory and—and everything."

Phoebe felt her stomach tighten. "Yes."

"I guess I was. Staring at her."

Phoebe's stomach clenched again. "Mallory's beautiful," she said evenly.

"Yeah, but." Benjamin sighed. "Yeah, but—Phoebe, I look at a lot of girls. I like to look, okay? It's, uh, it's what guys do. We look at girls. We think about them. We wonder. I do that with nearly every girl I see nowadays. Not just Mallory. It's just that maybe you haven't seen me doing it before now."

Benjamin looked even more awkward than before, but he continued determinedly. "Probably until I die, I'll be looking at girls. I really like looking. That's my point. I enjoy looking. So I look."

"I'm getting that." The knot in Phoebe's stomach was dissolving. This was interesting, but it wasn't one of Benjamin's worldview-shaking comments. "I think you've made your point three times. Or five. I lost count."

Benjamin actually laughed, a single snort. "Yeah, okay, but I'm still not done."

"All right. Sorry for interrupting. Go on." Phoebe rearranged her legs under her.

"Thank you very much. What I'm trying to say is it's like a fantasy. A girl I meet in person, like Mallory, is more real than some girl I'd see on, uh, on the Internet, but it's still just me looking and wondering, and, uh, fantasizing a little, which is just something I do, sort of on autopilot. I'm not saying it doesn't matter to me, because, uh, it does—"

"Because you enjoy looking."

"I'm talking here, remember? What I'm saying is that it's all in my head, which is where it belongs and where I like it, mostly. So when I was looking at your friend Mallory—your ex-friend Mallory, whatever—it wasn't because I fell in love with her at first sight or whatever it was you were thinking. I know she's your friend—*was* your friend—and that makes her more interesting to me than some random girl. But still. So you, uh, don't need to be jealous. I like looking at you more. Which is, in fact, my point."

And then Benjamin sat there, his eyes calm behind his glasses, and his big ears sticking out, and his knobby knees poking sharply through the fabric of his jeans, and his feet looking oddly large in his dirty sneakers, and his face ever so slightly red.

Everything is fine and normal, Phoebe thought in shock. Everything is fine and normal, and then Benjamin goes and says the thing that changes everything. Just like he always has. He's always the same. How could I forget?

But maybe what he had said this time didn't mean—maybe Benjamin didn't mean—what she had instantly thought he meant.

She sat up straight. Her voice cracked a little. "Jealous? I wasn't jealous!"

"Okay," said Benjamin. "Fine."

She put on anger that she didn't feel. "That's a pretty arrogant thing to assume—"

"I know. Sorry. We don't have to discuss it. I'm not sure I even want to discuss it. Not right now, anyway. I was just saying it, because you need to know I'm not interested in Mallory. Except for liking to look—"

"You enjoy looking at girls. I got that part."

Phoebe had been astonished, and now she was aghast and even a little frightened. Did all this mean—did Benjamin have a crush on her? Was that his point? Or was he saying that he thought she had a crush on him?

It had always been such an easy friendship. Biking. Birds. Honest talk, yes, but no hint before of—of—and he was younger than she was, and . . . and compared to Ryland, Benjamin was a *boy*. So he couldn't think that she—that they—could he?

"I'm not jealous," Phoebe said.

"Okay."

"It's—it's—" Abruptly, she realized that she didn't want to tell Benjamin about Ryland, even if she could have done so without breaking her word about keeping it secret. You couldn't say to a sixteen-year-old boy (okay, nearly seventeen) who might be in love with you, or at least have a crush on you, or even just think that you had a crush on him, that he couldn't compare to this twenty-four-year old man you loved.

She thought of the painted bunting, preening for the female bunting who wasn't and never would be there.

"If I seemed jealous of you and Mallory," Phoebe said carefully, "it was probably because of how bad it is between me and Mallory these days. We're not friends anymore. Well, you guessed that. And I don't see how it can be fixed. I'm not actually sure I want it fixed."

Benjamin turned toward her. "What went wrong?" He said it quickly, as if he too was relieved to have a change of subject.

"Mallory's changed," she said.

"How?"

Suddenly Phoebe was eager to pour it all out, and not only to leave the dangerous subject behind of what Benjamin might or might not feel for her. That gift of truth that Benjamin had—she needed it now, for this, for Mallory.

"She said something awful to me not long ago," Phoebe said. "And I realized she doesn't think much of me." She tried to choose the exact right words to convey to Benjamin what Mallory had said.

"So," she finished, "here's my best friend—my best girlfriend—telling me that I'm a bratty toddler and an empty name." She stopped for a breath; it was amazing how much it still hurt to say this aloud. "And that there's nothing even remotely special about me as an individual." She stopped for another breath. "Well, so, that's it. Anyway."

Benjamin patted her shoulder, and Phoebe had the sense that if she were to turn to him—just turn to the left and face him, and lean in—

But she didn't. Of course she didn't. Phoebe was appalled that the thought had even crossed her mind. *Ryland,* she thought. *Ryland. He's the only one I should be kissing.* She sat up straight and swiped at her eyes with the heels of her hands. "Sorry. I'll stop now. It just—it hurt. That's all."

"Yeah," said Benjamin.

"Do you . . . do you—" Phoebe stumbled over the question. It was ridiculous, she knew it was ridiculous, but she suddenly couldn't ask Benjamin why he was her friend. Whether he thought she was special.

But then she didn't have to ask.

Benjamin said, "I'll tell you why you're special to me. It's because you treat me like I matter, and you always have."

"Well, you do matter." Phoebe contained her disappointment. So, Benjamin hadn't noticed something amazing about her, something that she never had noticed herself but would instantly know was true. Basically, he liked her because she liked him. At least it was more than what Mallory had said.

"Why wouldn't you matter?" she said. "Everybody matters, right?"

"Really? Does everyone believe that?"

Phoebe sighed. "Well, everybody matters to somebody. Everybody's special to somebody, even if they're not special to anybody else." She waved a hand in the air, trying to work out what she thought. "Okay. There's being special in the ordinary way, the particular way, in your own little circle of family and friends. Then there's being special in the world, like my mother is. Very few people have that. And Mallory was saying that I don't have that special-in-the-world thing and never will, and you know what? I guess she's right. And that's okay. I mean, it sort of hurts that she believes that, and part of me thinks, who is she to judge what I might be someday, when I grow up? Who can know? Don't people grow into themselves as they mature? But it's okay. Probably it's true. Probably I'm never going to be truly special like my mother.

"But I'm not special to Mallory. That's what I learned,

simple as that. And I can't stand it. Which maybe is shallow of me. But she—she's special to me. And it has nothing to do with whether or not she's, you know, special-in-the-world special. Or wait, what was that word from her story about Mayer and his sons? Extraordinary. I don't need to be extraordinary, and I don't need anybody else to be. You can be special without being extraordinary." She tried to laugh. "Maybe that was what hurt, about her story. She's judging me against my ancestors, and I come up short."

Phoebe knew she was babbling. She hardly made sense even to herself. She was groping for some thought that was out of reach.

"Phoebe?"

She looked up to see that Benjamin was frowning.

He said, "I've got a question for you."

There it was again: that thoughtful, focused note in Benjamin's voice. It arrested Phoebe, even though in the back of her mind she thought that maybe she couldn't stand and did not want a second big revelation today. She sighed. She leaned toward him anyway. "What?"

"I'm just wondering," Benjamin said. "Mallory's been thinking about your family a lot, and she's even done research on it. Assuming she got it right, about Mayer and his five sons and all?"

"Yes," said Phoebe. "Mayer existed, and so did the five sons. Excuse me. The five extraordinary sons."

"Well," said Benjamin. "I knew basically about your family, but I didn't know any of that. I wonder why she's so interested. Why would anybody go and make up a fairy tale about your family? It was a lot of work. And she told it like—well, Pheeb, you actually said this last night. It was like she was Scheherazade and her life depended on her story. She was a pro."

"What are you saying?"

"Only that it means something; that Mallory is obsessed with your family and made up that fairy tale and did it so well. She had a reason. It's all pretty weird. Don't you think?"

"Last night," said Phoebe slowly, "I thought she was just trying to entertain my parents. And they loved it, they really did."

"But it's you she was watching," said Benjamin.

"Really?"

"Yeah. I was watching her watching you."

Phoebe chewed her cheek thoughtfully. "If she wanted a reaction from me, she got it."

"You got angry. But was that what she wanted?"

"I don't know."

"I don't know either, but I don't think so. I think she wanted to finish the story, and she wanted you to hear it. When you got angry, that stopped her. She didn't want to finish it without you there."

"It doesn't make any sense," said Phoebe.

"I didn't say it did."

They lapsed into silence.

"Palm warbler," said Benjamin conversationally after a minute. "Over there by the reeds."

Phoebe lifted her binoculars, failed to locate the warbler, and lowered them.

"I'm baffled," said Benjamin. "But I think we want the end of the story."

"Yeah."

"Phoebe? Why did the story make you so angry?"

Phoebe rubbed her temples. "I don't know if you can understand, Benjamin. You're not Jewish."

"So?" said Benjamin. "*Your* parents are Jewish, and religious to some extent, and they weren't upset by what Mallory had to say. And anyway, Phoebe, you always used to tell me you thought religious differences just made trouble in the world by encouraging people to hate each other."

Phoebe sighed. She said, "You're right. I do still think that. But it's a cultural thing too, being Jewish. It's like remembering and honoring your roots. And it was important to Mayer and his sons that their families stay Jewish. And the daughters too, of course."

"There were daughters?"

"Yes, five of them. But anyway, the family did not marry non-Jews, period. It was a huge deal, until you know, very recent generations. That faerie-worship nonsense completely undercuts everything that Mayer was and that he believed, and also what the family was about. They were Jewish! Not pagan! And that matters!"

"You need to calm down again."

"Sorry. It just upsets me."

"Yeah. I see that. I just wonder if there's some other reason you're upset too."

"Isn't that enough?"

Benjamin shrugged.

"I mean, Mayer was an extraordinary man, and one of the ways in which he was extraordinary was that he was loyal. He didn't get rich and powerful and ditch his people, all right? He identified as a Jew and was proud of it, and that's just how it is." Phoebe was talking rapidly. "Imagine if Mallory had said in her story that Mayer secretly converted to Catholicism. That would be offensive, right? So she said he worshipped the faerie queen. It's just the same."

"Don't get mad at me, but I'd be more convinced if your mother had taken offense, too."

"Benjamin—"

"You didn't want to listen to Mallory, Pheeb. Maybe because you were hurting over that word *extraordinary*. She mentions these extraordinary Rothschild sons and she'd just told you that you *weren't* extraordinary. So you blew up."

"When did you become a psychiatrist?"

"I'm just saying."

Phoebe felt exhausted. Benjamin's thinking was flawlessly logical and she didn't know how to explain that nonetheless he was wrong. She had blown up because—because—she didn't really fully understand why, but Benjamin was still wrong. Well-meaning, but wrong.

"Are you mad at me now?" Benjamin asked.

"I'm confused. But I already said I'd let Mallory tell the end of her story. I'll let her tell it even if I have to put a gag in my mouth the whole time." Phoebe thought suddenly that she'd been wrong earlier: Benjamin wasn't in love with her. He'd been talking just now like the friend he'd always been.

It was a relief.

"You know something?" she said. "When I was a kid, I thought extraordinary ought to mean somebody who was even more ordinary than usual. Extra-ordinary. Get it?"

"Got it. And I guess that means we're done with the heavy stuff?"

"Yes."

"Okay." Benjamin lifted his binoculars again. "And I think that was another palm warbler just now. But it flew." He got up. "I'm going to get the scope, so we can get some real birding in before we go back."

"I'll hang out here," said Phoebe. She was glad of the alone time. She closed her eyes and put her head down into her arms.

She never knew quite how long it was—but only minutes—

before she heard Benjamin shouting her name, and then crashing loudly down the path in a way he never did when he was birding. She was on her feet without even thinking about it, because somehow, somehow, she knew. And she knew it was bad.

chapter 24

Benjamin had his scope slung over his shoulder but had neglected to steady it with his other hand. It was as if he hardly realized he was carrying it. "Phoebe, your mom—"

His face was so pale that his freckles stood out on it. "Phoebe, come out to the parking lot. My parents are here in the car. They need to talk to you."

"What? But—" Phoebe put her hand to her pocket where her phone was. Benjamin had a phone too. Why hadn't they just called? Half a dozen confused thoughts raced through her mind. She turned and ran back toward the bikes. She could hear Benjamin right behind her.

She burst out into the little parking lot. Benjamin's parents, Gina and Justin Michaud, were waiting for her, and so was—she was shocked to see—Ryland. He was standing a little behind the Michauds and leaning against their car. He was watching her with a serious face.

What was Ryland doing here? How could he possibly be here?

She ignored him; she had to. She thought her heart had never beaten so fast and so frantically; she could feel it in her throat. She looked right at Benjamin's parents.

It was Gina Michaud who spoke, although Phoebe was unable to take in more than fragments.

"Phoebe, there's been an accident. Your mom seems to have fallen—hit her head—we're not really sure what happened, but she's being airlifted to a hospital in Boston now. Your dad's with her. We won't lie to you, it seems to be serious, but there's hope—"

Phoebe felt Gina Michaud's arms close around her, as if they could make her safe. "Come on," Gina said. "We told your dad we'd get you up to Boston as quickly as possible."

But Phoebe twisted around in her arms. "Mallory," she said. "Where's Mallory? Did she come here with Ryland? Is she back at the cottage?"

"Your friend?" asked Gina. "I don't know. Maybe she went with your father? No, wait, nobody else went with him on the helicopter. Don't worry about her, Phoebe, we'll find her. But now we've got to get you to your parents. We'll take care of everything."

"Ryland," Phoebe said. "He can get Mallory." She turned and craned her neck, but now Ryland wasn't in sight.

"What? Who?" said Justin Michaud.

“Mallory’s brother, Ryland,” said Phoebe. “He’s with you, isn’t he? I just saw him.” Doubt suddenly filled her as she remembered the previous night, on the stoop. She turned back to the Michauds. “I thought I just saw him,” she said. “But now I think I imagined it.”

“No wonder,” said Gina compassionately. “You’re in shock.” She put her arm around Phoebe’s shoulders.

Phoebe twisted around one final time to search for Ryland. Then she allowed Gina to draw her compassionately away.

Conversation with the Faerie Queen, 13

"Child, you have disobeyed your brother. And you have betrayed us. You attempted to warn the girl."

"Yes, Your Majesty."

"And now you stand before me with no protest or defense?"

"I don't have an excuse. You already know why I did what I did."

"Love for humans is dangerous. You were in their world too long. You became vulnerable."

"I became—torn. I know you can't excuse it."

"I cannot. You put the girl's welfare before that of your own people."

"Only for a moment, Your Majesty. It's over now. And I—I deserve whatever punishment you wish. But please, Your Majesty, I have to ask a favor. Just one. It's not for me. Please. Please!"

"What is it?"

"It's for the woman who thinks she's my mother.

She still needs my care. May I stay in the human realm and continue to help her?"

"Why? Once your brother has secured the girl and brought her to us so that we may be renewed, the woman will be on her own. This you know."

"It's just that I'd like her to have me for what time is left, however little. I'll stay with her. I'll keep away from Phoebe. I won't even go to school."

"The girl will have nothing to do with you now anyway. She is firmly in your brother's keeping. Without her parents, she depends upon him utterly."

"Yes, Your Majesty. It's actually a relief to me that my brother's in charge now. I know he can be trusted to put our people first."

"Where you cannot."

"No, I—I can't be. It hasn't been . . . pleasant for me to feel this way. Please, Your Majesty. May I do this one small thing for the woman? As you just said, it wouldn't be for long."

"I have rarely said no to you, child. But this time, I must. You have lost track of who you are. You say it yourself: You have become torn. Damaged. It is the hazard of all changelings, and a great sorrow to me; for once you were so strong. But now you blindly ask for freedom to make the same mistake a second time. I say to you, no."

"Not blindly! With open eyes. I beg you, Your Majesty. It's for the woman, not me. In her way, she has given us so much. For us all, I want to give back. It's balance."

"Do not speak to me of balance! Your mission is finished. Now you must retake your real name and place. Mallory Tolliver was always an illusion. Leave her and her so-called responsibilities behind. They were never yours."

"But this one last favor, Your Majesty. I ask."

"Your insistence both tires and angers me."

"I'm sorry. And yet, I still ask. No, I beg. On my knees, I beg you. Your Majesty, I beg you—"

"Stop! How dare you keep asking? How dare you—it is to me—to us—that you owe love and care—not that woman—we are dying—you have become mad—wild, untrustworthy—your logic is twisted—you think you see balance but you cannot—once you were so loyal and now—"

"Your Majesty! I didn't mean—I will get help. I'm so sorry. Forgive me."

chapter 25

In the weeks that followed, Phoebe's world narrowed into a tight noose of home, school, Ryland, and the hospital in Boston, where Catherine was in Critical Care and where Drew was also now practically living. Phoebe joined her father there as often as she was allowed.

Sometimes, even frequently, she was glad to be at the hospital. It was better than being alone and worrying. And in a strange way, it could be comforting to sit by her mother's bed and hold her hand and speak to her the way she'd been told she ought to, conversationally, talking about her day, pretending everything was more or less okay and that they were just waiting confidently for Catherine to wake up and rejoin them.

But sometimes it was not comforting at all. Sometimes Phoebe felt like she was barely managing to cling to a vertical rock ledge.

Phoebe had originally offered to be the contact person for

relatives and friends. About this too her feelings gyrated. At first it felt good to hear from so many people—the cousins scattered around Europe and the U.S. had all rallied round. It was good to know that they cared, even though there was little anybody could do to help right now.

But after a short time all the caring calls and emails and text messages became unbearable. Phoebe would see a relative's name on her phone and not answer. She waited longer and longer before responding. And then one day she called her mother's assistant, who was handling everything at Catherine's office, and begged her to take over, hugely relieved when the assistant promptly and efficiently set up a private website to post updates and exchange information.

After a week Phoebe understood that she simply could not know from one half hour to the next how she was going to feel. In fact, if not for Ryland, who was entirely kind and tender and loving and available to her through it all, Phoebe had no idea how she would have managed to stay sane.

Only when she was with Ryland did Phoebe feel like her world made some kind of sense. It was as if Ryland's apartment, and his arms and body—even his calm voice on the phone when she snatched an opportunity to call—made an island away from the fear and uncertainty that otherwise threatened to swamp her. Her very pulse seemed to slow when she was with him, and her worries would recede almost magically. In his presence, she could sleep deeply for a while, before he would awaken her. And although even with him she could not really stand to eat much, she was still grateful that he tried to make her. He never said another word about her needing to lose weight. Once he even made her a big goopy grilled cheese, but she could only pick at it.

She was also grateful for the opportunity to talk things out with him. Ryland was so interesting to talk to, so smart and insightful. He always made such sense, and came at things from such a unique angle. Phoebe could rely on his sense, his wisdom. She could trust him, she knew.

Just like she used to trust Mallory.

But she didn't want to think about Mallory. Thinking about Mallory and how it used to be with her—and how much Phoebe secretly wished for her, even now, even though she had Ryland instead—hurt almost as much as thinking about Catherine. The best way to navigate the present was to *stay* in the present. To simply put one foot in front of the other and do whatever needed doing, while waiting for the next time with Ryland when she could put the burden down for a little while.

Or most of the burden. Not quite all. Never all.

Catherine's condition, a coma caused by an unclassifiable brain injury, had the doctors poring over test results and frowning in puzzlement. Nobody understood what had happened. Catherine had been discovered unconscious on the floor of the kitchen that morning. Had she had a stroke? Had she fallen and hit her head? Examinations and tests had been done and they were weirdly contradictory and finally inconclusive.

"It could be," said the lead neurologist, "that Ms. Rothschild will simply wake up tomorrow. Her brain is swollen; she's sustained some sort of brain injury, but we don't know what or why. Unfortunately, we don't know everything we would like to about the brain. A sudden onset like the one Ms. Rothschild has sustained is odd, but it's not entirely unprecedented. The human body can be baffling. And people do recover from all sorts of things. Sometimes a recovery is even more mysterious than the condition itself. We can hope. There's always hope."

Everyone at the hospital, from the department directors down to the nurses and interns, was careful to refer to Catherine formally, as Ms. Rothschild. At first they had tried to call her Mrs. Rothschild, or Mrs. Vale, or even Catherine, but Drew had corrected them sharply. Phoebe wondered if it reassured her father to hear the powerful, individual name. Maybe it made him feel that his wife was not entirely helpless. That, even as she lay unconscious in a hospital bed in the center of a maze of machines, she was still Catherine Rothschild. *The* Catherine Rothschild.

One evening, nearly three weeks after Catherine's accident, Phoebe was lying on the futon sofa at Ryland's apartment, curled up on her side with her head on his lap. He was stroking her hair. His fingers were a little too cool on her brow, but she loved the feeling of being close to him and it was worth paying for it with some discomfort. Especially today.

It had been tough at the hospital this afternoon, harder even than usual. She had come upon her father crying, and he had not even tried to stop or to turn away when he saw Phoebe. In fact, he had hardly seemed to recognize her.

That was new, and frightening. It had been such a relief to come to Ryland and be held. Being held was unspeakably wonderful, incredibly healing, even if—well.

Even if she was an utter failure at sex. Even if, when they had tried—because Ryland had said it would help her feel better, help her feel more connected and loved—it had just not worked.

The awful truth was that Phoebe had felt positively repulsed. She'd concealed this, of course; she'd said she just couldn't right now, she wasn't ready.

But she knew. Inside, she knew. And she wondered what was wrong with her.

Ryland had smiled kindly, though. He had told her not to worry about it. He'd said he understood and that they'd try again when she felt better. He'd been wonderful.

But secretly, she didn't actually want to try again. Not anytime soon.

Phoebe knew this was her own fault; it had to be. It might be her inexperience. Or it might be that she was just not able to turn her mind off; was unable right now truly to focus on Ryland and on what they were doing. The worst part was that this meant she had a secret from Ryland too, since she needed to pretend she wasn't anxious about him . . . about sex . . . and about the bitter truth that she'd lose *him* too if she couldn't fix herself in this area. If she couldn't force herself to be grown up.

It was rather horrible to realize—as she did, in small flashes that she then repressed as well—that she was good at pretending. She was good at tucking what she really felt deep, deep down in her mind.

She needed to be loved; she needed Ryland; that was what was most important. It even made sense, that she would not feel sexual right now. And if she wondered once or twice why Ryland would not understand that, would not hold back for her—well, that also was a thought to be pushed down. She needed Ryland, on whatever terms. She needed human contact, and comfort.

She was so afraid. A world without Catherine—and maybe also without Drew—it was as if the floor had dropped away from beneath her feet. Even talking to Benjamin on the phone couldn't begin to fill the hole. Phoebe knew because she had tried. Maybe if Benjamin had been physically present. But he wasn't.

Except for Ryland, she was alone.

"I was thinking," Phoebe said to Ryland suddenly, diffidently. "I'd like to tell my father about us. I know that we agreed to keep things secret from my parents. But now, because of my mother, it's all changed." This thought had just popped into her mind. All at once it felt urgent.

"How have things changed?" Ryland's voice was calm, interested.

To Phoebe it seemed obvious. She groped for words. "Well, I want there to be honesty between us. Me and my dad, I mean. My dad trusts me. For example, he thinks I'm at home right now. I haven't actually lied to him in so many words, but it's still lying. When I hugged him today, after I found him crying, I realized—it's almost like I'm using my mother's situation to conceal what I'm doing with you. I never meant to do that, but that's what's happened. Do you see?"

"Yes. But here's a question. It's the only relevant question, in my view, although of course you are free to differ. And we know you're confused right now. So, what's best for your father in this situation? Not best for *you*."

"He'd want things right between him and me," Phoebe said. "No matter what, he'd want that. My dad would feel I was lying to him by keeping this secret. So would my mother. So—so do I."

Ryland tapped Phoebe's nose briefly. "I understand. But take yourself and your feelings out of the picture for a minute. Think about your father only. Think like an adult."

Phoebe felt herself go very still. Then she sat up. "I'm already trying," she said, "to be an adult. I—I wish you hadn't said that."

She heard Ryland sigh. She gnawed the inside of her cheek.

He said, in a very gentle, very patient voice, "All right. Let me put it a different way. Ask yourself what you can do—or not do—to help get your father through this horrible time until your mother wakes up."

"Do you think my mother *will* wake up? Really?" Phoebe found that she was holding her breath, waiting for Ryland's opinion, her gaze clinging to his face.

Ryland's eyes narrowed. Then he nodded. "Yes. I do."

Phoebe breathed. "Really?"

"Really." He reached out a hand and she let him pull her to him and hold her. She relaxed, again feeling loved and cared for, again feeling as if there might be a floor beneath her, even if it had gone soft and spongy for a few seconds.

Ryland said, "Your mother is fighting a battle in there, by herself. But she doesn't give up easily. You know that about her. I think she'll fight into waking up in the end. She's an unusually strong person, and she has a lot to live for, and she knows it."

"Yes," said Phoebe. "That's all true. If anybody can force herself to wake up, it would be her. Thank you. You don't know how much it helps me to hear you believe that."

Ryland's breath tickled her ear; it was warmer than his skin. "I just don't see your mother *agreeing* to die," said Ryland, which almost made Phoebe smile.

"No," she said. "Absolutely not."

"I wonder what sort of person would agree to die," said

Ryland. "Someone for whom life was very bad, obviously. Who else? What other reasons might make that happen, do you think? What would make you give up that way, Phoebe?"

"I don't know," said Phoebe. She could feel that Ryland's body had gone still against hers; he felt like that sometimes, hard, alien. After a while she realized he was truly waiting for a reply from her. "If life was bad," she said feebly, repeating what he'd said, not wanting to think about it. "Hopeless."

"Have *you* ever felt that way?" asked Ryland. "Hopeless?"

Phoebe buried her face in Ryland's shoulder, fighting a sudden sense of vertigo, which it made no sense she should feel. But she did. *Now*, she thought. *Right now. Don't you know that?*

"You just told me to hope," she managed to say.

"Yes, I did, didn't I?" said Ryland thoughtfully. "Even when it's not reasonable, one should hope."

"Are you—not reasonable—but don't you think—before, you said—"

Ryland interrupted smoothly. "But before we got sidetracked, we were talking about your father. And it was an important conversation, so I want to go back to it, sweetheart. Okay? We can talk later about how hopeless you're feeling. Your father—he's just barely hanging on, isn't that right? Didn't you say that? That he hardly recognized you today?"

Phoebe nodded against Ryland's chest. "Yes." She winced, remembering. Drew's face was as lined now as if he had aged ten years.

"So, and this is just a question, Phoebe. You wanted to tell him about us, but would it help him in any way to cope with life right now, if he knew about you and me?"

"I don't know," Phoebe said. "Maybe. Maybe he'd feel better able to cope if he knew that you were taking such good care of me?" But even she could hear the uncertainty in her voice.

Ryland smiled. "Well. If he knew me, and trusted me. Maybe. But since he doesn't, I honestly think it would add to his worries. Remember all the things we talked about originally? My age? Your youth?"

Phoebe felt so tired, and yet, at the same time, so knotted up. She leaned into Ryland. "Oh. Right. You're so smart. All right, then. I won't tell him. I don't—I don't even remember why I thought it was a good idea." And she didn't, although it had been something about honesty. Something about feeling the floor beneath her—but wait, Ryland was her floor. And honesty didn't matter; there were things that mattered more. Being held and having someone. Even just one person could hold you up—keep you from falling—one person was all you needed. Just the one right person.

Ryland nodded. "Good." He held Phoebe even closer. "It's so interesting," he said thoughtfully, after another moment. "The more time I spend with you, the more I think about what Mallory said about you. And how true it is."

chapter 26

Phoebe pushed back away from Ryland, so she could see his face. "What do you mean? That I'm not special? That I'm not—" The word from Mallory's fairy tale came to her. "Not *extraordinary*?"

Why did this particular topic keep coming up? She didn't understand. And why did it hurt more, each time it did?

"Well, yes, but—"

"Stop it!" said Phoebe. "Stop it!"

It was as if a tiny pinprick had been bored into her skin, something that would have healed on its own without too much trouble, except that it wasn't being allowed to scab over. Instead it was being poked, irritated, enlarged, and made worse. First Mallory. Now Ryland.

Phoebe spoke rapidly. "What Mallory said was that I'm nothing without, you know, my family and money and—you know. Whereas my mother, well, she's so amazing just all on her own. Extraordinary. My mother's extraordinary. I know that!"

Ryland cupped Phoebe's face. "Do you believe Mallory, then? That you're *not* extraordinary?"

His eyes had never been so intense.

"I guess," Phoebe said slowly.

"So you're ordinary. Just say it, in so many words. You'll feel better."

Phoebe chewed on the inside of her cheek. She had talked with Benjamin about this, and she had been calm then. She could be calm now. She had to be. She had to explain to Ryland what she really thought. She had to make him understand. It felt so—so vital.

She reached automatically for her inhaler. She felt him watching her, still calmly, as she had her puffs and then, a few minutes later, she returned to the conversation, groping again for words, the right words.

She said, "Spending all this time with my mother at the hospital . . . I've had time to think about her. And about us—me and her, our family."

"And what have you thought?"

"*She* thinks I'm special. My mother. I'm not, okay, maybe I agree with Mallory that I'm not very amazing, in the larger sense, not extraordinary. But my mother thinks I am—my dad too, of course—and that, well, that does something to me. I can't really explain it."

"Try."

Oddly, as Phoebe searched now for words to explain how safe she had always felt in her family, it was as if she was herself rebuilding that shaky floor beneath her feet.

"My parents love me," she said. "And that gives me something foundational, a confidence that's very basic. It has nothing to do with money or an impressive family. That's what Mallory didn't understand." *Or you, either*. "It's just about love, *unearned* love, even."

"What do you mean, unearned love? Say more."

"Well, I guess it's basic," she said. "Think of babies. There's no reason to love a baby for anything but the fact that it's there. The baby doesn't do anything to earn love, except being little and cute, which all babies are automatically. So, the baby is ordinary, right? But it feels special and fabulous before it even understands language, just because everybody is cooing over it and cuddling it and feeding it and loving it."

Phoebe paused. "If somebody loves the baby and takes care of it, then automatically, the baby believes it's special. And that conviction gets, sort of, baked permanently into its feelings."

"But then the baby grows up," Ryland said. "And finds out it's not special. It's just a regular human being like millions of others. Nothing extraordinary. What then?"

Phoebe dug deeper and, miraculously, found an answer. "Well, that's the thing. Maybe life teaches the baby—not a baby anymore—that he or she isn't extraordinary. But because of all that love right from the start, deep inside, he or she can never really believe it completely. He or she is secretly convinced of his specialness. That's what early parental love gives to you. It's primal. It's probably why the human race survives."

She had said it. She knew she had somehow blundered her way into the truth, or at least, her own truth. She drew in a deep breath that she felt all the way to the bottom of her lungs.

Ryland said nothing.

"It's pretty amazing, isn't it?" said Phoebe. She smiled shyly. "I sit there by my mother's bedside, and I know that I'll be the first thing she wants to see when she opens her eyes. She gave me this primal belief in my specialness when I was an infant, just by loving me. I don't deserve it, I completely don't deserve it, but I have it anyway."

"And nothing can take it away?" Ryland reached out. He stroked Phoebe's back. It felt good, but she had the fleeting thought it was the kind of indifferent caress you might give a stray cat.

"That's where I keep landing on this," said Phoebe. She laughed a little; but now there was a sob in it too. "I'm absolutely nothing special and I know it. Mallory's right." *You're right.* "But deeper down, my ego doesn't believe that, and, well, that's just how it is."

"So. Because your extraordinary mom loved you when you were a baby, that set your own value high within yourself, is what you're saying."

Phoebe frowned. He hadn't understood after all. But she now knew how to explain. "No, not exactly. I didn't know my mother was Catherine Rothschild. I was a baby, I knew squat."

Then Phoebe had a thought and it was this: Even if Catherine died tomorrow, even if Drew did also, she would still have had their love. Nothing that happened in the past could be taken away. This was an amazing gift. The past was done and over and settled; you couldn't get it back, but still, whatever good you had gotten from it, spiritually, emotionally, would be yours for your lifetime.

Phoebe discovered that she was babbling this out, in a flurry of excitement. "God," she finished. "I'm totally incoherent, but do you see what I'm saying? *Do you?*"

She looked up into Ryland's impassive face.

He did not reply for a full minute. Then, slowly, he nodded. "I believe so." He spoke drily. "You're saying that my sister's words about you not being worthy of your mother and family resonate in you. You know they're true. But at the same time you have a—sorry, Phoebe—a stupid infantile ego that stubbornly refuses to face reality."

Phoebe blinked. Then she laughed. It was a shocked, uncertain laugh. She searched Ryland's face. Was he joking? "I—I guess you can look at it that way. That wasn't quite what I meant. At least, I don't think it was. Maybe—maybe it's true."

There was silence. The good feeling—the floor—that Phoebe had had as she thought about her parents' love was rapidly receding again, replaced by uncertainty. She tried to cuddle up close to Ryland.

"Ryland?" she asked tentatively. "What are you thinking?"

It took him a moment to respond. "I'm remembering something else my sister said about you, before I met you. It fits in with what you were just saying."

Phoebe now just felt tired. So tired and empty. "What is it?"

"She said that the big psychological struggle of your life was your relationship with your mother and, in a more abstract sense, with the Rothschild family history. She said that you would use every excuse you could find to not look at it straight on and take it seriously."

Phoebe sat up. "I am taking it seriously. That's what I was just talking about. It's nothing to do with the Rothschilds—I was talking about parents and children and love and how in any family—"

"No, actually. It seemed to me you were still talking about how you could be a bratty toddler—just as my sister said—and that was okay."

Phoebe was very, very still. Then she got up. "No," she managed. "You totally misunderstood me." Suddenly she felt as if she were alone with a total stranger.

A hostile stranger. But why? *Why?* Was what she had said so terrible? It must have been. Even if she couldn't understand why.

Was he right after all? Was Mallory?

She couldn't stop herself from talking. "Look," she said desperately. "I don't understand why Mallory harped on this and I—I don't understand why you are now too."

Then fury overtook her.

"The big psychological struggle of my life, Ryland? I mean, seriously? The way I feel now, if I get to be intimidated by my mother and worry about living up to her expectations, that would be a wonderful problem to have and I hope I get to have it, and her, for thirty or forty more years."

She glared.

"I see," said Ryland.

But then, abruptly, the fight went out of Phoebe. Did he really think she was a bratty toddler? Why hadn't he understood her? Was she wrong? Stupid?

"Phoebe," said Ryland. His voice was very soft.

She looked at him. Then she turned away and looked for her backpack. Finally she spotted it on the kitchen counter. She went there and picked it up. And then, when she turned toward the door, meaning to leave, she found that Ryland was up also, and he was standing directly in her path. With his arms out.

She couldn't help herself. She burst into tears and flung herself, wordless, fully into his arms. He could say anything he wanted to. Anything he needed to. She would listen. If only he would hold her, if only he would be there for her, she would listen.

"Phoebe," he said quietly. "Let's go to bed. I think I'll be better able to communicate with you there."

Phoebe felt herself go very still.

"Please, Phoebe. Let's try again."

"I don't know . . ."

"Phoebe."

It felt so good to be in his arms. To be held like this. And he did love her. She knew he did.

"All right," Phoebe said tentatively.

Conversation with the Faerie Queen, 14

"You should not try to speak, my queen. I have been given permission to say a few words, just to reassure you. All is well. I am making progress, if slowly, with the girl. I am almost there. And my sister remains at the house quietly with the woman, taking care of her, just as she was doing before you collapsed. My sister may have taken advantage of the situation, but she is being entirely useful and obedient at last. Are you not, sister?"

"Yes, Your Majesty. It's just the way my brother says. And I apologize again for upsetting you the last time we spoke. And to promise that I will only stay in the human realm for a little longer to care for the woman."

"We must leave now. My queen, be calm. Everything is proceeding as it ought. The girl has been fighting me, it's true. She is strangely strong, just as my sister said she was. But she is alone now, confused, vulnerable, and very near to complete despair. I am pushing her hard. She will break soon. Very soon. I can feel it. Very soon, she will give us what we need."

chapter 27

It was in the fifth week of Catherine's coma, just after noon on a fiercely, hurtfully bright Sunday morning. Phoebe had been at the hospital with her father until the small hours of the morning, and had then left her mother's bedside and gone with her father across the street to the hotel suite he'd rented. But even though she was tired, Phoebe was unable to sleep. She eventually left Drew a note, pulled on a short, dark, sleeveless dress, which was the only thing she had at the hotel that wasn't dirty, and come back to Catherine.

She had been there, alone, ever since.

To call Catherine's room "private" was stretching a point. Like the other rooms in Critical Care, it had a wall of glass where it faced the nurses' station. But Phoebe had long since stopped noticing or caring that her every move could be observed. She washed her hands and forearms carefully at the sink, counting to thirty as she rubbed with the antiseptic soap. Then she pulled a chair up next to where Catherine was lying in bed at the center of a bewildering number of attached machines, kicked off her silly high heels, and put her hand loosely, stroking, on Catherine's upper arm.

"Hi, Mom," she whispered. "It's me." Phoebe thought of that poor swollen brain inside her mother's head, and added, "It's Phoebe. Your daughter. Who loves you." Catherine might have memory issues. Brain injury was tricky that way. Phoebe wasn't sure if these memory problems came into play only after the comatose person woke up, or during the coma itself, but there was no harm in playing it safe.

"Dad's sleeping," Phoebe said. "That's your husband, my father, Drew. Drew Vale. I hope he's sleeping, anyway. It's pretty early in the morning. Sunday morning."

She transferred her grip to her mother's hand, squeezing it gently. It was hard to believe that her mother would need these little extra prompts about who was who. Why wouldn't Catherine Rothschild be the sharpest coma patient there ever was?

Beyond the anxiety that lived in Phoebe always these days, she was aware of restlessness and of a desire for something she couldn't name. She began the sort of typical aimless chatter she'd been using lately with her mother.

"Your heartbeat looks good, Mom. And your blood pressure.

You'd be amazed how much I've learned about reading these machines. I know exactly what all of them do and I know what your readings ought to be.

"I watch everybody and everything all the time here. I'm like a hawk. The other day, on grand rounds? One of the interns was going to peel back your eyelid. I know—icky. But that wasn't the problem. If they have to check your eyes, they have to check your eyes. It was that he didn't put on gloves! So I stopped him. He said he'd just washed, but I didn't care. How was I supposed to know that for sure? You can never be too careful, I told him, and he agreed with me. And he put on gloves." Phoebe trailed off. The last thing she'd meant to do was describe her new obsession with germs. There was no reason to risk getting Catherine all bothered about it too. "Anyway."

She hadn't liked watching that intern peel back Catherine's eyelid. For some reason, it was worse than seeing somebody take Catherine's blood, or even do things to Catherine's feeding tube. She squeezed her mother's hand again. And then suddenly, vividly, she had a flashback to being in the bathroom in the house on Nantucket that last night, when she had not confided in her mother about Ryland, even though she had sort of wanted to.

She looked down at her mother's face. It was one of those times when Catherine didn't look as if she were in a peaceful slumber. Her forehead was deeply creased and her neck muscles looked tight, as if she, herself, were being prevented from speaking.

Catherine's eyelids twitched. For a moment it was almost as if she were going to open them. "Mom?" said Phoebe. "Mom?"

Nothing happened.

Phoebe counted the lines across Catherine's forehead and at the corners of her mouth. She touched her mother's soft cheek, cupping it in her hand. "Mom," she said, softly, uncertainly. "Oh, Mom. I miss you."

An urgent feeling swelled in her. Catherine was fifty-nine years old. She was in a coma. What if they had no more time? What if there would never again be a real conversation? What if this opportunity to tell her about Ryland was the only one Phoebe would ever have? If Phoebe grabbed this chance, did that make her selfish, immature, unethical, small, stupid, and just plain wrong?

"I need to tell you something, Mom," Phoebe said aloud. "I wanted to tell you before. When we were in the bathroom on Nantucket, and you said that thing about how sometimes it's a boy that comes between best girlfriends? Remember that?

"Well, maybe you knew and maybe you didn't. Maybe you were guessing. But you were right. There is a boy—a man—in my life, and it caused problems between me and Mallory. My best friend, Mallory Tolliver, remember her? We're not friends anymore. Can you imagine that, Mom? Mallory's not even coming to school these days. I hear she's home taking care of her mother. And she's being homeschooled over the Internet or something.

"But you know what, Mom? I keep expecting Mallory to show up here, at the hospital. To sit here with me and Dad. She was like my sister. And I can't believe she doesn't care enough about you to come. Or even to call and ask me how you are! Not that I'd take the call.

"I know I was wrong in how I acted with her. I lied to her. But it's not really about that. It's about how she sees me. She doesn't actually like me much. But you know what? The person I always thought she was—that person would have understood me. And she'd, you know. She'd still care about me. But she doesn't, so that means she was never who I thought she was."

Phoebe discovered she was crying. "I'm sorry to bother you with this, Mom," she said. "Please don't think I care as much about Mallory as I do about you. You're the main person I'm worried about. You're the main person I love. It's just that I miss her too." She got up. "I have to go get a tissue. I'll be right back." She went back to the sink, where she blew her nose and then carefully washed up again, including rinsing her face. She caught the eye of a nurse who stopped in the doorway.

"Everything okay?" said the nurse.

Phoebe nodded. "Fine. Thanks." She stood back while the nurse entered and began checking Catherine's vital signs.

"Your mother is holding her own here," said the nurse. "And it would be good if you got some rest. It doesn't help your mother if you don't. You have to keep your chin up."

Phoebe hated that expression. "Thanks," she said, but did not move. When the nurse left, Phoebe went back to Catherine's side. She pulled the chair close and put her head down on the bed as close to her mother's as possible and held her hand again. Now, she realized, she was tired. So tired.

But she still hadn't told her mother about Ryland. She had ended up talking about Mallory instead. And—oh, God. How could this be? She didn't want to talk about Ryland. The very thought made her feel empty. She reviewed all the words in her head. The right words to tell Catherine.

I have a boyfriend. I love him. I know I do. But—but—he keeps trying—I keep trying—and it's not working out, and last night he said to me—he said—

She couldn't say it out loud. But still it had happened. Things had been said that she knew were true. Everything Ryland had said to her was true.

It's not the things that are happening with your mother that cause you to be this way, Phoebe. And it's not inexperience. The problem is you, Phoebe. You have to face it.

There's just something really wrong with you.

Phoebe had been absolutely naked when he'd said this.

It shouldn't have hurt like it had—like it did—it shouldn't have—but—but—

If only she could tell someone.

If only she could tell her mother.

She clenched her mother's hand in hers. "I know you love me, Mom," she said softly. Then the words began to pour out. Different words, but words she meant. "I want you to know how wonderful your love has always made me feel. I know I'm not really special and wonderful. I mean, as a person.

"No, don't disagree with me. I know you'll want to. I love you for that. But just listen. I'm coming to understand something. It's that you can be made to feel special and extraordinary by someone else, when they love you. But that doesn't actually *make* you special and extraordinary. Not for real."

Phoebe leaned in close, close. She dropped her voice to an even softer whisper. "I was thinking at first that it couldn't be taken away. But now I'm not sure. Because the truth is—Mom? The truth is that I'm not those things. I'm not extraordinary like you. I'm only special to you and Dad. I see that now. Alone, I'm ordinary."

Then something very odd happened. All Phoebe's agitation suddenly drained away. A strange, fatalistic calm filled her. She sat up. She released her mother's hand.

It felt almost a relief to have said it out loud, at last. It felt as if she had just become unstuck. And maybe the truth was ugly, but if it was, in fact, the truth, well then. It had to be faced.

"I'm ordinary," she whispered again.

And having said it, she felt the truth of it. She felt it to her bones.

She was actually worse than ordinary; she was sort of nothing.

chapter 28

The next second, Phoebe was desperate to see Ryland. Why, exactly, she didn't know. But suddenly she felt she couldn't survive another hour without seeing him, talking to him, telling him that she finally got it. She had finally grown up and faced the truth about herself.

She knew with everything in her that it would please him to hear it. And she wanted to please him—it was all that was left—

When Ryland didn't respond to a text message, or to a call, she found that, for once, she could not simply wait for him to get back to her.

She got into her car and went by Ryland's apartment. But his car was not there, and when Phoebe squinted up from the street at his window, she could see that the apartment was dark. Once more, she tried calling; once more, he didn't respond. She pressed the disconnect button in frustration.

She ought to have gone home then. For a few minutes, Phoebe even believed she was doing exactly that. But instead, some internal robot took over the driving, and she found she had turned her car toward the neighborhood where Mallory and her mother lived, thinking that Ryland might be there with them.

She slowed down just before the Tollivers' house. Light gleamed softly behind its drawn living room curtains, and Ryland's car sat next to his mother's in the driveway. So, he *was* there. They were all there. A complete family.

Phoebe parked across the street, where she had a good view of the house. She turned off the motor and the lights, and sat with her arms crossed on the steering wheel and her cheek resting on her arms, watching the house and feeling her heart beat just a little faster than normal in her chest. After a minute or two, without even thinking about it, she reached for her inhaler and automatically took a couple of long, steadying puffs. Then she got out of her car. Somehow she was on the Tollivers' front steps, somehow she was reaching, not to press the doorbell, but for the doorknob. And then she was turning that doorknob, and finding the house unlocked.

By now, her heart was racing; she could literally hear her pulse thudding in her ears. "Hello?" she called out as she came through the door. "It's Phoebe." Her voice was shaky.

"Hello!" Phoebe said again. She was in the foyer now, looking over into the living room.

“Hello, Phoebe,” Mrs. Tolliver replied serenely. She sat on a big cushion on the floor, with three magazines open in front of her, and a large pile of Skittles in a candy dish to her left. She didn’t seem surprised to see Phoebe, or perturbed. She looked pleased. She even smiled. She said, “Come on in!”

A quick look around told Phoebe that Mrs. Tolliver was alone in the room.

“Oh, nobody else is here,” said Mrs. Tolliver. “They’re off . . . you know. To that place where they go.” She reached to pull a nearby cushion invitingly closer. “Have a seat. Skittle?” She held up the candy dish. She added perkily, “They think I don’t know all about them, but I do.”

Never had Phoebe seen Mrs. Tolliver smile so much. In fact, Mrs. Tolliver appeared more lucid and, well, normal, than ever before.

The part of Phoebe that had been driving her toward Ryland suddenly eased up. It was enough to be nearby.

Phoebe sat down on the cushion across from Mrs. Tolliver. She took a Skittle to be polite.

“Try the sour raspberry,” Mrs. Tolliver said, pointing.

Phoebe wondered how much, if anything, Mrs. Tolliver knew about what was going on with Catherine. But this was still Mrs. Tolliver, who, even if she knew, would never lean forward and touch Phoebe and say, “How are you, dear?”

Mrs. Tolliver popped a sour raspberry Skittle into her own mouth, smiled again, and then held up one of her magazines. “I was just thinking about that place, you know, the place where they go, because I was looking at this picture."

Phoebe took the magazine—a gardening magazine—and looked. Her hand tightened on the magazine. Her breath caught in her throat as she stared.

The picture was of a small garden glade, spring-like, enclosed by flower beds, framed by trees, and with a pretty upholstered chair in the middle. Phoebe gazed at it in shock. Then she looked back up, straight into Mrs. Tolliver's utterly clear, utterly understanding, and utterly knowledgeable eyes.

"The place where they go," echoed Phoebe. She stared at Mrs. Tolliver, and Mrs. Tolliver smiled at her, and then Phoebe looked again at the magazine picture.

The upholstered chair in the picture was not the throne that Phoebe had seen, or hallucinated, the last time she had been in this house. This magazine picture was merely an advertisement for furniture, and the chair was upholstered in a flowery fabric, intended to imply that buying this chair would make you feel like you were sitting in a bower. It was not what Phoebe had seen. This was not Ryland's bedroom, or anyone else's. It was a magazine fantasy.

But the composition of the picture was a dead ringer, and Mrs. Tolliver's oddly sparkling eyes were now telling Phoebe the impossible: that she too had found the garden.

Mrs. Tolliver clasped her hands. "It is there, isn't it? I knew it! You've seen it too. I can tell by your face." She leaned forward confidentially. "You won't tell on me, will you? I'm not supposed to know it's there. But I do know. That's where they're from. And there's a gateway to it right here in my house."

Mrs. Tolliver nodded her head decisively. "They're faeries. Both of them. What I don't know is what they're doing here. Besides pretending to be my children, that is."

Conversation with the Faerie Queen, 15

"My queen, please. Don't try to speak. Please—"

"No, Ryland, let her talk. Can't you see that she needs to? Your Majesty, try again. Just a little louder and I will hear you—"

"She is near."

"What? Your Majesty? Who is near?"

"I can feel her. The girl. She is ready. Bring her to me."

"No, she's not ready. She has to admit that she's ordinary. She hasn't. Not yet. Ryland said she wouldn't even say it last night when he—"

"It is done. She has said the words, just not to Ryland. But they are said, and they were meant."

chapter 29

Phoebe sat with her mouth agape.

A wistful look passed over Mrs. Tolliver's face. "Do you know what I'm hoping, Phoebe? What I've been hoping for all this time? That if I'm very good, and if I keep pretending, then they'll give me back my own Mallory someday. The faeries must have her, don't you think? They must have made it seem like she died, but that didn't really happen. The faeries took her. They saved my Mallory from leukemia and they gave me the other Mallory in exchange.

"But one day they'll have what they came for and then they'll go away and give me back my own daughter. Don't you think, Phoebe? So I help them all I can, by pretending. I'm just what they want me to be."

She's not well, Phoebe thought to herself. Mrs. Tolliver is not well. Whatever she's babbling about, I don't have to listen. She's—Phoebe reached for a word Catherine might have used—she's psychotic. I'll get up. I'll walk away.

But she didn't move.

Mrs. Tolliver traced the edge of the candy dish with a loving fingertip. "The Skittles are my secret weapon. I remember better when I eat them." She giggled. "I think it's because Skittles are so sugary. Dark chocolate doesn't work. Twizzlers do, but I hate them, don't you? I think any refined sugar will do the trick, really, but I stick with my Skittles."

Crazy as a loon, Phoebe thought. She began to push herself up from the floor. She was suddenly frantic to escape. "I actually came here looking for Ryland, but since he's not here, I can't stay. Thank you for—"

"No!" Mrs. Tolliver grabbed for the candy dish with one hand and with the other reached across to take hold of Phoebe by the front of her dress. Phoebe found a Skittle pressed to her lips. She opened her mouth to protest and the candy was within, melting a little in her mouth.

"Don't go," said Mrs. Tolliver. "I have more to tell you!"

Phoebe's instinct was to spit out the Skittle, but she didn't. She had no conscious awareness of deciding to settle back onto the cushion, but there she sat. Then carefully, consciously, she chewed and swallowed the Skittle, although the candy seemed to fight her throat as it went down and a moment later, her stomach roiled. She pressed her lips shut.

"Thank you." Mrs. Tolliver put her hand to her throat.

"Who knows when I'll be able to talk to you again? Maybe never. And it's such a relief. You're probably the one person who knows I'm not crazy."

Phoebe managed a small, polite nod. She felt cold. So cold. This *was* craziness; it had to be. She twisted her hands together.

"You're such a nice girl," Mrs. Tolliver said. "You were always good to my Mallory. Wait. Not my Mallory. The other Mallory. It's confusing, isn't it? She was in such a terrible place when she met you. So vulnerable and scared. And I couldn't do anything. I needed to pretend not to notice. You can't know how terrible it is, to be helpless concerning your children. I mean, not my child at all. But she looked like my Mallory. Then, she did. Not now. But she's always been nice to me. Well, maybe not always. But mostly. She tried. Which the other one—you know, the man—he's never bothered. Not that he's been here long. They think I'm stupid, but I'd never forget I had a son! I didn't. I only had a daughter. My Mallory. But I pretended. I always pretend."

Mrs. Tolliver paused for another Skittle. "The other Mallory. You helped her fit in; you helped her stay here. And so, you helped me. You have no idea how grateful I was. I will always be grateful. Especially if in the end I get my Mallory back!"

Now Mrs. Tolliver was looking confused. "I'm drifting," she muttered. Her hand hovered over the candy dish, and then attacked it and retrieved five Skittles. She put them in her mouth and chewed quickly.

"I was glad to help Mallory," said Phoebe uncertainly. "And I want you to know that I was aware she needed help. My whole family knew. My mother knew." Her voice stumbled over the reference to Catherine. "We wanted to help," she said. "Mallory needed a friend."

"I'm starting to feel sick," Mrs. Tolliver said. "There's no sense in my finishing these, even." She dumped the Skittles back into the candy dish. They left colored smudges on her palm.

Phoebe saw her escape route. "Let me help you to bed. And I'll get you your medication if you tell me what to do."

A visual memory formed in Phoebe's mind. Mallory, that very first day, with the cheap fairy wings hanging drearily from the shoulders of her costume. She'd been wearing clothing she'd gotten from her mother, Phoebe recalled.

Suddenly the rational explanation came to her. The young Mallory, sane where her mother was insane, had occupied her time playacting, going along with her mother's faerie lunacy. It was a wonder Mallory hadn't gone insane too.

Fury filled Phoebe. At Mrs. Tolliver, a little, but mostly at Ryland. Why hadn't he done something? Why hadn't he protected his sister at least, and been there for her?

Phoebe had a moment of desperately wishing for *her* mother, who was so much the opposite of this passive, loony creature. But there was no sense in that.

"Let me get you to bed. Come on." Decisively, Phoebe got up, and five minutes later, she had gotten Mrs. Tolliver off the floor, down the hallway, and into her own bed.

But what to do next? Mrs. Tolliver had reverted to mumbling incoherence, but also seemed sincerely in pain, abdominal pain that was increasing every minute. Phoebe retreated to the bathroom to look at the row of prescription medications lined up there. She looked at medication names, she looked at dates, but she had no idea what would help.

Finally, she pulled out her phone to try Ryland again. Of course he still wasn't responding. And so, the next second, she tried calling Mallory. And when Mallory too did not pick up, Phoebe impulsively left a message.

"Mallory, it's Phoebe. I'm with your mother right now, at your house. She's sick. I don't know what to do. She's in pretty bad shape, a lot of pain. It might be nothing—she's been into a lot of Skittles—but I can't take the risk. So if I don't hear back from you in five minutes, I'm going to call 911. I know you're mad at me and I'm mad at you, but this is about your mother. Call me the second you get this, okay?"

It didn't even cross Phoebe's mind to leave a similar message for Ryland. He had umpteen messages from her already today. She looked at her watch to note the time and returned to Mrs. Tolliver's room to check on her.

And found her passed out and snoring like a hibernating bear. Beside her, rolling on the floor next to the bed, was a bottle of ordinary non-prescription Tylenol PM.

"Well," said Phoebe aloud. "So much for that." She hesitated, in case it only looked like Mrs. Tolliver was all right. But that snore announced health in just about the loudest possible terms.

There was a further safety precaution to make, to put Mrs. Tolliver on her side, just in case she vomited and choked while she slept. Phoebe heaved her into place and propped some pillows around her.

Now she could leave, drive home, collapse into bed, and forget she'd ever come here. Her only regret was that she'd left that telltale message for Mallory. She'd have to call and leave another, explaining and telling her not to worry. And then leave a long explanatory message for Ryland too.

What a tangled mess. At least she was breathing okay.

And she no longer felt that she desperately needed to see Ryland. That had been odd, that feeling . . .

Faeries! She had to get away, out of this house . . .

After one last check of Mrs. Tolliver, Phoebe headed back down the hallway toward the exit. But her feet slowed and then stopped halfway down the hall, in front of the closed door of the room that belonged to Ryland.

She could close her eyes now and see her hallucination from before. The little walled garden. And then Mrs. Tolliver's magazine picture of what was essentially the same thing.

There was a logical explanation. Of course there was.

But she still couldn't move on past the door. Her hand twitched. She wanted to open it. She wanted just to check. Just to see.

Behind her, she could still hear the regular, stentorian notes of Mrs. Tolliver's snores. Phoebe thought of all the stupid heroines in horror books and movies who went into the haunted house, where they met their deaths. But she knew this was an ordinary room. She knew it. This was the real world. In the real world, there was plenty of horror of the regular kind involving war and famine and floods and disease and crime. And mothers in comas from which they might never wake up.

But there were no faeries.

She would prove it right now.

Phoebe turned to face the door to Ryland's room, grasped the knob, and threw the door open.

And came face-to-face with Mallory, panting, one hand extended as if to open the door from the other side, her phone in the other hand, and, behind her—

Behind Mallory was Faerie.

chapter 30

Phoebe was filled with cold, hard fury. All right, then. The impossible was not only possible, but true.

She wasted not a second more on doubt. She launched herself at Mallory in a full tackle, overturning her onto the cobbled stone path and landing on top of her where she could hold her down and grab her arms and scream directly into her face.

"You lied to me! From the very first, you lied! Homeschooling, yeah, right, absolutely. Clinically depressed mother! Brother in Australia! Everything about your brother! Both of you, liars! What about that legend that says faeries never lie? They can trick people but they never directly lie? It's not true, is it? I can prove it! You both lied to me. And to my parents!

"And why? That's what I really want to know. Is it about my mother's money? I may be a Rothschild, but beyond that we both know I'm nothing special. I admit it, I'm ordinary. So what? Why was that so important for me to realize? To say? Did you tell your brother I was an easy mark for—for whatever it is you're up to?

"You know, I wondered at first how he could possibly be interested in me. I wanted to believe it, so I did. I was an idiot, okay, granted, but I'm not one anymore. He never cared about me, the real me, any more than you ever did, right? You've both used me! It was all about some faerie thing. Something to do with that crazy story you told us on Nantucket about Mayer Rothschild. Right? Well, now I'm sorry I missed the end. Would it have made a difference if I'd listened to the whole thing? Or would we still be here now, only I'd know why you've betrayed me, not to mention my mother—my mother—

"My mother—that mysterious coma—I saw your brother on Nantucket. Both of you were there! Did you put my mother in that coma? You did, didn't you? Both of you! Why? *Why*? What do you want from us? From me? Whatever it is, why didn't you just come out and ask for it? My mother—she was never anything but good to you! My dad—he's a wreck—you—you—evil—"

Phoebe didn't know when, during this rant, she began to cry. She didn't know when she realized that Mallory, although tense beneath her, wasn't fighting back, and had not even tried to say anything. But these realizations came to Phoebe when she paused, panting, for breath. And then she looked down into Mallory's tense face, felt Mallory's tight muscles under her hands and body, and came back fully into herself. And all the words she had just said washed back over her in a flood of understanding.

If she had said all those things, if she had asked those questions now, then she must believe all of it. And that meant she either was insane and deep in a hallucination (and strapped down and/or drugged in a mental hospital somewhere), or she was truly in Faerie, having entered through a portal in Ryland's bedroom, and there really were faeries, and Mallory and Ryland were amongst them, and they had entered her life wanting something from the human realm and from the Rothschild family, and/or from Phoebe herself.

Fayne, Phoebe thought. Fay equals Fey equals Faerie. How ironic. She remembered having made that very connection once, laughing about it to Mallory, even. Actually, it had been Mallory who brought it up. But of course Phoebe had not been paying any serious attention. Because she wasn't, like, a certifiable nutcase.

Until now.

Phoebe rolled off Mallory and scrambled a few feet away. Vaguely, she became aware that Mallory was wearing something that glimmered. But she didn't look closely. She was shaking all over her body and didn't dare try to stand up. She grabbed her knees with her arms instead. The door to the hall was only a short distance away; beyond it she could see the gray Berber pattern of the hallway carpet and where the white paint had chipped away from the molding of the doorway. The real world, just outside the door. She could race for it, and leave all of this craziness behind her. And she would, as soon as her legs would support her, and her breath calmed down.

Around her and in all directions was the gorgeous, mysterious landscape of Faerie. Flowers, brighter and more fragrant than normal flowers. Birdsong, more harmonic than its earthly counterpart, but somehow for this very reason grating to Phoebe's ear, which had been trained by Benjamin.

She didn't want to look down into the glade, to see if the throne was still there. The throne with the books about the Rothschilds piled up beside it.

Later she could blame herself for all her mistakes. For loving and trusting where she was not trusted and loved—or cared for at all—in return. But now was not the time.

If she ran back through the doorway and slammed the door shut, would the nightmare end? If she set the house on fire, if it burned to the ground with Mrs. Tolliver and Mallory and this gateway to Faerie inside it, would that take care of things? Would Catherine then wake up and be okay? Phoebe would probably have to go to jail for arson and murder, but it would be worth it. Maybe she'd be able to claim insanity. It wouldn't necessarily be a lie.

All of these rushing thoughts had taken only a few seconds. Mallory was sitting up now too. When she spoke, her voice was quiet but clear, and held a bone-deep tiredness. "There is a reason for my behavior, Phoebe. Not one that will excuse me to you, but nonetheless, it exists."

"You were never my friend," said Phoebe. "You were acting the whole time. You know what hurts the most, after what you did to my mother? It's that you manipulated me from the start. You were my friend for some reason that had nothing to do with liking me, weren't you?"

"Yes," said Mallory simply.

For some reason, that single word stopped Phoebe cold. She had nothing more to say. Mallory had admitted it. She stared at Mallory, looking for some sign of—something—on her face, but found nothing. She had even temporarily forgotten her intention to make a run for it.

After a minute, Mallory said quietly, "Before—all this. You left me a message. Something about uh, Mrs. Tolliver."

"What? You receive messages in here?" said Phoebe nastily. "Who handles the network, AT&T? The monthly charges must be huge."

"My mother—that is, Mrs. Tolliver—"

"You're a little confused about who she is, huh? Or is it that you're confused about who *you* are? But it's good to know you care about someone. Unless you're faking it again. You're good at that. Well, don't worry. That's her in the next room, snoring. Can't you hear?"

They listened.

Mallory said formally, "Thank you. It sounds like she's

all right. Or she will be as long as she sleeps." It was as if this were a regular conversation. It was surreal, but it helped Phoebe calm down a little.

"She took some Tylenol PM," Phoebe said. "On top of a lot of Skittles." Amazing how easy it still felt to talk to Mallory. She gathered her fury protectively around her again. "She knows all about you, by the way. She's not fooled. She's been going along hoping to get her real daughter back."

Mallory—or whoever she was—went very still.

"What did you do to the real Mallory? Sacrifice her in some faerie ritual? Or is she alive and there's some small chance that your—Mrs. Tolliver—can have her back?"

Mallory—Phoebe wished she could think of her by some other name, but she could not—winced. "Her daughter can't come back. She died of leukemia. We had nothing to do with it."

"Why should I believe you?"

"No reason."

"Tell me, is your mo—is Mrs. Tolliver really sick? Really depressed? Or do you do something to keep her dependent and helpless? Did you *make* her crazy?"

As Phoebe narrowed her eyes at Mallory, Mallory's appearance penetrated fully for the first time. She was awfully thin; thin, not slender. Also, she was wearing a soft-looking dress that glinted and glimmered with sparkles in the Faerie sunlight. But there was something peculiar about the dress; it wasn't quite beautiful. The fabric was too shiny, like polyester, and the starry glints, on closer examination, came from cheap sequins that had been sewn on with a less than expert hand.

"Incidentally," Phoebe said, "that dress isn't what I'd have thought a faerie would wear. It's a little, uh, ragged. And you look pale and, uh, sick."

"We've been encountering some difficulties lately, here in Faerie," Mallory said politely. "This is the best I can do right now."

Phoebe's breath was coming easier now. It was time to leave. Past time. And she would. Carefully. She just needed to keep Mallory talking until she was closer to the door and could outrun her—slam the door behind her—figure out where to go to be safe—Benjamin, she could go to Benjamin, he'd listen—or no, Mallory knew all about Benjamin, Phoebe couldn't endanger him—maybe one of her Rothschild relatives—but how to protect her mother—father—maybe she really should set the house on fire. She would turn on all the burners on the gas stove. She'd pull Mrs. Tolliver with her, somehow.

"Do these difficulties have something to do with why you've interfered with Mrs. Tolliver and with my family?" Phoebe kept her voice conversational. She slid her butt a half inch nearer the door.

"You were always smarter than you gave yourself credit for."

Another inch. "Really? That's a change, coming from you. And in fact, I'm feeling exceedingly stupid. It seems to me that I was very easy for you to fool. Wouldn't you agree?"

Mallory's voice was soft. "Yes, actually. From the first, you were very credulous and trusting."

It shouldn't have hurt, because it was not news. But it did. *I loved you!* Phoebe wanted to scream back. But she needed to remember that the friend she loved had been an illusion. A made-up Mallory. This creature was not her.

Another inch.

"Did you know your mother—Mrs. Tolliver—was on to you?" And another.

A pause. "No," said Mallory.

"Then you're not so infallible, are you?" Phoebe matched her calm, even tone to Mallory's as she scooted another inch. At this rate, she might make it to the door by midnight. Could she speed it up? Why not? Mallory had made no move to stop her. Yes, it was time. Phoebe would scramble to her feet and run like the wind. She'd grab Mrs. Tolliver; she'd set that fire—

"I have never," said Mallory, "felt infallible."

Phoebe tensed her muscles. Now—it was now!

She jumped to her feet and headed for the door.

chapter 31

Phoebe crashed into a stone wall that materialized before her. The crash knocked the wind out of her and she leaned against the wall, feeling its solidity against her bruised shoulders.

"Don't bother, Phoebe," said Mallory. "It's too late. The queen has summoned you. You have to go to her. It's over, Phoebe. And for what it's worth, I'm sorry."

Phoebe ignored her. She put out both hands and touched the wall with her palms. It felt like old stone; mossy, somewhat worn. The wall looked old too; its stones irregular in size and fitted together precisely, without the use of mortar. It could have been there for centuries. She pressed here and there, frantically, as if she would find some secret touchstone that would magically make the wall an open doorway again.

She turned back to Mallory. She could literally taste fear now, acid at the back of her throat.

She would not collapse. She would not allow it. She stood up straight.

"Now you will go see the queen," said Mallory again. "She's expecting you."

Phoebe had a sudden, vivid memory of Mallory describing the Queen of Faerie as Mayer Rothschild had seen her. *Hair the yellow of a bee's fur, the russet of a fox's pelt, the white of a dandelion gone to seed, and the shiny black of a songbird's eye. Skin formed of leaves. As much akin to trees and plants as to humankind.*

She shuddered.

"You have to understand something, Phoebe," said Mallory. "It really is nothing to do with me anymore. My part is done."

"You've got me wishing I was Christian," Phoebe said. "So I could call you a Judas." She took in one long, deep breath.

And then, shocked, another, as a new realization dawned on her. By now, if history was any guide, she should have been having a very serious asthma attack. But she wasn't. There wasn't even the slightest rattle to her breathing, and her lungs were filling up with air to a depth that was totally unfamiliar and should, for Phoebe, have been physically impossible.

Phoebe breathed in again, to make sure. She frowned.

"Health comes to any human in Faerie," said Mallory quietly. "Your lungs are already healing. When you were here before, you left too abruptly, and that was what triggered that attack."

"Am I supposed to be grateful?"

"No. Just—point of information."

Mallory got up from the ground and dusted off her tawdry little dress. "I have to go. My mother—Mrs. Tolliver—I need to check on her. And, I repeat, you have to go too." She pointed down lower into the garden. "Follow the path on the far side of the clearing. Ryland will be waiting for you. He'll take you to the queen."

Ryland. Phoebe thought of the last time she had seen him—of being in his arms—of begging him to give her another chance.

Bile rose again forcefully in her throat. It was less easily swallowed back than before.

"Terrific," Phoebe managed.

Mallory shrugged. "Good-bye."

"Mallory," Phoebe began. She stopped talking because she saw that Mallory had raised her hands and was shaking her head back and forth, almost violently.

"Don't start," said Mallory. "Just don't. I have to go!"

Possibly the worst thing of all about this moment—worse than the panic and terror and the unbelievable knowledge of betrayal—was that Phoebe wanted to beg her ex-friend, her betrayer. *Don't leave me! Be by my side. Please. Don't leave me all alone. Don't abandon me to your brother! Stay with me.*

She didn't say any of it. She looked at Mallory instead. Just looked.

"I told you, it's nothing to do with me anymore!" Mallory shouted.

"Mallory . . ."

"No, Phoebe, I—"

"All right. All right! But can you just tell me the end of the story?"

Mallory blinked.

"The end of the story about Mayer Rothschild," Phoebe said steadily. "Just take a few minutes. You were going to tell me on Nantucket, so what's wrong with doing it now? Don't you at least owe me that?"

Mallory didn't answer.

"A short version." Phoebe tried to keep the pleading out of her voice. She tried simply to speak normally. "Come on. Mayer joined the dance. He was naked. He was worshipping the faerie queen, paying tribute to her, being part of her court. And then . . ."

The two girls locked eyes.

Mallory sighed. She shut her eyes tightly for a moment.

Then they snapped open. "All right," she said to Phoebe. "I actually now have permission to tell you. Someone else would have to explain it to you later anyway, now that you're here. So Ryland will wait."

"Thank you," Phoebe said uncertainly. She was freaked out, a little, by what Mallory had just said about permission.

Mallory hesitated another moment. Then she began. But this time her voice wasn't slow, mesmerizing, but rapid and angry.

"Hours passed, while Mayer danced with the faerie court. It was solstice, and he had seen the court and the queen as they really are. He had eaten no faerie food. He was not beguiled or enchanted or enslaved. And yet he gave voluntary tribute, with a full and joyful heart, without doubt or hesitation. He danced with the full attention of his body and his mind and his heart and his soul. This had never happened before with any human. It has never, incidentally, happened since.

"The queen is rarely surprised and even more rarely pleased, especially by a human. But Mayer had both surprised and pleased her, with this gift of his full self. And she—she wanted him."

Phoebe blinked.

"It's not unusual," Mallory said. "The queen has had many lovers over the ages, some of whom have been human. And while Mayer was not the handsomest human male to ever come her way—and that had been her usual method of selection, for she is very sensitive to beauty—the marks of his strong character and mind made him attractive in his own distinctive way. He was as exotic to her as she was to him. And so when the dancing ended, the queen held out her hand to Mayer, and he took it, and I don't suppose I need to be explicit about what happened next, Phoebe."

"No," said Phoebe harshly. She tried to suppress a compulsive thought of herself with Ryland. It was not the same. She had been beguiled and used, for reasons still unclear, and anyhow it had not worked, it had never worked, and the memory was bitter and humiliating.

Except. Except that Phoebe could now admit quietly and fully to herself that she had not—

She had not actually *wanted* Ryland. She had just wanted to want him. But it had not been real, because—

The realization broke over her. Because she had been too afraid. Deep down inside her, where she kept secrets even from herself, Phoebe had been afraid of Ryland.

And she'd known it too. If she had only been able to listen to her body—her body had told her. Her body had known what her mind refused to understand. Her body had—peculiarly, or maybe wonderfully—tried to protect her.

It was her mind that had failed her. Her mind, which had kept coming up with excuses; her mind, which had been so very desperate to believe she was loved.

She wrapped her arms around herself.

"Phoebe?" said Mallory uncertainly.

"Go on," said Phoebe.

Mallory's eyes were sharp, but she nodded. "All right. So. The queen would have kept Mayer forever, and he would still be alive and part of the court to this day, if he had wished. He pleased the queen that much. But he was present of his own choice, and so she left him free to decide his future. To stay with her, or to return to human existence.

"Mayer did not hesitate. He kissed the queen, and then he chose his wife and his life and his coming son. He explained to the queen that he needed to find some way to protect his family—that it had been thoughts about this that had driven him to the forest that night. And he told her that his experience with the faeries had changed him forever. Now, he said, he would fight back, he would change his fate, and he would use every gift he possessed to do so.

"The queen was intrigued. She asked question after question, for though she had a vague awareness that humans worshipped their God in various ways, she knew no details. And while she had heard the term Christianity, she did not know what it meant and she had never heard of Jews—or, indeed, of Muslims, or Buddhists, or of the various divisions between Catholics and Protestants. And of course my story is not concerned with all of the world's religions and what the faeries know or think about them. But it was a good thing that time is not the same in faerie as in the human realm, because the queen had many detailed questions, and required many detailed answers. But finally she was satisfied.

"And she said to Mayer that, if he would accept, she would make sure that he got the thing he most wanted. She said to him, 'You shall have five sons, the sons that you need. They will inherit minds like yours, and determination like yours, and they will understand your vision, and you shall not be disappointed in them. And together, you and your sons will make your family safe from those who would destroy you, and that safety shall last many, many generations.'

"Mayer leaned forward eagerly, but the queen held up one hand and shook her head.

"'Be still,' she said. 'For nothing comes without a price. It must be that way so that the earth stays in balance.'"

"Mayer nodded. We must not forget he was a businessman. 'Of course,' he said. 'What is the price?'

"'In exchange for your five extraordinary sons,' said the Queen of Faerie, 'you must promise me one daughter.'"

chapter 32

Mallory paused and bit her lip, and glanced at Phoebe.

"*What?*" exclaimed Phoebe.

"You heard me," said Mallory. "In exchange for five extraordinary sons, one daughter. One Rothschild daughter."

"But—"

"Listen to the rest," said Mallory tensely. "Just listen, Phoebe."

Somehow, Phoebe managed to contain herself. She would not have thought it possible for her stomach to churn more than it had already been churning, but . . .

One Rothschild daughter?

"The queen smiled," said Mallory. "'Come, Mayer Rothschild,' she said. 'You cannot claim it a hardship, or unfair. It is sons you value; sons you long for. What is one girl to you?'

"Yet Mayer hesitated. 'What would become of the girl?' he asked.

"The queen studied Mayer's face. Finally she said, 'I spoke before of balance. Suffice it to say that I will draw from the earth to give you what you want, for this I have the power to do. But the earth must be repaid for its generosity. I can assure you, however, that the rite is sacred. No disrespect is involved, and great honor is given. We, unlike you, value daughters.'

"'You are saying that the girl would become a valued member of your people? Your family?' asked Mayer.

"'No,' said the queen, and she said it compassionately, but clearly. 'No, that is not what would occur. We take from the earth. We give back to the earth. You understand me.'

"And he did," said Mallory steadily. "He did understand."

Phoebe found that she was leaning against the stone wall, and that it was supporting her weight entirely.

"'I see,' said Mayer Rothschild at last. 'And I thank you. I am indeed honored. My family is honored. Your offer is most generous.'

"But he did not agree," said Mallory. "And here we must again remember that Mayer Rothschild was not simply a businessman, but one of the greatest businessmen of all time. The proof of it came in this negotiation, the most important of his life.

"He took the queen's hands in his. 'You are not wrong about my feelings, and certainly sons such as you describe are worth a serious sacrifice. But here is my dilemma. I fear losing a daughter would break my wife's heart, and although such a thing could happen naturally, for children die for many reasons and leave their parents in sorrow, yet I could not bear to be the cause of pain to my wife. No, even if she is not aware that I am responsible. I must decline. I will instead take my natural chances in life with my children, as all men do.'

"But he did not drop the queen's hands, and both of them knew," said Mallory, "that this was not a true turn-down, but instead a move upon the chessboard. And so the queen listened, and thought, and finally responded.

"'I like your consideration for your wife. Perhaps you are less dismissive of your womenfolk than I had thought. Very well, then. I will make you a compromise, as the earth is patient and we have some time to repay it. I offer this: the girl shall not be your daughter, nor even your granddaughter. It will be from a future generation that we shall take our exchange. Your wife need never know, and never grieve.'

"'That is a concession indeed,'" said Mayer. 'I thank you. I shall accept with gratitude, if we come to terms in the end. However . . .'"

Mallory broke off, her voice impatient. "Phoebe, why are you making that face? You asked me to tell you the whole story."

"It's a *racist* story," said Phoebe. Her stomach had not ceased to churn, but to her astonishment, her mind had also not ceased to work. And what Mallory was saying—

"What?"

"Come on, Mallory!" Phoebe exploded. "Maybe your Queen

of Faerie two hundred-plus years ago knew nothing about the history of anti-Semitism, and had to have it all explained to her. But you can't claim the same! You've had the same education I've had! You've been to synagogue with my family, and you've been invited to our Passover seder every year since I met you, and you know about the Holocaust . . . We even analyzed *The Merchant of Venice* last year in English class. And right now you're making Mayer out to be some Shylock character, bargaining away his own flesh and blood, wheeling and dealing, a complete stereotype—and a completely offensive stereotype, let me add. Bargaining the exact terms for a sacrifice of his—his daughter!"

It felt good to be angry, the anger an effective counterweight to the fear. "Don't deny it, Mallory," said Phoebe, staring at her with hot eyes. "Your little Mayer Rothschild fairy tale is just plain racist and anti-Semitic." She paused. "And anti-feminist."

Mallory took in a tight little breath. "We don't have time for your tantrums. This isn't just a story, okay? It's what actually happened. And if you'll take my advice, which frankly you ought to, you'll do your little sensitivity analysis on your own time." She stopped for a second, and Phoebe thought she was done, but then Mallory swept on, her voice rising, the words pouring out of her as if she too were furious, as if she too couldn't help herself.

"Also, may I remind you, this was 1772, and a man who

didn't have the luxury of a lot of choice. Look, sometimes people in desperate circumstances do desperate things! Sometimes—" And now Mallory's voice was like a whip. "They even do bad things, okay? Things they would rather not do. Sometimes it's just one loyalty pitted against another, and there you are, trapped, and you have to choose. Maybe, Phoebe, you're just a little bit lacking in compassion for your great-great-great-whatever-grandfather, who you claim to admire so much. Life is complicated. Sometimes people really do get trapped, and why should it be bad for them to use whatever they happen to have, whatever skills, to try to make a bad situation a little bit better? Nobody can look out for absolutely everybody else in the world, can they? Don't we all have to look after our own, first and foremost?"

Now it was Phoebe who was staring at Mallory.

Mallory drew in the kind of ragged, harsh, wheezing breath that might once have come from Phoebe.

After a minute of silence, in a much altered tone, she muttered, "Sorry."

"No," Phoebe managed. "I see—I see what you're saying. Only—"

"Only we don't have time," interrupted Mallory. "Can we—please—can I just go on with the story?"

Silence.

"Go on," said Phoebe heavily.

After a few seconds, Mallory did.

"'One daughter,' said Mayer thoughtfully. He raised first the queen's left hand to his lips, and then the right. 'Let me be sure I understand. In exchange for giving me five extraordinary sons, you shall receive one daughter of my line. She is not to be taken from either my own or my children's children, but from a generation after that.'

"'Yes,' said the queen.

"'But here is one final clause that I suggest,' said Mayer. 'To balance the fact that my sons will be extraordinary, the daughter must be commonplace. You said, remember, that any child of my line would do. So, this daughter shall qualify herself when, at an age of sufficient maturity to judge herself and her capabilities, she sincerely and accurately feels herself to be ordinary.'

"'Interesting,' said the queen.

"'These are my terms,' said Mayer.

"'And to these terms you freely agree?' said the queen.

"'To these exact terms,' said Mayer, 'I freely agree.'

"So," said Mallory, "the contract was made on Midsummer night 1772, between the Queen of Faerie and Mayer Rothschild. The queen kept her word. But in all the time since, the Rothschild family has not produced that one ordinary daughter that is owed to Faerie."

Phoebe's mouth was so dry she could hardly get her question out. "Why not?"

For a second, Phoebe could see in Mallory's expression a

flash of the old witty, insightful, familiar friend she once had had.

"Honestly, Phoebe? I've decided Mayer must have been planning on it. Remember the terms? *She must sincerely judge herself to be ordinary*. He figured no child of his line, female though she might be, would do that. Whether they were ordinary or not." An expression approaching compassion crept into Mallory's gaze. "Until you, Phoebe."

Phoebe was silent. She was thinking of Catherine, imagining what she might have been like at Phoebe's age. The awkward, homely, socially maladapted young Catherine. Would that Catherine, with all her personal problems, have agreed that she was ordinary?

Never. And no one could have made her, either.

"And now," said Mallory to Phoebe, "I really have to go. And so do you."

"But—but—" Phoebe could hardly think. "I don't think *badly* of myself, I really don't—"

Mallory was turning away. "I know it's a lot to take in, but this is what has to happen now." She pointed. "Go that way. You don't have a choice. I mean, you could stay here in the glade after I leave, but then Ryland would come get you and force you. My brother—well. We have all been waiting a long time. Patience is short. You don't want him to come get you. You want to be dignified."

"I might be the most ordinary Rothschild ever, but I can

still have dignity?" Phoebe managed a trace of sarcasm.

Mallory shrugged uncomfortably. "I don't know. At least now you understand. Phoebe—this is where we say good-bye. So. Good-bye. Stand away from the wall now, and let me pass. I still have to take care of—of my mother."

Phoebe didn't move.

"I know what you're thinking," said Mallory steadily. "But the wall won't let you through now. Only me. Go. They're waiting." She pointed again toward the path.

Under Mallory's anxious gaze, Phoebe finally stepped away from the stone wall. She had a plan: She'd throw herself on top of Mallory and hurtle them both through the gateway when it opened.

But when Mallory reached one hand out to the wall and it began to dissolve, and Phoebe moved closer, Mallory turned. Phoebe got one last glimpse of her face. It was desperate, half feral, and wholly defiant. The face swung close for just a moment.

Then Mallory reached out with her other hand and shoved Phoebe hard, with strength, accuracy, and efficiency.

Phoebe landed on her butt on the ground, within Faerie. A second later, Mallory had disappeared through the gateway to the Tollivers' house. Then the gateway resolved itself instantaneously back into an impenetrable stone wall.

chapter 33

Phoebe sat on the ground for a minute. Ordinary.

Ordinary.

It was almost like the punch line to a joke, she thought. When were humility and modesty a great big mistake? When you were a Rothschild. Except she couldn't find any humor in it.

Had Mayer really been so sure that none of his female descendants would be ordinary, as Mallory speculated? Or had he merely been counting on egotism and arrogance? Phoebe wondered briefly about some of her aunts. She didn't know them all that well; the family was too scattered. But Phoebe would swear that none of them, nowadays, were truly extraordinary, like Catherine or like the five sons. But then again, they had their businesses and charities and their lives, and yes, they all appeared to think well of themselves, and who knew? Who really knew? Maybe they *were* all special and she, Phoebe, wasn't, and that was just the truth.

And did it matter about them? No, because she, ordinary Phoebe, was here, trapped in Faerie, and they weren't.

Oh, and incidentally, she'd been betrayed by her best friend *and* by her supposed boyfriend. Which at least made her stupid, if not ordinary. She'd been betrayed into some kind of human sacrifice . . . she had *allowed* herself to be betrayed . . . It was all still so hard to believe. Even as she looked at the magical stone wall, even as she looked around at the Faerie garden and inhaled its fragrance, even as she felt bruising on her shoulders from Mallory's shove and on her hands from their earlier struggle, she couldn't help thinking that in a minute or two, she would wake up and find she'd been having a nightmare. She might even wake up in Ryland's arms and—

Speaking of nightmares. Ryland.

Phoebe shuddered, and in that second she knew that it couldn't be a dream. She could tell by the violent way her whole body now reacted at even the thought of him. It turned out to be true that the mere thought of somebody could make you physically sick.

If she could have thrown herself into boiling water at that moment, if she could have scraped her skin from her very bones, she would have. Anything, anything to feel clean. How could she have made such a mistake? How could she have thought he cared about her, when instead he was attempting to trick her into dying? And when she remembered—no, no, no, she would not remember. Not now. She would not let herself remember all the little things. The things she had said and done, begging, and that he must have been laughing at her—

And now there were tears too, trying to force themselves up from behind her eyes.

Both of them. Ryland and Mallory. Luring her, lying to her, manipulating her. Wanting her dead. And Catherine—they had involved her mother, they were killing her mother—

It was good to feel anger. Much better than humiliation and shame and self-pity and fear.

Was there, at least, some way to get them to release Catherine from her coma? If they had caused it? Could she bargain? Like Mayer? Was she enough of a Rothschild for that? Could she use what little she had, to try to win?

Or was she just too ordinary?

Phoebe got to her feet. The air felt piercingly sweet as she inhaled. She closed her eyes and breathed deeply, more deeply than she would ever have felt possible. So, this was what healthy lungs felt like. She smiled sourly; she almost wished she could have an asthma attack right here and now, which at least might mean dying on her own terms. Would it help them if she were to die on her own? Or did they need to be the ones to kill her? Maybe she could thwart them yet.

Except she really didn't want to die. And there was Catherine, and the little idea, the tiny idea she'd just had, about bargaining for her. If she could at least save Catherine, that would be something. Even if her mother and father never knew what had happened to Phoebe, it would be something Phoebe could do to atone for how—she lashed herself—how *stupid* she had been about Mallory, about Ryland.

One more deep breath. Then Phoebe dusted herself off and grimly began walking deeper into Faerie, as Mallory had told her to do.

The path was supposedly located just beyond the central garden. Phoebe hurried through the garden, not taking the time to do more than glance at the throne that dominated the space, although she did note that its table was now empty of books. Perhaps the books had belonged to the faerie queen, rather than Ryland. No doubt she had kept tabs on the Rothschild family and its varied branches all these years, as she waited for one of the daughters to be as ordinary as Phoebe.

But it hadn't just been that she was ordinary, Phoebe thought. It was that she had been gullible. Yes, she had been deliberately manipulated by others—by both Mallory and Ryland—into saying she was ordinary. But she also had to take responsibility for her own actions, and her own mistakes, and for where they had led her. She couldn't simply blame them.

She had known, deep in her own heart, for example, that keeping her involvement with Ryland secret from her parents was wrong. What if she had told? Would that have changed things?

Catherine would say that you couldn't learn without errors

and misjudgments. That you learned better when you made mistakes than if you did things perfectly. But what if you didn't live long enough to learn from your mistakes?

Now Phoebe could see an opening in some trees ahead; maybe that was where the path was. She trudged toward it, her pace steady and measured. And while she trudged forward, she kept thinking, trying to stay logical and calm, as Catherine would.

Here was the path. It was a little trail that wound through a substantial copse, almost a forest, of thick white ash trees. The walkway was bordered by soft mosses of various greens. Tiny purple flowers peeked through the moss. Phoebe could not see what lay beyond the trees; only that the path wound downhill through the trees. Doggedly, she walked. She barely noticed the trees around her, or the faint breeze that moved the green leaves that formed a canopy above her head, or the beautiful, flute-like song of a wood thrush somewhere in the canopy.

At last, Phoebe emerged from the ash trees and was confronted by a lake. Its waters were black and flat, and it stretched wide to left and right. But Phoebe's path ended directly ahead, at the base of a dock that stretched out onto the lake. At the end of the dock bobbed a little gray rowboat that looked considerably less than trustworthy.

Phoebe's heart stopped for the space of an indrawn breath, and then it took to beating in her chest as frantically as the wings of a hummingbird. Standing on the dock above the rowboat, facing Phoebe, handsome and unsmiling, was Ryland Fayne.

Phoebe turned, bent, and neatly, directly on top of a lady's slipper, threw up.

chapter 34

Ryland had come near—Phoebe could feel him even though she wasn't looking at him—but he made no move to touch her.

"I know," he said to her downturned head, "that you have spoken with my sister."

Phoebe opened her eyes. Throwing up had made her feel better. If it was not quite the decontamination she had wanted, it was something akin to it. She now felt empty and clear. She could function.

Also, her old desire to please Ryland—the power of his effect on her—was simply gone.

For a moment she wondered at herself. After all, Ryland was inches away and only yesterday—mere hours ago—she had craved him and his approval like a flower craves sun and rain.

It was as if, deep inside her, an electrical switch had been thrown. Emotions clamored inside her, but not one was about him. For Ryland, for her ex-boyfriend, for the love and understanding she had believed in and now understood to have been false, her own body had just delivered the final verdict. As, indeed, it had tried to do all along, if she had been able to listen.

She spared a second to be glad, glad, *glad* that she had never actually made love to him. It was worth the horrible things he had said to her about it, to have that knowledge now.

She straightened and looked Ryland in the eye. She was aware of the volume of things that were unsaid between them, but she felt the need to speak only one. And she said it simply and quietly and surely.

"I never loved you."

He said, "True."

"I thought I did."

"Yes."

"A magic potion, something like that?"

Ryland looked thoughtful. "Glamour, we call it. But it was hardly necessary. There was willingness. You wanted to love me."

Phoebe winced. "Because of Mallory."

It wasn't a question, but he answered as if it were. "In part."

Despite herself, Phoebe was curious. "And the other part?"

"It was time for you. It's not as if any man would have done—not quite—but after all, you are a normal young woman."

"You mean an ordinary young woman." Phoebe had not

meant to let bitterness escape, but it did. However, Ryland only nodded and shrugged.

"In this case," he said, "they are just the same."

That was all. He could have been a complete stranger. In fact, Phoebe thought, he *was* a complete stranger. She knew nothing about him as an individual whatsoever, and did not care to learn. She was done with him.

Except for the pesky little business of effectively being his prisoner.

In the silence that followed, Ryland offered Phoebe a handkerchief. It was a silk handkerchief from another century; pretty, delicate, meant to be dabbed gently in the corner of a lady's eye. But the handkerchief was faded and fraying with wear, fragile as an ancient cobweb. For all Phoebe knew, it was indeed a cobweb in disguise. After a second she shrugged and accepted it anyway, and used it to wipe her mouth. She then took a vicious little bit of pleasure in handing it back to Ryland, even though he took it without a flicker of disgust and, incredibly, simply tucked it away in the pocket of his pair of remarkably threadbare—and dirty—linen pants.

Phoebe looked at him, then, really looked at him. First his clothes and body, and then his face. She frowned, because this was not the gorgeous, carefully dressed Ryland that she had known. He was alarmingly thin, and his clothes hung on him as on a scarecrow. And his face was drawn and gaunt, and, well, yellowish.

Mallory hadn't looked well either, come to think of it.

Huh.

"Are you finished?" Ryland made a vague gesture toward the flower that Phoebe had assaulted by throwing up on it.

"Yes," she said politely. "I think so."

"Then we have to leave. But we go by boat, which might upset your stomach more." Phoebe followed his gaze back toward the lake and the dock that he'd been standing on when she first saw him.

"I'll be fine." Deep inside Phoebe, an unexpected emotion joined the orchestra of anxiety and humiliation and rage and bitterness and terrible, terrible fear.

Curiosity.

Ryland offered Phoebe his arm to walk down the dock; she ignored it and instead walked just ahead of him, feeling the dock's wooden planks give dangerously beneath each step, for it, like the handkerchief, seemed to be on the verge of falling apart. When they came to the end of the dock and found the shabby little rowboat tied up to it, Phoebe allowed Ryland to hand her into it. He did this expertly, so that not a drop of water touched her, even though the boat sat a little too low in the water for her taste.

Phoebe sat in the stern and watched Ryland untie the boat and slip into place facing her. He began rowing them across the lake. Despite his thinness and the appearance of weakness, Ryland's movements were strong and smooth. Shoulders, arms, working together. Once upon a time, she'd have taken pleasure in watching. Now she wondered if his human-like appearance was even real. Would he, like the faeries in the story Mallory had told about Mayer, prove in his real form to have skin of tree bark? Or would there be horns on his head?

What did Mallory really look like?

Were the handkerchief, the dock, and the rowboat too, all illusions that were cracking?

Neither Ryland nor Phoebe spoke for a time. With the back of her mind, Phoebe identified the chatter of a kingfisher coming from somewhere nearby. That made her wonder if birds crossed freely between the human and faerie realms, and if so, how. At least the landscape itself, around them, seemed firm and healthy.

"You don't have any questions for me?" said Ryland, when they'd reached halfway across the lake and Phoebe had still not spoken.

"Yes," said Phoebe. "As it happens, I do. What about my mother? You were responsible for what happened to her, right?"

"Yes."

"So will she wake up now, and be able to go on with her life?"

Ryland glanced behind him and reoriented his rowing. "That is a question," he said, "that you will have to discuss with the queen."

"But—"

"Because I don't actually know the answer," said Ryland.

"Even though you were the one who harmed her."

"Yes."

Phoebe chewed on the inside of her cheek.

"We could try another question," said Ryland, with that same tone of careful courtesy.

"That's okay," said Phoebe.

She kept her eyes open. She tried to take in everything she saw, just in case it proved useful.

But as they rowed onward, a fog descended on them, hiding the view, so that Phoebe couldn't see the land around the lake, and then could barely see a foot in any direction around the rowboat. When the boat finally bumped gently up against another dock, she started, and then strained to try to see where they had landed. But all she could see was the gray dock itself. It seemed to be a very long dock, built over shallow, murky water.

Ryland helped Phoebe out with continued civility. She glanced up at him, wondering if he could possibly be nervous. There was tension in him, she could feel it.

"I have a question now," she said. "What happens next?"

"Just come." Ryland offered Phoebe his arm.

She took his elbow, grasping tightly on purpose, and now she could feel the vast difference in his arm from how it had been before; the lack of muscle, the bone directly beneath the skin. He was a walking skeleton. By contrast, Phoebe felt plump and round and healthy . . . positively juicy. And this even though she had lost some weight to anxiety, these last weeks with Catherine so sick.

She reached again for her curiosity, to wear it as she would armor.

She let herself be guided down the dock. With each step, the fog grew denser around them, limiting visibility. Phoebe could literally feel the tiny droplets of water massing in the air. Goose bumps formed on the skin of her exposed arms. After a time, the dark was complete.

"I can't see anything." Phoebe tried but failed to keep an alarmed squeak out of her voice.

Ryland pulled her in closer, and kept her walking by his side, and she let him. Another few moments of walking carefully in the dark, and the soft, rotting wooden boards of the dock ended. Now they were on rock; it was hard beneath the thin soles of Phoebe's ridiculously high-heeled shoes. And the air felt distinctly colder.

"Is this a cave?"

Ryland didn't respond. He put his arm fully around Phoebe's shoulders now, guiding her in what had become pitch-black, not allowing her to slow down and move as carefully as she wanted to. The slope of the rock below their feet changed too, heading downward, and he quickened their pace. She could both feel and hear his breathing now, and it was ragged—more so than her own.

Even though Phoebe could still walk upright, Ryland was now stooping. He had one hand over the top of her head as if ready to push her lower too. The rock beneath their feet tilted even more steeply downward—their pace increased—and they took an abrupt turn to the left, and then another, and then one to the right, and then Ryland was making her duck down low, and then there was another turn, and another, until Phoebe became completely disoriented, turning, stooping, walking, stooping, turning, walking—faster, faster, faster.

And Ryland's breathing near her ear, was nearly as bad as Phoebe's once had been.

She was healed, but he had sickened?

Some primordial sense told Phoebe when they emerged from the tunnel into a wider, more open space. Though she still couldn't see, she could feel the openness ahead, smell it in the air. Then Ryland's hand slid from the top of her head to her shoulder. She felt his harsh breath on her cheek as he said, "Almost there."

Then they were out again in the open air, though still standing on rocky ground, and directly ahead was a circle of nine standing stones that reared high against a brightening sky as the sun began to come into view above the horizon.

It was dawn? Phoebe was bewildered. Where had the day and the night gone? What day was it?

But she could not dwell on the puzzle for more than a second. Surrounding them were figures, numbering at least a couple of dozen. Phoebe took the group in with a single comprehensive glance, getting a vague impression of heads and bodies that were human-like but definitely not human. She saw horns and animal ears and extra limbs and fur and feathers. But she was too frightened to look closely, because they were all looking right back at her, and the impact of their hungry and desperate gazes was immediate and unspeakable.

But then Phoebe gathered herself. She gritted her teeth together and she straightened her shoulders, and then she looked at them all, straight on, in the beautiful growing light of the rising sun.

And then she saw with shock that the faeries were like Ryland, only worse. They were thin and frail and shaking. They were as skeletal as end-stage cancer patients or as—the thought sprang compulsively into Phoebe's mind—concentration camp victims.

All of them.

Conversation with the Faerie Queen, 16

"So this is the girl at last."

"Yes, my queen."

"Thank you, Ryland, for your good and faithful service. We all thank you. It is hard to believe we shall have relief at last. The knowledge of that has strengthened us somewhat, for the moment. It is interesting. She looks nothing like Mayer. She—"

"Stop talking about me like I'm not here!"

chapter 35

Phoebe's ferocious tone crackled across the rocky landscape, surprising even her with its force. She stepped forward, her fists clenched involuntarily.

When in danger or in doubt, run in circles, scream and shout. This silly advice from childhood had inexplicably popped into Phoebe's mind, and though she couldn't run, since Ryland still had firm hold of her arm, she could at least shout, and she had. It was something to do while she figured out what to do. Which she would. Soon. Any second now.

"Don't you dare," Phoebe continued rapidly. "Don't any of you *dare* talk about me as if I'm not here." She was suddenly truly indignant about it, not faking. She sent a separate glare to each and every one of the skeleton-like creatures who were gathering more and more tightly around her. She ended by locking eyes with the extraordinary female figure who sat directly before her, and who had been speaking to Ryland about Phoebe as if Phoebe had no ears or mind or will of her own, as if that were the measure of an ordinary girl.

Which it was not. At least, Phoebe thought, it was not the measure of her, ordinary or not.

This female was unmistakably the faerie queen. Yet, how different she looked from the way that Mallory had portrayed her, from the way that she had been when she met Mayer. She wore a crown of vivid tiger lilies, but the flowers' beauty and vibrancy served only to emphasize that the queen herself was neither. The unearthly, waving, living, colorful hair that Mallory had described now hung lank and thin; the skin that had once been formed of the green and soft leaves of early spring was now brown and cracked. And though the queen was seated on a throne-like chair, one that was not dissimilar to the throne that Phoebe had seen when she first invaded Ryland's bedroom, this throne was much smaller and lighter, woven from the flexible living limbs of a young willow, and sized as for a child.

It was hard for Phoebe to picture how she could ever have been the stunning, regal creature that Mayer Rothschild had supposedly worshipped. Indeed, it was hard to believe that this tiny, shriveled figure was any kind of threat at all. Phoebe felt almost as if she could simply shout her to death. Just now, when Phoebe yelled, the queen had visibly winced.

But now, at least, Phoebe had her direct attention. She decided to assume this was progress.

Automatically, she moderated her tone, and continued speaking as words came to her. She was trying to buy a little more time in which to think. "Also," she said, "Ryland does not speak for me. Neither, by the way, does Mallory." She could not resist a quick, compulsive glance to reaffirm that Mallory was not among the group of faeries, that she lacked even the dubious comfort of her ex-friend's familiar presence. It was so.

"I speak for myself," she went on. "Also, my name is Phoebe, not 'the girl.'"

Vaguely, she was proud of herself. Mallory had told her to behave with dignity. She was trying.

But the skeletal figures drew even closer. They were listening, but more, they were watching. Without looking at any of them directly, Phoebe could sense their fixed gazes almost as tangibly as she could feel Ryland's cool fingers tightening around her elbow.

Then one of the fey shuffled into her field of vision just to the left of the queen. He—or she—or it—was a short, thick, curiously stump-like being covered with grayish, drooping fronds, each of which was tipped with a tiny lidless eye. For an instant the fronds parted and Phoebe had a glimpse of a large opening edged with bark, and within, a long flexible pink tongue that flicked out between sharp teeth.

Phoebe clamped her own mouth shut and glared even more ferociously at the queen.

"Phoebe, then," said the queen. Her voice, though weakly pitched, had the brittle quality of an icy wind as it threatened to break a tree. This made Phoebe reconsider what she had just thought about the queen's powerlessness. "You understand that you are promised to us, Phoebe Rothschild. The bargain with your ancestor was explained to you."

The queen had come directly to the point, without camouflage or pretty talk. Phoebe's stomach clenched. She had to respond, but how?

She must do, must say, the right thing.

If only she knew what that was.

She could feel the fey eyes on her. All their hungry eyes.

What would Mayer do? What would Catherine do?

She wasn't either of them. They were extraordinary; she was not.

Still, Phoebe dredged up a courteous smile. "No," she said. "I don't understand that. What I understand is that I have been betrayed and manipulated. What I understand is that my mother has been made sick. But I have promised nothing to anyone here. And I won't."

"The promise was made on your behalf by your ancestor."

"A story," said Phoebe. "A fairy tale."

"The truth," said the queen formally. "We gave much to

Mayer, to his family. We helped him change his destiny. And now, Phoebe"—the queen pronounced the name strangely, overemphasizing the second syllable—"his family must give back what was promised."

It sounded so logical. So final. Phoebe looked into the desiccated face of the faerie queen, met the deeply brown round eyes that contained no hint of white, and no hint of mercy, either. The circle of fey around her was tight, close. Ryland's fingers had turned viselike.

What if she could break free of him? What if they were all as weak as they looked and she could somehow escape, despite their numbers? What if she ran? What did she have to lose? Since she was not Mayer or Catherine, she wasn't going to be able to talk herself out of this.

She wrenched her arm suddenly, breaking free from Ryland—

Then she staggered, off balance. Thin strong bands of spring willow had come from nowhere and twisted themselves around her torso like living rope, binding her arms to her sides and her legs close together. She was saved from falling to the ground only by Ryland's hands.

"Phoebe," said the queen again. Her voice was patient, even kind, and she looked very small and very frail upon her throne. "You have declared yourself ordinary. You are a Rothschild daughter. There is no more to be said, and no reason for delay.

Tonight, at moonrise, we shall rebalance the debt. You will either be willing, or shall be forced to perform the ceremony. To us, it can make no difference."

"Wait," said Phoebe. "What about my mother?" She lifted her chin. Where the strength to speak came from, she didn't know. Despair had filled her, crowding out disbelief. This was real. She knew it was real. But still—

"My mother," she said urgently. "You put my mother in a coma. If you—if I do what you want, what happens to my mother? Will you release her? Will she wake up and be all right again?"

The queen's eyelids closed briefly and then opened. "Yes," she said simply. Was there a hint of compassion now in her eyes? "We will then have the strength to reverse your mother's injury. I will be frank. If the ceremony does not occur, we will not, and she will remain as she is."

"You promise?" The words came from Phoebe's lips like bullets.

The queen nodded. "Yes." She seemed to gather strength into herself, enough strength to speak more fully. "It is a promise. Your mother will awaken and be herself again. This we will do."

Phoebe exhaled.

Now the queen was no longer even looking at Phoebe. "Make her comfortable, Ryland," she said. "For this next little while. Answer any questions she may ask. Give her whatever she wants, so far as it is possible. Be—be kind." Then she spoke to her subjects.

"Only a few hours more, and then it shall be done, and we shall all be healed, and I shall at last be able to thank all of you for your patience. Back away now, all of you. Return at first moonlight."

The queen's eyes closed, and she slumped.

chapter 36

Before Phoebe's eyes, the faerie folk seemed to melt away and disappear into the landscape. Now only Phoebe, Ryland, the queen, and one other individual were left.

This was a tall, broad-shouldered male creature with long, thick, twisted antlers on his head, and a grayish pelt of fur covering nearly all of his body. Large and powerful though he appeared at first glance, at a second Phoebe could see that his fur was as thin and flat as an ancient, moth-eaten rug.

The antlered man stooped before the queen, reaching for her, lifting her. She looked even more tiny and frail in his arms, and her limbs dangled. She couldn't have weighed very much, but still the antlered man staggered, making small adjustments until he could manage to hold her. Moving carefully, he straightened back to his full height, with the queen safely cradled in his arms, and turned.

It was then Phoebe saw that the antlered man wore a circlet

on his head, formed of ivy and oak leaves entwined around—and growing from—the base of his antlers. The green wreath made a stark contrast with the tattered fur on his head. Yet it was part of him, alive and budding, even though beneath it the rest of him was withering and weakening.

For the first time Phoebe thought to wonder if there was a king as well as a queen. Mallory had not spoken of a king in her story, and there had been no hint of infidelity in the way she had spoken of the queen having been with Mayer Rothschild or her other lovers. She had also described the queen in such a way that had made Phoebe believe that the queen held sole power. Indeed, in her audience before the queen just now, Phoebe had seen no hint that this was not so.

But the antlered man held the queen not like a subject, but like a lover and a full partner, while for her part the queen rested trustfully, vulnerably, in the antlered man's arms. They were a pair, Phoebe knew suddenly and for sure; a deeply bonded pair, even if the rules of their union were something she didn't understand, even if, as in a game of chess, the king's power was limited next to the queen's. They were held together by a history and understanding and culture of which she knew nothing, but which was nonetheless palpable in the simple way in which, despite great weakness, their bodies were clinging together, dependent on each other. No—not dependent. Interdependent.

No sooner had Phoebe had this thought than the antlered

man turned his head to meet her gaze. His eyes were slits in his animal face. There was no possibility of reading his thoughts, even though his eyes held Phoebe's for a long moment, steadily. She looked back at him just as steadily, with a curiosity that she made no attempt to hide.

Then, slowly, Phoebe ducked her head respectfully toward the antlered man. She made no decision to do this; she simply did it and it felt right. She was still trussed up in the willow bands like a big plucked bird being prepared for the rotisserie, with only Ryland's harsh, indifferent hands keeping her upright. But she felt compelled to acknowledge something that she could not put into words. She thought of her ancestor Mayer, seeing the queen all those hundreds of years ago, and being filled with awe. As she looked at the antlered man, Phoebe understood in her bones and blood some of the reason Mayer had joined the primal dance.

The least she could do was nod.

To her surprise, the king nodded back, inclining his head just as respectfully to Phoebe, though his expression remained unreadable. Then he turned and, bearing his wife—the only word Phoebe felt was remotely appropriate—he disappeared, leaving Phoebe alone in the clearing with Ryland.

"Come," Ryland said. "You will spend the next hours at the glade. I'll bring you there." He put out his arms as if he was going to lift her into them, just as the king had lifted the queen, but Phoebe jerked herself away, hopping backward, managing somehow to keep her balance, even with her heels on. “Don’t touch me.” She had to keep hopping in order to stay upright. Hop. What was it Mallory had said about dignity? Hop. Glaring at Ryland and indicating the willow bands, she said, “The queen,” hop, “told you,” hop, “to make me,” hop, “comfortable.”

Hop.

The willow bands disappeared from around her arms and thighs so suddenly that Phoebe fell. She landed painfully on her left hipbone and then saw that Ryland had also fallen and was on the ground beside her. Writhing.

She stared at him in disbelief.

Between one moment and the next, Ryland had shrunk in on himself even more. The bones of his face were suddenly so sharp and prominent that they seemed as if they would slice through his skin. He was breathing hard too, as if he’d been running . . . no, as if he had asthma. Automatically, Phoebe groped in her dress pocket for her inhaler. Then, realizing how stupid that was, she jerked her hand away and kept watching as he breathed, or tried to.

It was strange to have him be the one gasping. Strange to watch his chest rise and fall unsteadily.

“You’re dying,” said Phoebe quietly. The words came out of her with conviction and all the pieces came together in her mind as they should have earlier. “Not just you, Ryland. All of you. Weak and dying. All of you . . . faeries.”

Ryland turned away from Phoebe in one convulsive move and curled up on the ground with his face hidden. His back seemed to hump, as if his spine were shifting shape beneath his shirt and skin, and then the muscle followed along with the bones, distorting, transforming. Phoebe put one hand to her mouth and instinctively scooted a few inches away in the dirt.

It was as if another creature were inside Ryland, trying to break free.

Then she realized that if she was going to run, this was the time to do it. Phoebe got shakily to her feet. Could she find her way back through the dark maze of the rock tunnel? And then over the lake in that rowboat? She swiveled back to face the cavern opening, to run, but stopped in shock. She could not see it. Instead, the rocky plain on which they stood now seemed to stretch endlessly in every direction.

No escape.

At that moment she understood, with horror, that she was relieved. She could not run. She could not, because she had already made a decision.

In exchange for Phoebe's cooperation, the queen had promised Catherine's life. Phoebe believed the queen would keep her word. So, she would trade. She would trade herself for her mother.

She thought briefly, sourly, of all the stories in history about parents sacrificing for their children. Were there any in which the opposite happened? She could think of none. It might be that this was the kind of story nobody wanted to tell, and nobody wanted to hear . . . however real it might be.

Phoebe sank back to a sitting position on the ground next to the writhing figure that was Ryland. She wrapped her arms around her knees, hugging them tightly, and watched him.

He had coiled completely in on himself, and he was still wheezing. Phoebe discovered that she was holding her inhaler tightly in one fist, though she had no memory of pulling it from her pocket. She supposed, with grim humor, that her inhaler had become like a baby's security blanket or teddy bear for her. She might as well hold it tight.

She listened with a professional ear and could tell that Ryland's breathing was settling into something that, if it was not normal, at least did not sound quite so desperate. Phoebe bit her lip. Then, sighing, she reached out very consciously and pressed her inhaler into what was now only partially a humanoid hand. She heard the creature whisper, in a voice deep and rough and utterly unlike Ryland's, "That won't help me." Nonetheless, and weirdly, the elongated claws wrapped around the inhaler.

As his breathing settled more, the creature rolled back to face Phoebe.

He was both larger and smaller than the man he had been, because he was now clearly part feline. But only part. What Phoebe now saw was a human head on a lion's body. It was a monstrous, beautiful, and still pitifully skeletal lion's body, with a head and face that was entirely Ryland. A sphinx? But no, it had wings! Then, a moment later, Phoebe saw its tail, and it was not a lion's tail but the thick, muscular, and unmistakable tail of an entirely imaginary—or so she had thought—creature. A dragon.

That detail told her all. She recognized the creature from her reading: a manticore.

Phoebe flinched, but only a little. After all, that her ex-boyfriend should turn out to be a hellish creature of myth was neither the strangest nor the most devastating thing that had happened today.

The manticore's claws released the inhaler. He said, "I'll be better now, in this shape. Using magic to loosen your bonds was one thing too many. The illusion of being human became too much for me to maintain."

That human speech would come from this creature of legend and nightmare seemed crazy. But again, it was no crazier than what had already happened.

"This is your true self?" asked Phoebe.

The manticore nodded.

"You look pretty sick."

"I am dying," said the manticore. "We are all dying, as you said a moment ago. The vast majority of us were too weak even to attend the queen's council and meet you. Some—many—have already died."

Phoebe nodded. She hugged her knees. "I understand now,"

she said. "It's because of Mayer Rothschild's bargain with the queen, right? She drew some sort of power from the earth to give Mayer the sons he wanted, and in exchange he promised an 'ordinary' female descendent. Except there wasn't one. For hundreds of years, there wasn't one."

The creature who had been Ryland simply folded his paws beneath him and tilted his human head to the side.

"So, in the meantime," Phoebe said, "you've gotten weaker and weaker, waiting. And then, I guess, you decided it wasn't going to work, to wait and hope for that ordinary Rothschild girl. You decided to force the issue. You and Mallory."

The manticore nodded. How strange. It had Ryland's features, more or less, but to Phoebe, it didn't look at all like him now. Although of course it was the other way around. The Ryland she had known was the unreal creature, the illusion.

She wondered what Mallory's true appearance was. Was she also a manticore?

"So now you have me," said Phoebe. "I said those words out loud. I said I'm ordinary. I guess that was what you wanted, right?" She did not need the manticore's nod for confirmation, though he gave it.

"But you also have my mother for insurance, to force me to do what you want. Which is, I'm assuming"—and Phoebe discovered that she did, after all, have to draw in a little breath before she could pronounce the word—"to die."

"At the ceremony," said the manticore. "Tonight."

"After which the balance—wasn't that what the queen called it? The balance will be restored and you will all return to health and happiness. Probably you'll have one of those big dancing parties like the one Mayer went to."

"Yes," said the manticore. His human eyelids flickered. He said, "I'm sorry, Phoebe."

"Like hell you are," said Phoebe.

A moment.

"I can feel two things at once," said the manticore. "Sorry for you, but glad that we will be saved. I picked my people over you. Of course I did."

"And your sister did too," said Phoebe.

"In our place," said the manticore, "would you not do exactly the same? Isn't that what your ancestor Mayer Rothschild did, all those years ago? He picked his family and his people, and left us to suffer and die."

"He didn't know!" snapped Phoebe. "How could he have known?"

"Perhaps he did and perhaps he didn't," said the manticore. "But what if he had known? Would he have chosen differently? Would he have made a different bargain? Would he have sacrificed his family and his people for us? Would you?"

"Probably not," whispered Phoebe, after a minute or two.

"We had to force you," said the manticore. "It was the only way." He extended his front paw. For one ludicrous moment Phoebe thought he was offering to shake hands. But then she saw that he was holding the inhaler out to her. Its casing was cracked.

Phoebe took the inhaler and tucked it into her pocket.

Then she pulled her knees up to her chest once more and encircled them with her arms, and sat beside the manticore in silence.

Conversation with the Faerie Queen, 17

"I'm not asking permission, Your Majesty. I'm telling you. I've already brought him into Faerie and I'll bring him to Phoebe. She needs someone with her while she waits today. Someone who loves her. The human boy, Benjamin, is all she has now. He's willing."

"No! I forbid this."

"With the greatest respect, Your Majesty, you haven't got the power to stop me."

"It was not for this that we siphoned so much of our remaining power to you all these years."

"I'm sorry. After tonight, when she is dead and our people are alive and healthy, you can punish me as you see fit."

"You have betrayed us in so many ways, I have lost count. And now you carelessly reveal our realm to this boy."

"Later, we can have him forget where he's been and what he's seen. After tonight I will submit again and forever to your rule, Your Majesty. But Phoebe will have her friend with her for her last hours. And if I have to suffer or die for this later, I will."

"No."

"She is my friend, Your Majesty. I have to do this for her. It's all I can do."

"Phoebe must die, child."

"I know. Believe me, I know."

chapter 37

The manticore conducted Phoebe back to the pretty little garden that she had first seen ten hundred million years ago, when she peeked behind the door of Ryland's bedroom. This time, getting there involved only a ten-minute walk on a raised earthen bank across a cattail marsh. When Phoebe asked, with only a little sarcasm in her voice, why it was that previously they had needed to row across a lake and then thread through a cavernous maze to go between the two locations, the manticore shrugged his gaunt feline shoulders.

"Coming and going are two completely different things. Haven't you noticed that traveling back is always shorter than traveling out?"

"It feels that way sometimes, but—" Phoebe stopped. There was no point in arguing human time and space with a faerie manticore. She looked hopelessly around the garden that had once seemed so beautiful. There was the same glorious profusion of flowers, the same curving path, the same archway, and the same thick stone wall that had materialized with such finality behind Mallory when she abandoned Phoebe once and for all. She remembered hearing about a garden in England in which all the plantings were poisonous.

She sat abruptly on one of the low walls that edged the central garden. Here she had a view of the hazy mountains in the distance and of the flowers, from which a couple of worker bees were busy collecting pollen because, after all, their world was not about to end. Maybe they were faerie bees. Phoebe had a brief, violent fantasy of killing them—smashing them with her shoe or even with her bare hands—and then blinked in astonishment. Normally, she was a little afraid of bees, and she was not violent. Was her personality transforming too, along with her lungs?

The manticore sank down to the ground at Phoebe's feet, much the way a large pet would. But a pet would never watch her the way he did. "Have you any more questions?" he asked. "I am instructed to answer."

Phoebe's primary question was still the old one. How could he—how could Mallory—have done what they had to her? It was evil. Her incomprehension kept rising like bile in her throat. She wanted to batter him, to scream her rage, to shame him. And Mallory. But she knew their answer. It should not matter to her anymore, anyway. They were what they were. They had done what they had done. They felt they were justified.

Would she have done the same as they, in their place? She didn't know. She thought hypothetically for a moment of Benjamin. Would she betray him to his death, to save, say, her mother? She didn't think she would. She thought she would talk to Benjamin instead and try with him to find another way for her mother. But she didn't really know.

And what if the survival of an entire race hung in the balance? What if there was no other way? Was murder always murder? Was killing someone innocent ever justifiable?

She just couldn't believe that it was.

Phoebe said, very calmly, "Tell me how exactly I'm going to be murdered."

The manticore turned his large, mild, unblinking eyes on Phoebe. "You will drink poison."

Even as she winced, Phoebe thought that poison sounded better than a knife across her throat.

Maybe. Unless it was slow . . .

"Will it hurt?" she asked, still calm.

The manticore shifted position. "The poison will not hurt. It will numb you."

"Wait. The poison won't kill me?"

"No," said the manticore. "You will lift the goblet to your

lips yourself, and swallow. Before this, you will say aloud to all of us that you are the descendant of Mayer Rothschild, and that you are ordinary. The queen will tell you what to say."

"What if I don't do it?" said Phoebe. "What if I refuse to say those things and drink the poison?"

He shrugged again. "As the queen said, you can be forced. You have already said the words once. That gives her power over you."

"And once I'm numb? What happens then? A knife across the throat?"

"You will not be afraid," said the manticore. "And it will not hurt."

"Oh," said Phoebe in a small voice.

Should she fight to the end? She thought of the queen's promise that, if Phoebe cooperated, her mother would live.

And the faerie people too. Was that important? A whole people. A whole people and culture threatened with extermination. All of Phoebe's Jewish roots whispered to her that this *was* important.

But she wasn't doing anything to them. They had brought it on themselves. Or rather, the queen had. Or could you say that Mayer had, although unintentionally? Did that make Phoebe responsible now?

She couldn't sort it all out.

She looked bleakly back into the manticore's eyes. And saw them narrow, change; saw them focus sharply on something behind her a second before he sprang to his feet, spine arched. Phoebe turned her head, following his gaze.

The wall between the faerie world and the real world had again vanished. Once more, Mallory stood in the newly opened portal. She was now fully as thin and starved-looking as the other faeries, her clothing even more ragged.

But Phoebe only focused on Mallory for an instant, because standing beside her was Benjamin. And though afterward Phoebe had no memory of getting up or of running, suddenly she was all the way across the clearing and flinging herself at him.

Benjamin stumbled a little from the impact, but recovered. "Pheeb." He hugged her hard. "Pheeb."

Phoebe hugged back with force. He was solid, real, and a little sweaty. Maybe also in need of a shower. But miraculously, miraculously, he was here with her.

Or not so miraculously.

Phoebe turned her head to the side and there was Mallory a few steps away. Mallory, with her eyes unreadable and her face immobile. Mallory, with the portal now firmly closed again behind her.

Mallory had brought Benjamin. Alarm surged through Phoebe. Why? Was he another hostage to make sure Phoebe did as she was told? How dare they? Benjamin had nothing to do with anything—his only crime was in being Phoebe's friend. Would they hurt him, kill him too?

She swung fully away from Benjamin to face her former

friend. But her thoughts must have been written all over her face, because Mallory spoke before Phoebe could say a word.

"Don't worry, Phoebe. No harm of any kind is intended toward Benjamin. He's just here for you. When everything's over, I'll take him home. He'll be safe."

When everything's over. Phoebe clenched her fists. "Call it what it is, Mallory. When I'm dead. That's what you mean. Unless you're lying about this too."

"I—yes. That's what I mean. And I am not lying."

"Really? You're not using him to blackmail me? Manipulate me? Torture me?"

"No!"

"Why should I believe you?" Phoebe didn't wait for an answer. She turned again to Benjamin. She put her cheek against his skinny chest and tightened her arms around him again, and felt his tighten again around her.

But extra tension had entered his body at her words. He whispered in her ear, "Pheeb, I never thought of her manipulating you. She told me that I could come and be here for you, that you needed a friend now. That's what she said."

"She's a liar," Phoebe said, her voice muffled. "She's always been a liar. But I'm still glad to see you. I can't believe you came."

"Of course I came. When she told me—once I believed her—well, of course I'm here."

Phoebe thought that there was no such thing as *of course*. You never knew, with people. A friend might or might not be for real. Only a crisis would tell.

But he was for real. He was Benjamin, her friend.

chapter 38

They had the whole afternoon together. By the time Phoebe managed to step slightly away from Benjamin—and an inch was all the distance she could bear—Mallory had vanished. Then the manticore withdrew, without words, to the far end of the clearing, and though he still kept watch, the distance was enough to provide Phoebe and Benjamin with a small illusion of privacy.

They sat down immediately by the portal. Phoebe felt shaky with emotion, but the real problem was that Benjamin was wearing ankle shackles. They were made of soft moss, but a few attempts of Phoebe's to tear them away proved their strength. "Ouch!" she said involuntarily, and rubbed her bruised fingers.

"Resistance is futile," Benjamin quoted nerdily, and smiled almost shyly at Phoebe. "Hello," he said then.

"Hello," said Phoebe.

They looked at each other. Then they looked away. Then back.

Benjamin leaned up against the wall, muttering something about keeping near it, just in case they had an opportunity to escape. Phoebe smiled bleakly. She harbored no hope of escape for herself. And whether Benjamin was an intentional hostage or not didn't matter. Like her mother, that was what he was. She prayed Mallory had been telling the truth about Benjamin's eventual safety. She prayed he would get to go home to Nantucket. Which she would never see again.

But at least she had her friend with her—the friend who had never done her any harm. The knowledge filled her with grateful tears that Phoebe was determined to keep inside.

They sat close together, side by side, thighs and arms pressing against each other. Benjamin was talking softly, almost whispering in Phoebe's ear as he held her with one skinny arm, and eventually Phoebe was able to take in what he was saying: that Mallory had simply appeared by the side of the road in Nantucket, catching Benjamin as he was bicycling home from school, and told him the whole incredible story.

"You believed her?"

He looked a little defensive. "I don't know if I did or not. Maybe I decided to, uh, suspend disbelief. She said you needed me and that if I would step with her behind a particular tree—it was just an ordinary pine, Phoebe, not even a very old one—then I would see you." He shrugged. "She said there was a doorway between Nantucket and, uh, here. One step and I would be with you. So I went. And here you are. Unless I'm having a nightmare, which I sort of hope I am."

He shrugged awkwardly. "But I've been so worried about you. All these weeks, Pheeb, with your mother sick. And also I was worried that I—well, that I ruined things between us. By, you know, telling you I cared about you. I thought maybe that was why you weren't answering my emails very much. But it doesn't matter what I said, you know that, right? We're friends. We're always friends. And this stuff—this faerie stuff . . ." Benjamin's voice trailed off. He gestured at the garden, at the manticore, clearly at a loss for words.

"It's not a nightmare. It's real," Phoebe said. She too kept her voice low. "But if you want, you can try pinching yourself, and me, to see if it goes away. If we'll wake up."

Benjamin said hesitantly, "And this stuff about you, uh, dying . . . ?"

"The faeries think they have to sacrifice me to survive. I thought you said Mallory explained it all."

"Yes. But like you said, she's a liar. Even if she weren't, I'd want to hear what you have to say. Tell me what happened. Everything. We need to go over it. There's got to be a way out."

"Oh," Phoebe said. "Well. All right. Um. Keep in mind that

probably we're being listened to. I can't imagine that anything we say here isn't overheard."

Benjamin nodded.

Phoebe told him everything that had happened since she had talked to Mrs. Tolliver, including the conclusion of Mallory's tale about Mayer Rothschild, and ending with what had happened when Phoebe met the faerie queen. As usual, Benjamin listened without interrupting, though for the first time Phoebe could feel from the way his body tensed that he was having trouble forcing himself to remain silent.

When she had finished and turned fully to face him—it had helped her, in telling the story, to remain side by side, in physical contact but without seeing his face directly—she found he was crying. But even though his face was distorted, it wasn't from the tears, but from what she recognized incredulously as pure rage.

"Let them die," he said. "Phoebe, just refuse. Let them all die."

"But refusing won't work. They said that. And my mother—"

"*Let them die!* Let's at least try this. Don't drink their poison. Don't repeat their so-called ritual words. Maybe they can't make you, after all. Who knows? And if they all die, that might release your mother too." Benjamin's voice rose. "And you know what else? You're not ordinary! How could you ever say that or think it? That's another one of Mallory's lies—not to mention that . . . that other one. They talked you into it. You get that, right? You're wonderful, Phoebe. Kind, thoughtful, smart, fun. A good friend, all these years. And it's nothing to do with your family, either. It's just you."

"Benjamin, I—"

"And listen. Phoebe, I just have to say it. I love you. I just—I love you. I hope that doesn't offend you. I know it's not what you feel about me."

"I'm not offended," Phoebe said, once it was clear he had stopped talking. In fact, Phoebe felt so far from offended that she was vaguely astonished Benjamin would even think it a possibility.

"Oh. Good," said Benjamin. "I don't expect to talk about it. I don't even want to talk about it. I just want you to know. And now—" He set his jaw. "Now let's talk about getting you out of this. Suppose you just say you're extraordinary tonight, right to their faces. Say it like you mean it, instead of saying you're ordinary. Say it like you believe it, which you should. And then you don't drink their poison. Can you do that?"

"Do not go gentle into that good night," said Phoebe.

"What?"

"It's a poem. Dylan Thomas. *Old age should burn and rave at close of day / Rage, rage, against the dying of the light.* Not that I'm old. The point is that you should go down fighting. You shouldn't give in to death."

"That's what I'm talking about."

"And if my mother dies?" Or, Phoebe thought, if they kill you?

"I've been thinking about that. *They're* responsible for her being in a coma. Not you."

"But—"

"And she'd want you to fight. You know she would."

Phoebe did know.

"Don't you want to fight?"

"Only if I win," said Phoebe finally, softly. "Otherwise, I want my mom to live. And you. And—" She stopped.

"And what?"

"I don't like the thought of a whole people dying. I don't want to be responsible for that."

"But it's them or you, Phoebe. And Mallory and—that other one." The sharp inhale and the tightening of Benjamin's face, and the way he did not even so much as glance at the manticore, was the only opinion that Benjamin would ever utter to Phoebe about the creature who had been Ryland. "They deliberately set you up."

Phoebe sighed. "Look. I'm thinking it all over. But I need to know: Will you be with me tonight? Whatever happens? Whatever I decide to do or—or not do?"

A long, long moment of silence.

"That's why I came," said Benjamin bleakly. "That's what she asked me to do. She said you needed me."

"Mallory, you mean?"

"Mallory. May her soul rot in hell."

"That won't happen," said Phoebe. "She doesn't have one."

chapter 39

Evening came. There was no preventing it. The sun began to sink behind the mountains, sending out bands of orange and pink against the sky. Across the clearing from where Phoebe and Benjamin sat, the manticore got to his feet. As he stretched, the bones of his skeleton rose up from his thin pelt in stark, chilling silhouette.

Phoebe felt Benjamin's hand tighten where it cupped her shoulder, digging painfully into her skin. His face was rigid with fury and hate, directed at the manticore and perhaps also at the setting sun and the inescapable fact that time had run out. A second later he was struggling to stand. But the moss shackles had grown to cover even more of Benjamin's legs, so in the end Phoebe had to help him.

"Phoebe," Benjamin whispered. "What have you decided? Will you refuse? Will you fight?" His voice was urgent, demanding. He had no need to say again that this was what he thought she should do; it was utterly clear.

She loved him for it. But she didn't know if he was wrong or right. All afternoon, as she sat with Benjamin, first she had decided one way and then, the next minute, the other.

Phoebe shook her head. "I'm not sure." Then she added, "I'm sorry."

She heard Benjamin's wordless exhalation of impatience, of frustration. But he stayed close to her; he kept holding her, and she knew he would be there as long as possible.

And so they stood, leaning on each other, while across the clearing the sun sank lower and the manticore was gradually joined by others of his kind.

The new arrivals drifted into visibility like mist solidifying. First there was a group of four faeries by the manticore's side. Then there were eight, then ten, then twenty-one, and soon too many to count, many more than had gathered with the queen that morning. Phoebe turned slightly so that she could watch Benjamin's face as he took in the faerie folk in all their variegated glory. Fur, feathers, leathery skin, tree bark, spots. Two legs and four legs and in a couple of cases, eight. Tails. And yet they were so unmistakably humanoid too.

They were exactly as Mallory had described in the story of Mayer Rothschild and the faerie queen, which Benjamin too had heard on Nantucket. But seen in the flesh, they were also so much more. They were the creatures of myth and legend, of ancient pagan religion and power. They were the unearthly, the inhuman. The mysterious and the unutterable, that which cannot be mapped or known. They represented the limits of logic and rationality and the depths of the subconscious. Their very existence made you small. And somehow, at the same time, it made you large.

Despite everything, Phoebe's breath caught in her throat as she looked. Once more she understood why her ancestor had knelt. But this time, she also had a glimpse of something else: that perhaps his worship had not been entirely in contradiction to a love of the one God. For who was she—and who was Mayer—who were even the faeries—to understand the whole of the universe?

What would the world be without this physical manifestation of the ineffable living somewhere in it? If they died, what else might be destroyed along with them?

She saw Benjamin's eyes flicker behind his glasses—those intelligent eyes that she knew so well—as he looked from one faerie to the next to the next. She saw him understand fully what she had understood earlier: They weren't making it up. These people had been decimated by weakness, disease, powerlessness. They were truly on the verge of death.

She felt his breath in her ear as he whispered, "Let them die, Phoebe."

It was no longer a demand. It was a plea.

Perhaps he did not see all that she now did about them. Or perhaps he did, but still valued her life more. This too Phoebe couldn't know. There was no time to find out.

She thought: I am not smart enough or brave enough or strong enough to make this choice. I am not—she groped for the right word and found it—not *extraordinary* enough.

Across the clearing, the faerie folk formed themselves into a rough semicircle, facing Phoebe and Benjamin. Then, in the center of them all and taller than everyone, the antlered man appeared.

"The king," Phoebe whispered to Benjamin. He nodded. Phoebe inclined her head again when the king's gaze rested on her, but Benjamin didn't. Benjamin stood straight and grim, and Phoebe had a kind of double vision as she saw in him a glimpse of what he was going to be like when he was a man. Suddenly she knew that if she could have been so lucky as to pick one certain thing to happen in her future, it would be to still know Benjamin. To always know Benjamin.

The piping notes of a pan's flute twisted through the air.

The king approached, alone. He bowed to Phoebe deeply, and then he held out his arm, offering it silently to her. But Benjamin's arm was still around her shoulders and it tightened like a vise. He was shaking. So was Phoebe.

She could not help noticing that, in a fitted sling that hung over one shoulder, the king wore a knife. She could only see its shape, but that was enough to tell her that the knife was thick, with a curved tip that came to a point.

For one second she closed her eyes. Then determinedly, she turned swiftly within Benjamin's arm and faced him, and reached up with both hands for the sides of his head, cupping her palms against his cheeks. "Thank you," she said. "Thank you for being my friend. Thank you for being here. I wish I knew how to tell you what it means to me. And don't believe for a second that I didn't love you, Benjamin. I always did and I always will. I never understood how much until today. Until right now. I love you."

"Phoebe," said Benjamin.

"And now," said Phoebe steadily. "Let me go."

"Phoebe, no. No."

"Yes," said Phoebe. "My dear friend. My beloved friend. This is my decision to make. Please let me. Right or wrong." She saw the desperate question in Benjamin's eyes. "No. I still haven't figured out what I'll choose. But I'll know soon. And here's the thing. No one is forcing me into anything; not anymore. That's over and past, because I say so. This is just me now. Just me and my decision. So let me go. Let me go."

He did. His arms loosened and fell to his sides, though his eyes remained fixed on hers. After several long seconds, Phoebe let her hands fall from his face. She stepped away and, in silence, took the king's arm. "Wherever we're going now, my friend is coming too," she said to the king, and it was not a question, it was a command.

He nodded. A glance at Benjamin's legs, and the moss shackles fell away. Phoebe held out her other hand and Benjamin took it and stood once more beside her.

By now the sun was almost finished sinking below the horizon. Phoebe fixed her gaze on it in these precious remaining seconds—this final sunset—and watched the last of the orb disappear. Then, in the dusk, the fey in their semicircle held torches aloft. The fire from the torches lit the night. Though music still came only from the single pan's flute, now it seemed entirely to fill the clearing.

The faeries parted, making a pathway between them, with their torches lighting the way. Slowly, between the king and Benjamin, Phoebe walked with her head held high. Ryland trailed behind. Behind them came the flutist, playing. Walking in the dark, Phoebe could not see the landscape. What she saw, instead, were the eyes and the shapes of the faerie folk as they stood along the path that they lit for her. As she passed, those at either side fell in behind them, making a procession that grew in length and glowed with more and more light as it went on, and on, and on, until at last they came again to the rocky ground with its circle of standing stones, and to the throne of the faerie queen.

Torches that had been driven into the ground filled the circle with light. In the very center of the circle, the small, shrunken queen sat upon her throne. At her right hand stood Mallory. She was thin and wan, as before, but also straight, tall, and grave. And she was beautiful in the exact same way that, to Phoebe, she had always been.

chapter 40

Apart from that first glance, Phoebe didn't look at Mallory. As she and Benjamin and the king came forward, she fixed her gaze instead on the queen. Odd. The queen's eyes were no longer calm and unreadable, but instead held an emotion that Phoebe recognized. A very human emotion. Anxiety.

Then Phoebe was distracted by something else. The queen held a chalice on her lap.

The poison. Phoebe's grip would have tightened on Benjamin's hand, but he was already crunching the bones of her hand to near-numbness. On her other side, at her elbow, she felt the king's support. There was a moment when, without both of them holding her up, she would have fallen.

She could not look away from the chalice.

It was the size of a large wineglass, but was opaque, with a short, thick stem and a wide base. The queen held it between her hands, with its base resting on her thighs. Something about the way she cupped it made Phoebe think that it must be of considerable weight. Or maybe, she thought, it wasn't the chalice itself that the queen found heavy, but the death within it.

Staring at the chalice, seeing its physical reality, Phoebe suddenly could not imagine willingly lifting it to her lips.

But then again, hers was one life, and against it was an entire culture. Plus she had the assurance that Catherine would recover and Benjamin would return home safely.

What did Phoebe's small life matter against these things? It wasn't as if she had any extraordinary plans or dreams for herself; just ordinary ones that she had hardly even begun to articulate. True love. Good friends. Some fun. Some sort of satisfying work. Children?

Oh. Children.

Time had run out. Phoebe, the king, and Benjamin were standing directly before the queen. Behind them, the procession of faeries formed themselves into a wide ring, within and beyond the torches that lit the circle of stones. Their desperation and their hope and their expectation filled the atmosphere like thick smoke.

Beside her, Benjamin stooped to whisper, "Phoebe, believe me. You are not ordinary." But his words were lifted aloft by some acoustical quality of the standing stones, and echoed. *You are not ordinary—ordinary—ordinary.*

Phoebe tore her gaze from the chalice and fixed it on Benjamin. She didn't speak, but her eyes communicated again what she had told him before. *This is my decision to make*. She planted her feet and stood straight.

The queen turned to Mallory and said something that was not audible. But Mallory's reply was. "Yes, Your Majesty. That is the friend."

The queen lifted her voice so that it too was caught and enlarged. "The friend is welcome."

Benjamin spoke precipitously. "Yes, I'm the friend, and the friend thinks—"

Mallory interrupted. She sounded tired. "Benjamin. Stop. Your part now is only to witness. If you try to interfere, you won't be allowed to stay. Would you do that to Phoebe? She needs you here. Also, I remind you, you gave me your word."

"My word? When you cheated and lied—"

Mallory lifted her chin, and three faeries—hulking brutes of fur and claw—surrounded Benjamin. They hustled him a few yards away from Phoebe, and stood tight around him. Phoebe met his gaze again for one long wordless moment before she looked back at the queen and at Mallory.

Silence descended upon the gathering.

With Mallory assisting her, the queen struggled to her feet, careful to keep the chalice balanced. She took two, three, four steps to stand directly before Phoebe. The top of her head was barely level with Phoebe's chin. The bones of her outstretched arms looked as if they would snap beneath the weight of the chalice. It trembled in her hands.

The king released Phoebe and stepped forward too, reaching out as if to help support the queen instead. But with a movement so small it was almost imperceptible, she shook her head. His hand remained outstretched for a moment more before dropping to his side.

The queen said formally to Phoebe, "You are a descendant of Mayer Rothschild?"

Phoebe's body was shaking, but she found that her voice was steady, and as formal as the queen's. "I am Phoebe Rothschild. I am a descendant of Mayer Rothschild."

"You also understand," said the queen, "that your ancestor Mayer promised you to us."

"I know he promised you a daughter of his family," said Phoebe. "A daughter who is ordinary." She felt the faerie crowd stir restively at her careful wording.

"You are the promised one," said the queen. "There is no doubt."

"I have doubt." Phoebe cast the quickest look at Benjamin before refocusing on the queen. "And if you're honest, you do too. For hundreds of years, you've waited for an ordinary Rothschild daughter. But now you have no other option but me, and no more time. So you need to believe I am the one. You've tried to force me into that role."

Phoebe looked directly at Mallory, who was expressionless.

"I did say aloud that I was ordinary," said Phoebe, as much to Mallory as to the queen. "At that moment in time, when I said it, it felt true. But what I think and feel changes, and simply saying something out loud doesn't make it correct. The bigger truth, as I stand here now, is that I don't know. Also, I'm just barely an adult. Even if I'm ordinary today, will I be tomorrow?"

"This is sophistry," said the queen sharply. "You are either ordinary now, or you are not. That is all that matters."

But Phoebe answered, "What happens if I drink this poison, but I am not in fact ordinary? What happens to you if I die, but the condition of the bargain remains unfulfilled?"

There was silence.

"That is the risk we take," said the queen finally. "That you die uselessly, the earth does not accept the sacrifice, and so we die also." She paused. "It is a risk we *must* take, however. We have no choice. Nor do you, not anymore."

Slowly, deliberately, ceremonially, she extended the chalice to Phoebe. "Will you drink willingly?" she said. "Or shall we force you?"

Phoebe fisted her hands, feeling her nails dig into her palms. "My ancestor Mayer never meant this to happen. He wanted so much for his family, and for himself. But he never meant to harm you and your people."

Some kind of emotion moved behind the queen's eyes. She nodded. "I know. It was my mistake too. I was young. I misunderstood the balancing of powers and the risk, and I did not really understand humans, either. I acted rashly. It was pride."

Phoebe found herself shaking her head. "No, it wasn't pride. Or not only that. You wanted to help Mayer. And he believed you were all-powerful. Which you were not." She cleared her throat. "There's no sense in blaming anyone. He was needy. You were generous. And—and also . . ." She paused, but the words were there in her throat and they wanted to come out. "Also, there was love."

Suddenly the king was at the queen's back. She leaned on him. Her hands trembled, so that the chalice shook. "Yes," said the queen. There was the strangest look in her eyes now, as she stared at Phoebe. "There was love. You—I am surprised that you know this."

"Ordinary or extraordinary," said Phoebe, "I can recognize love."

She watched as the king reached around the queen, holding her, supporting her outstretched arms. Then she looked down, gathering herself; she had no business being moved by the queen and king. No business thinking that they reminded her of her parents. She had a point to make, and she knew at last what it was. One point. Or plea, really.

"But now here we are," said Phoebe. "Facing each other. And there's no love here, or anywhere, anymore. There's just force and threats and coercion and lies and death. How did we get here, when we started with love? Can you tell me?"

Renewed silence. Like a large shadow, the manticore slipped into place, padding on his lion's feet to stand, tautly, between Mallory and the queen, between Mallory and the chalice.

The queen's hands on the chalice trembled. She said, "I ask one last time, Phoebe Rothschild. Will you drink willingly?"

Phoebe closed her eyes. When she opened them, it was to look at Mallory.

"Answer her," said Mallory desperately. "Phoebe, you must reply! Will you drink willingly or be forced?"

And now, at last, Phoebe had her answer.

"Not willingly." She was grateful for the acoustics that made her sound stronger than she was. "I'm not willing and I won't say that I am. I want to live. But," she added quickly, "you don't need force, either." On impulse, she swiveled to face the multitude of faeries. She lifted her chin and scanned their faces. "Since your queen says that there isn't any other way, I'll take her word for it, and I will do this. Unwillingly. But I'll do it to save your lives and the lives of my mother and my friend. And we'll hope it works. We all know it might not."

The faeries stood as if frozen.

"One last thing," Phoebe said. "Thank you. Thank you, all of you, for what you have unwittingly sacrificed for my family, for so many years." She inclined her head; a slow, respectful gesture.

Then she turned back to the queen and king. She didn't

look at Benjamin; she couldn't bear to. She knew she needed to be swift or her decision would falter. She reached out and peeled the chalice away from the queen's oddly tight grip.

The chalice was indeed heavy.

Quick, now. Quick.

Phoebe raised the chalice to her lips.

chapter 41

"No!" cried Mallory. She leaped forward, and the manticore was a half second behind her. But he wasn't fast enough to stop her. She knocked the chalice from Phoebe's hands. It spun up into the air, rotating madly and spilling its contents. As it fell to the earth and broke, the manticore pinned Mallory to the ground. From beneath him, she shouted, "She's not ordinary! If she ever was, that's over. She's grown into herself and she just showed us who she is now. Don't you understand? Killing her won't save us. It's useless. We have to die." The stones took her words and amplified them sevenfold. They reverberated from stone to stone.

"We don't know that," snarled the manticore. "We have to try—and she's willing now—"

Then they weren't the only ones shouting; other voices joined theirs in a ferocious babble of noise and rage and panic and fear. The fey broke rank, crowding in tightly, and Phoebe, who had almost been knocked off her feet when Mallory attacked, somehow managed to stagger upright to find that, weirdly, no one was even looking at her right now, so divided were they. She scanned frantically for Benjamin—there he was, held fast by one of the furry guards, but the two others were in each other's faces, while around them the rest of the fey—

"Peace!"

Instantly, all noise and all movement ceased.

It was the king, and Phoebe realized that this was the first time she had heard him say anything at all. The antlered man strode to the center of the stone circle. He raised his arms high in a motion that was half command, half plea, and after a minute or two, it caused the near-mob of faeries to step back and reassemble, albeit more raggedly and with some grumbling. Then he turned back toward his wife, returning all attention to her.

The queen stood alone, small and shrunken. She waved one hand almost absently toward the manticore. "Let her up."

Reluctantly, the manticore moved aside. Mallory scrambled to her knees and then her feet. She was breathing heavily, her eyes were huge in her face, and her mouth was drawn into a severe, determined line. She didn't look at Phoebe.

But Phoebe looked at her. She kept looking, even as she felt two arms come tightly around her from behind and realized that Benjamin had slipped away from his captors. She leaned back against him. His chest was thudding, thudding.

The queen looked out on her people. "It is clear to me now that Phoebe is—is very much a descendant of Mayer Rothschild. Therefore she shall not die, for her death would not help us."

"Mayer tricked us," said the manticore bitterly. "He knew—he knew!—that there would never be an ordinary child of his line."

His sister narrowed her eyes at him. "How could he know that? He couldn't read the future. And besides, it's clear he had no such automatic pride. He believed he needed help to have extraordinary sons, didn't he?"

"Somehow he knew."

"No," said the queen quietly, "he did not know. Perhaps he hoped. Or perhaps—rare though truly extraordinary may be—there is no such thing as simply ordinary. Or perhaps there is always the capability of becoming extraordinary, buried inside any ordinary being. Perhaps, ironically, we were the ones to force Phoebe Rothschild to bloom. I do not know. It does not matter. It was my mistake. Now I must pay for it."

"We all must pay," said the manticore.

"Yes," said Mallory. "We must die. I suggest that we bear our fate with the same dignity and grace and generosity we have just been shown." Now she looked directly at Phoebe.

Slowly, gravely, she stepped forward. Then she inclined her head to Phoebe. Formally. Respectfully.

It was the very same gesture that Phoebe had used minutes before as she faced the fey.

Phoebe stood still in Benjamin's arms. She felt that if she moved, if she even breathed, her heart would shatter.

The fey were motionless as well, watching the two girls.

Finally, Phoebe nodded back.

Then, into the rippling pool of silence, the queen said, "Before we accept death, it comes to me that there is one last possibility. There is another sacrifice to the earth that might work. Phoebe Rothschild has by her example, and her talk of love, made me see it."

"No," said the antlered man. He spoke directly, forcefully, to his wife.

She looked at him for a long, long moment, and then tilted her head in query. "You knew this? All this time?"

He made a noncommittal move with his shoulders.

"Husband," she said gently, and held out her hands to him, palms up. He shook his head, but she kept her hands out, not withdrawing them even when he turned his back on her.

The queen and king were ignoring all the watchers, behaving as if they were in private. Her hands, outstretched. His back, turned. An invisible thread of awareness running palpably between them.

Phoebe had once more a sense of recognition. They were

a couple, as her parents were a couple. They needed very few words to understand each other.

Benjamin cupped one hand around his mouth and whispered into Phoebe's ear. "What's going on?"

Phoebe shrugged.

All the tension was back in Benjamin's body. "They can't have you, Pheeb."

She twisted slightly to whisper back. "Don't worry. That's over. This is something else. I don't know what."

"Maybe. Let's get out of here anyway."

Phoebe shook her head. She knew that she would not leave unless asked to do so. As a Rothschild, she belonged here at this moment, even if she didn't understand what was happening.

"We stay," she whispered to Benjamin. "We witness."

She heard him sigh. Then he squeezed her shoulder.

The queen was now approaching the king. Each step was almost beyond her strength. But she reached him at last, and as she did so he turned and faced her, and then suddenly he dropped to his knees and embraced her. He was so tall, and she so small, that in this position their heads were nearly level. Their foreheads rested on each other's. Their eyes were closed. He clutched her so tightly the sinews stood out on his arms. The queen's hands cupped the back of his neck and then ran gently over his head and the base of his antlers, before coming to rest on each side of his face.

"Don't ask this of me," he said.

"It must be you," she said.

He drew back and looked into her face. And then, finally, he nodded.

"Thank you, my love," the queen said. She drew away, and he let her go.

The queen addressed the group. "When I made the bargain with Mayer Rothschild, I used my body as the channel to take power and direct it elsewhere. It has come to me that I may be able to use my body to return that power." She paused. "The earth requires a sacrifice. It shall be me. It shall be now. And the sacrifice shall be offered with love."

Phoebe caught her breath in shock. For the briefest moment the queen glanced at her. Then she looked out again on her people.

"I do not know if this will save us. I do not know if my sacrifice will be acceptable. But it is the other way that Phoebe Rothschild asked about. The loving way. It is the only possibility I can think of, and the king, my husband, who it seems thought of it long ago, agrees that it may work. It is our last hope. And it is my responsibility, and only mine."

In the stunned silence that followed, Mallory was the first to speak. "No," she said. "No!"

The queen turned to her. "Child, hush. It must be. Surely you can see it."

Mallory was now on her knees. Her eyes were wild. She glanced at the manticore as if for support. But he shook his head.

"My queen," he said. "We honor you. We respect your decision. I know I speak for all."

"Indeed, I am sure you do," said the queen drily.

A strange sound began, a low and mournful ululation, a music that was composed of pure sound. There were no words while the music swelled high and full. Then, after a while, the pan's flute wound itself into the music, twisting round it, filling the air with haunting, frightening beauty.

Phoebe leaned back into Benjamin and felt him lean into her as well. Dread filled her. Dread—and awe. Together, they watched as the queen stood with her head bowed. The music filled the air and the torches flared brightly against the dark.

Dancing began around the queen. It was slow, and formal, and caught Phoebe in the throat with its intricacy and beauty.

Benjamin whispered to Phoebe, "Should we leave now?"

Again she shook her head.

He said, surprising her, "Should we dance?"

Phoebe hesitated. She looked at Mallory, who was not dancing. Mallory, who stood beside the king, both of them still. All of the others, including the manticore, danced.

Phoebe thought of her ancestor Mayer, dancing.

"No," she said. "We're visitors. Not participants. We should just—witness."

Time hung suspended while the flute played and the faeries danced. It could have been ten minutes, or ten hours. But at length the strange music ceased and silence filled the dark stone circle once more.

The king approached the queen. He had taken out his knife. It was indeed thick and curved, and Phoebe could see that it had a frightening, jagged edge. He held it with an ease that showed he knew exactly how to use it, but his face was rigid.

Benjamin was leaning on Phoebe as heavily as she was on him. If one of them had disappeared, the other would have fallen down. She heard him whisper again. "God, Phoebe. God." She herself had no voice at all. She would have closed her eyes if she hadn't felt, strongly, that it would be disrespectful.

We witness, she told herself. We witness.

The king came to the queen and held the knife out to her, handle first. She took it and examined it carefully before nodding. Then, with the knife in her left hand, she held out her right hand to Mallory. It was a command.

Phoebe thought that Mallory had never looked more agonized. But she came forward and took the queen's hand. She stood beside her, facing her people.

"I give you Queen Kethalia," said the queen formally. "My daughter. My heir."

Benjamin gasped. But what surprised Phoebe was that she felt no surprise. It was the very last puzzle piece about Mallory, slipping seamlessly into place.

Her name was Kethalia. She was the daughter of a queen.

The king lifted the crown of tiger lilies from his wife's head, moving to disentangle it from her long hair. It came away easily, as if it were willing. He set it upon Mallory's head, above her icy face with its panicked eyes. Then he turned to his wife.

Then, almost more quickly than Phoebe's eye could follow it, the queen sank to her knees. With the knife in both hands now, she extended it to her husband with a gesture that was nearly identical to the way in which she had earlier offered Phoebe the chalice of poison.

The king took it. The queen raised her head and they exchanged one long last glance. Then the queen offered her throat. In the next second the blade in her husband's hand had sliced swiftly, cleanly, spilling her blood onto the rocky ground.

The queen remained upright on her knees for fully twenty seconds. When she fell at last, her arms stretched out to embrace the earth.

Chapter 42 and Conversation with the Faerie Queen, 18

The exact moment at which the queen died—and her sacrifice was accepted—was unmistakable. Phoebe was looking at the king as he knelt by his wife, and so she saw his appearance begin to shift. It happened rapidly, the changes visible from one moment to the next as his fur grew in, dense and deep. Beneath it, his frame thickened with strength. Then he straightened, and he was taller than before too.

Involuntarily, she put a hand to her mouth.

Benjamin spoke into her ear. "Phoebe, look at them. Look at them all."

Phoebe tore her eyes from the king. In the flickering torchlight, all around them, the fey were shifting and strengthening as their link to the earth was renewed. Vines grew and flowered around the plant-like fey; muscle grew dense in the animal bodies. Even the shadows their figures threw onto the ground flexed with power and renewal.

And in the center of them stood Mallory. No, not Mallory. Kethalia.

Queen Kethalia.

Queen Kethalia, who glowed with the light of a hundred candles.

Like her mother before her, Kethalia's link to the earth was apparent in the soft leaves that formed her skin and in the strong, slender, willow-like curves of her arms and neck. She was elongated, taller than tall, and the lily crown that had been placed on her head by the king was now clearly alive, growing from her scalp and blooming as part of her head and her hair. Her hair was like and not like the hair that Mallory had described to Phoebe and Benjamin and Catherine and Drew as belonging to the previous queen. It was a thousand colors and textures of green and brown and orange; it was hair and fur and feather, and as Phoebe stared, a quarter-mask of reptilian skin grew from Queen Kethalia's forehead and settled gently, lovingly, around one eye and over her cheekbone, just as a small leopard-patterned gecko crawled out of her hair to rest inquisitively on her shoulder.

Then, as Kethalia moved slightly to place a clawed, commanding hand on the back of the now-hulking manticore that stood beside her, Phoebe saw that she was also winged. Kethalia's wings were feathered and strong and enormous. No gossamer fairy wings these; they were the strong wings of a hawk. They were meant to be used.

Phoebe knew exactly why it was that the wings brought tears to her eyes; why it was that the wings felt like the final piece of a complex puzzle sliding into place. They were tears of joy and of understanding—finally, finally, understanding. She blinked them back. She would pour them out later, in private, at home. For she would go home, she knew that now too. She and Benjamin would go home, and Catherine would wake up, and all would be well.

All would be well, but it would never be the way it had been before.

It was also the presence of the wings that made it so that, while awed, she wasn't afraid.

Deliberately, Phoebe stepped forward, aware that Benjamin came with her and glad of it, but not needing him. She inclined her head. She wanted to say Mallory's name, but it wouldn't come, because it was now the wrong name. And yet, she knew this glorious creature. This glorious creature had been and was still her friend. Mallory. Kethalia. Queen. Whoever and whatever she was, she had ultimately saved Phoebe's life, and at the end, had been willing to give her own life to do so.

Which, oddly, was what Phoebe had ended up offering as well.

So how could it be that Phoebe could stand here in the torchlight, facing her friend, and have nothing to say?

Phoebe lifted one hand helplessly.

"Leave us," said the queen. Her voice echoed in command. "All of you. Leave me alone with Phoebe Rothschild for a time. Later, when our visitors have left, I will call you all back."

In singles, in pairs, in groups, the fey melted away. Last to go were the king—was he now the ex-king?—and the manticore, who in fact needed one more sharp order from the queen before he skulked away.

"He's going to be trouble for you," said Benjamin conversationally. Only a slight hesitation in his voice betrayed any nervousness or awe. "Your brother, that is. Uh, can I ask something? Is he really your brother? You don't look a thing alike."

It was so strange to hear Mallory's voice coming from the queen. "Our family trees are constructed in a very different way from yours," she said. "But *brother* is as good a human word as any to describe our relationship. Yes, you're correct. He is going to be trouble. I'll manage, though. Somehow." That was definitely Mallory's laugh, trilling out suddenly, and then sobering just as quickly. "Actually, while it might be difficult for you to believe, he's not without a kind of wisdom. I imagine there will be times in the future when I'll be glad of his advice. But as for now—Benjamin? May I ask you one last favor?"

"I won't leave this place without Phoebe. I'm staying as long as she is, and when I go, she goes with me."

"I understand. I ask only that you step to the other side of the clearing so that Phoebe and I can talk in private for a few minutes. She'll be in your sight the whole time."

"It's all right, Benjamin," said Phoebe. She smiled reassuringly. "I want to talk to—to the queen alone too."

It was a few moments before Benjamin nodded. A few more

passed while Phoebe and the queen watched him stride lankily away to stand, uneasily, hands in pockets, at enough of a distance to give them the privacy that the queen had requested.

But then Phoebe wasn't sure what to say. She was relieved when the queen spoke first, and then surprised when Mallory's voice came out sounding just as awkward as Phoebe felt. "Thanks for being willing to talk to me."

It was like a cork had been pulled out of Phoebe. "Willing?!" she said. "Are you joking? I was hoping you'd want—be able—to talk. I'd have asked if you didn't. At least, I hope I would have. I was just working up my nerve."

"Phoebe? Would you call me Mallory still? At least here and now. For this conversation?"

"Gladly. Mallory?"

"What?"

"I need to tell you something. I had no idea what you were going through. If I had known, I would have behaved differently. But I don't suppose there was any way you would ever have trusted me enough to tell me the truth about yourself and your—your people."

"How could I, Phoebe? I needed you to die. That was my mission. To break you down and make you willing to die. Don't look at me with those big misty, forgiving eyes—don't you dare do that, okay? You were the only person who ever loved me for no other reason than because she chose to. I was special to you for no reason at all! And I went and betrayed that, betrayed you, betrayed my best friend to her death. And it's not due to me that you're still alive. *You* did that."

"Mallory. Stop. You're too harsh."

"No, actually, I'm not. It's true, Phoebe. Don't forget it! Don't ever forget what I am and what I did."

"Then tell me this: Who was it that knocked the poison away from me at the last minute?"

"Don't mock me."

"I'm not. You saved me at the end, and it cost you. My mother is alive, Mallory, and I get to go home to her today. But yours—yours—you've lost both your mothers now. Don't pretend to me you don't care. I know you better than that. At least, I do now. Mallory, I am so very sorry."

"Oh. Well. Phoebe, since you bring it up . . . when I asked to talk, one of the things . . . that is, I was wondering about my other mother. Mrs. Tolliver. This is a huge favor to ask, and I don't deserve it, but would you look out for her? It wouldn't be for me, but for her."

"Of course I'll do it. For you *and* for her."

"Thank you. I hurt her so much, you see. I did her great harm."

"You also loved her. And I'm thinking it could help her to talk about it with me, to know that I believe her and she's not crazy. I don't think she's as fragile as we thought."

"She's not. I was responsible for keeping her helpless, remember? I can't believe you're being so good to me, Phoebe.

You know everything now. But you always had a soft heart."

"You say that like it's a bad thing. Earlier you said just the opposite."

"Sometimes it's bad. It opens you to hurt. Let me be clear. I don't deserve your kindness. Are you forgetting my brother? I let him have you! I betrayed you!"

"Well, I don't know about that. I have to take some personal responsibility."

"You were glamoured by my brother, Phoebe. You had absolutely no way to resist."

"Maybe. But I made my own bad choices as well. If you betrayed me, I also betrayed you."

"You didn't."

"Yes, I did. I turned my back on my best friend. I chose lies and sneaking around. I knew better, Mallory. Faerie glamour or no, I knew better."

"Well. You'll manage love better next time, Phoebe. I hope you know that. And I—I know it's not my business, Phoebe, and I imagine you're not ready at this point to try having a boyfriend again. But Benjamin . . ."

"You're right. I'm not ready."

"I'm just saying. When you are. He's going to be amazing someday."

"He already is. And I—well, that was something I wanted to say. Thank you for bringing him to me. You didn't have to do that."

"Yes, I did."

"So you're not all bad, are you?"

"Phoebe."

"What is it, Mallory?"

"I'm so sorry. So sorry for everything I did to you."

"I understand. It doesn't matter anymore. It's over."

"Easy to say that. But what about what happened with you and my brother? Don't just smile and say that didn't affect you. You can't just declare yourself all better and healed. I know my brother, okay?"

"I—well, I—it was—that will take time. I actually don't want to think about it too much right now. I know I—I'm strong."

"Yes, you are. But I'm so sorry. I'd undo it if I could."

"I don't want it undone. I'm not saying I'm happy about—about the bad parts, Mallory. But I'm also not sorry to be who I am now. I keep thinking about that moment when I was willing to die. How I felt at that moment. I was strong when I needed to be, Mallory, and I didn't know that about myself before then. And now I know I can be . . . bigger than I really am. I'm not describing this well."

"No, you are. You forget, I was watching you. You were—truly—extraordinary."

"Mallory? Is being . . . extraordinary—maybe it's not about being that way all the time, every minute of life? Because that's not really possible. Not even my mother is that. But maybe it's about learning that you have something deep inside that you can reach for when you really need it. Strength. Strength that helps you do whatever it is you need to do, when you need to do it."

"I hope that's true. Because if it's not, I can't do what I have to do now."

"You mean, be queen. But you will, Mallory. You'll be wonderful at it."

"How do you know?"

"Because I know you better than anyone. Even though I hardly know you. I love you, Mallory. And I—oh, Mallory. It's all right. Cry if you need to. You don't have to be strong with me."

"I—how can I ever say good-bye to you, Phoebe?"

"We'll never see each other again?"

"I don't think we will. Phoebe, can I ask you something? Do you remember that very first day? When you asked me to be your friend?"

"I'll never forget it."

"I made the right choice, Phoebe. I just want to say it. Choosing you then. Choosing those few years we had. And just now, at the ceremony, choosing you once more."

"You chose me over your mother."

"It was right, my friend. My best friend."

"Mallory. Oh, Mallory."

"Go quickly, now, Phoebe. Go with Benjamin. Go to your

mother. She'll wake up soon, and she'll be scared. She will have seen some of what has happened to you in her dreams. Nightmares. But she'll be fine, I promise, and you must be there, with your father, so that yours are the first faces she sees. Go, before I keep you here with me forever. Go."

"Good-bye, Mallory."

"Good-bye, my friend. Good-bye."

Author's Note

Mayer Rothschild, his wife, Gutle, and their five extraordinary sons were real, but of course the meeting between Mayer and the faerie queen is entirely a figment of my imagination. Catherine Rothschild is likewise fictional, and for that reason, I deliberately kept Catherine's exact connection to the present-day Rothschild family vague.

Readers interested in Mayer Rothschild might like to read *Founder: A Portrait of the First Rothschild and His Times,* by Amos Elon. To find out more about the family business and its involvement in and effect upon European politics, see the two-volume *The House of Rothschild* by Niall Ferguson. And for a chronicle of a real-life Rothschild love story, as well as a fascinating window into Victorian society, politics, and anti-Semitism in the mid-1800s, see *Charlotte and Lionel* by Stanley Weintraub, which is about Mayer's grandchildren.

However, despite the importance of the Rothschild family history in the shaping of *Extraordinary,* my original inspiration for the novel did not come from there. Stories beget stories; art inspires more art. And so for me, *Extraordinary* is a daughter of the remarkable novel *Wicked* by Gregory Maguire (itself a child of *The Wizard of Oz*), and of its musical adaptation (book by Winnie Holzman), and of the beautiful song "For Good," music and lyrics by Stephen Schwartz. These varied magical works moved me to want to write my own magical story about the soul-changing effect that one friend can have upon another . . . for good.

Acknowledgments

I am grateful to my first- and second-draft readers for their thoughtful critiques and commentary: Franny Billingsley, Jane Kurtz, Dian Curtis Regan, Joanne Stanbridge, Deborah Wiles, Melissa Wyatt, Alexis Canfield, my terrific agent Ginger Knowlton (who is owed thanks for much more than being a reader), and, perhaps most importantly, Jennifer Richard Jacobson, whose early suggestions had a significant effect upon this novel's structure.

For fellowship and laughter along the way, my thanks go to: Sarah Aronson, Toni Buzzeo, A. M. Jenkins, Jacqueline Briggs Martin, and Tanya Lee Stone.

As with all of my previous novels, *Extraordinary* was edited by Lauri Hornik. This time I want to thank Lauri especially for her trust in me. I have never yet figured out how I got so lucky.

Thanks also go in great heaps to the folks at Penguin and Puffin Books for their creative and imaginative efforts on behalf of my books. I appreciate it, and all of them, more than I can say.

And I will end by thanking my husband, Jim McCoy, for everything.

Keep reading for a glimpse of

Nancy Werlin's bestselling novel

impossible

prologue

On the evening of Lucy Scarborough's seventh birthday, after the biggest party the neighborhood had seen since, well, Lucy's sixth birthday, Lucy got one last unexpected gift. It was a handwritten letter from her mother—her real mother, Miranda. It was not a birthday letter, or at least, not one in the usual sense. It was a letter from the past, written by Miranda to her daughter before Lucy was born, and it had been hidden in the hope that Lucy would find it in time for it to help her.

It would be many years, however, before Lucy would have a prayer of understanding this. It was typical of Miranda Scarborough's terrible luck that her daughter would discover much too early the letter she had left for her. At seven, Lucy barely knew of Miranda's existence and didn't miss even the idea of her, because she had a perfectly wonderful substitute mother, and father too. She did not even know that, once upon a time before she was born, her mother had slept for a few months in the same bedroom that today belonged to Lucy.

So, when Lucy found the hidden letter, she was not capable of recognizing who it was from or that it was a letter at all.

Lucy had been in the process of taking possession of the bottom shelf of the built-in bookcase in her bedroom. Previously, the shelf had been crammed tight with books belonging to her foster mother. "Overflow storage," Soledad Markowitz called it. And recently, she had said to Lucy, "I stuffed my college books in there when we first moved into this house, when your bedroom was a spare room. One day soon I'll move them down to the basement office so you can have that space for your things."

One day soon had not yet arrived, however, and so Lucy had decided to take care of it herself. Her birthday—although it had not included the longed-for present of a little black poodle puppy—had brought her many books, including *Harry Potter and the Sorcerer's Stone* and a complete set of *The Chronicles of Narnia,* and she wanted to arrange them all perfectly to wait for the day when she would be old enough to read them by herself.

It was only after Lucy had gotten all of Soledad's books out of the bookshelf that she noticed the bottom shelf was not quite steady. A moment later, she discovered it could be lifted completely away to reveal three shallow inches of dusty, secret space between the bottom shelf and the floor.

At seventeen, rediscovering the secret space, Lucy would see what she did not see at seven: The nails that originally held the shelf in place had been painstakingly pried out. Then she would understand that Miranda had done this. But at seven, all Lucy knew or cared about was that she had found a secret compartment. An actual secret compartment!

Lucy leaned in to see better, and then felt around inside with both hands. The only thing she found, besides dust, was a sheaf of yellowing paper covered with tiny handwriting.

She pulled the pages out and fanned them in her hands. They were not very exciting to her, although the pages did have a ragged edge, as if they had been ripped out of a book, which was somewhat interesting. But the handwriting on the pages was faded, and it was also so small and cramped and tight that it would have been hard to read even if Lucy was accustomed to cursive. Which she wasn't.

She had a moment of frustration. Why couldn't whoever had written the words on the pages have typed them on a computer and printed them out, like a sensible person?

Then she had an idea. It could be that the pages were really old. They might even be from before there were computers. Maybe the pages were ancient, and maybe also the words on them were magical spells. That would explain why they had been hidden. And it would mean that she had found a treasure in her secret compartment after all.

She wanted this to be true for good reason. If Lucy really did have a secret compartment, and magical spells, she already knew what she wanted to do with them.

In fact, it almost felt like an emergency.

Lucy sorted through her pile of birthday presents until

she found the one from her oldest friend, Zach Greenfield, who lived next door. It was a Red Sox T-shirt that he had claimed, today at the party, to have bought for her with his own money. On the back, above the number eight, it said "Yastrzemski." Every Red Sox fan in Boston knew the name, even if they weren't sure how to spell it. Lucy had been touched at first with the gift. Yaz was one of the players from the past that Zach just loved.

The problem was that the T-shirt was an adult medium, too big for Lucy to wear, which meant Zach wasn't really paying attention to her, only pretending to. Or even, possibly, that he had gotten it for himself (Zach wore his T-shirts large), and decided to give it to Lucy at the last minute, because he'd forgotten about her birthday.

Lucy, despite her willingness to believe in magic spells, was mostly a realistic child, so she believed this was probably the case. Lately, Zach had been busy with his other friends, the ones who were closer to his age, which was nine and a half. He had not played with Lucy much at all, and at school, he hardly even said hello.

Which hurt.

Filled with a sense of magical possibility, Lucy folded the T-shirt carefully and laid it down on the floor inside the secret compartment. Then she picked up the sheaf of pages with the cramped writing on them, and, by concentrating, managed to sound out a sentence located about halfway down the first page. The ink in which this sentence had been written was a little darker than the rest, as if the person writing had pressed down hard with the pen. Lucy decided that this sentence would be enough to start the magic. It would have to be, because she wasn't up to reading more. And, she told herself, it wasn't cheating to include only one sentence, because it wasn't as if it was a short sentence.

She read it out loud, softly, not sure she was pronouncing all the words correctly, and quite sure she didn't understand them.

"I look in the mirror now and see my mother and I am so afraid you will end like us: doomed, cursed . . . all sorts of melodramatic, ridiculous, but true things."

Saying the sentence out loud gave Lucy a distinctly unpleasant feeling. She had an impulse to call her foster parents to look at the pages and the secret compartment.

Everything would have been different if Lucy had done that.

Or possibly not.

She didn't, in the end. She wanted the magic too badly. Instead, Lucy added her own magic words: "Abracadabra! Bibbidi-bobbidi-boo! Yastrzemski!" She tucked the handwritten pages into a fold of the T-shirt inside the secret compartment. Then she put the shelf back in place on top, and arranged her new books on the shelf just as she had originally planned.

The magic spell would work, she knew it. Even if she had not said the words right, or had selected the wrong sentence to read out loud, the magical pages were inside the T-shirt, touching it, so they would do their job. Plus, she would be patient. She would not expect Zach to change back overnight. But once she was old enough to wear the T-shirt he had given her, Zach would remember to be her friend again.

She planned how she would check the magic compartment on her next birthday. She would try on the shirt. Maybe by then, she would be able to read the entire magical spell.

But by the time her eighth birthday arrived, Lucy had forgotten all about the secret compartment and the T-shirt, and about the mysterious papers with the faded, tight, urgent handwriting. She would be seventeen, and in deep trouble, before she remembered.

chapter one

Ten minutes after the last class of the day, Lucy got a text message from her best friend, Sarah Hebert. "Need u," it said.

"2 mins," Lucy texted back. She sighed. Then she hefted her backpack and headed to the girls' locker room, where, she knew, Sarah would be. Nothing and nobody, not even Jeff Mundy, got in the way of track practice.

Because of course this problem of Sarah's would be about Jeff. Lucy had seen him at lunch period, leaning flirtatiously over an adorable freshman girl. Maybe this time Sarah would have had it with him for good. Lucy hoped so.

But still, it was delicate. And it wasn't like Lucy had a lot of experience to guide her friend with. Or any, really, if you didn't count Gray Spencer, which you couldn't, not yet, anyway. No, she didn't have experience, Lucy thought fiercely, but she did have years of understanding about who, exactly, Sarah was and what made her happy. And also, frankly, some basic common sense.

Which Sarah had totally lost.

Lucy found Sarah already changed and sitting on a bench by Lucy's locker. "Are you all right?" Lucy asked.

"Yeah. It's just—it's not Jeff, it's me. I'm the one with the problem." Sarah made a little motion with her hand. "But now we have to go to practice."

Lucy put an arm around her and squeezed. "There'll be plenty of time to talk later if you want."

Sarah nodded and tried to smile.

Lucy turned to change. Then they walked out together toward the school's track, moving to the infield to stretch. Lucy's practice routine as a hurdler was different from Sarah's distance training, but they always did as much together as they could.

When they were side by side doing leg stretches, Sarah was finally able to talk. Lucy listened patiently to all of it, even the parts she'd heard many times before. But when Sarah said, "We both agreed from the start that we weren't serious and Jeff's right that it truly is my problem that I'm so jealous, not his, because he's not doing anything wrong," Lucy couldn't help herself. She cut in.

"Sarah, please. It's not a problem that you want something more serious than Jeff does. There's nothing wrong with you that you want that! And there's also nothing wrong that he doesn't. Can't you see? It's just that you're fundamentally incompatible. You should just say so and move on."

"But I don't want to move on! He's such fun and so smart and good-looking and I just love him and if I could only control the way I feel when—"

"Then be his friend. But that's it. For more, look around

for somebody who's not going to hurt you all the time. Even if Jeff doesn't mean to hurt you, it's still pain, right?"

Lucy grabbed one foot, and, standing on the other leg, pulled the foot behind her to stretch her quad muscles. She decided not to say that Jeff knew perfectly well he was hurting Sarah, and didn't care, so long as he got to do what he wanted to do, which included being with Sarah whenever he felt like it.

Sarah was silent for a minute, concentrating on her own quad stretch. Then she said, "Lucy, I don't think you understand. I can't really control how I feel. I can't just look around for somebody else. I want what I want. Who I want."

Lucy switched legs. She chose her words carefully. "But this is hurting you so much. It can't be right."

"Love hurts," said Sarah simply. "That's okay. It's supposed to."

"I don't believe it," Lucy said. "Look at Soledad and Leo."

"People who've been married umpteen years like your foster parents are different," said Sarah impatiently. "When you first fall in love, it's supposed to be awful. Awful, uncertain, scary, wonderful, confusing, all at once. That's how you know it's real. You have to care deeply. Passionately. That hurts."

Lucy got down on the ground, stretched her legs to each side, and began pressing her head and torso out to the left. "I don't know." As she switched to the right side, she found that Sarah had gotten down too, and was looking her in the face from three inches away.

"Lucy, look. You can't just make a list of what qualities would be compatible for you and pick somebody based on that. You have to, well, consult your heart. And if love doesn't hurt sometimes, well, then." Sarah actually put a hand over her heart. "Then maybe you don't truly care."

"Oh, please!" Lucy sat up. "Can't you consult both your heart *and* your head? Shouldn't they be in agreement? And, also, I'm telling you, I continue to not like the pain thing. Continued pain is a signal to the body that there's something wrong, not right."

"But we're talking about the heart, not the body."

"Why should that be different? Pain is to be avoided."

At this, Sarah laughed. "Really? That's your philosophy? Tell me that after practice today."

Lucy went to the left on her stretch again. "I don't *like* interval training! I just do it. Anyway, that's not the same kind of pain, and you know it."

It was good to hear Sarah laugh, she thought, even though she knew that the abrupt change of subject meant that Sarah was done, wanted no more advice, and would, no doubt, go right on breaking her heart over Jeff Mundy.

Well, all right. Lucy had said what she had to say. And she would say it again if and when she was asked.

Or possibly even if she wasn't asked.

Sarah, who was done with her stretching, stood up.

"Listen, Lucy. Now that you've got this kind-of-sort-of-maybe dating thing about to happen with Gray Spencer, with the prom and all, I'm thinking that pretty soon you'll start to see what I'm talking about."

Lucy snorted. "I like Gray, but hello? Were you listening to me at all? About pain?"

"If you're expecting a walk in the park—"

They were interrupted by the coach calling the track team around and assigning them their workouts. "Call me later," Sarah said. Lucy nodded, and Sarah went off on her run. Lucy and the other two hurdlers began doing drills with tightly spaced hurdles, practicing alternating their lead legs.

Lucy worked out hard. She always did; it was her strongest point as an athlete. She was good, but she didn't have any truly extraordinary level of talent, and she knew it. What she did have was will and determination. And next year, if she kept it up and was lucky, she thought she might have a shot at going to states and maybe also at some college scholarship money, which would be a big help to her foster parents. That was her real goal. Even though her parents had told her not to worry about college costs, that they would figure it out, she wanted to help all she could. Wonderful as they were, and loved as Lucy had always felt, she never lost a certain consciousness that she was indebted to them. She tried her best to be perfect for Soledad and Leo Markowitz.

Here it was really no problem, though. She loved

hurdling. When it went well, when she got her striding length and her pace and her hurdles just right, there was nothing like it. Nothing like how competent and powerful and whole it made her feel.

Lucy didn't know exactly what made her lose her focus during that practice. A prickly feeling on the back of her neck? The creeping conviction that she was being watched?

But suddenly she lost her rhythm and messed up her hurdle. She landed hard on the track on one knee, with the hurdle coming down beside her. And she looked up to see her mother. Not her foster mother, Soledad, but her real mother, Miranda.

It was unmistakably her.